LIBERATOR OF METALHAVEN
METAL AND BLOOD
BOOK 3

G J OGDEN

Copyright © 2024 by G J Ogden
All rights reserved.

No part of this book may be reproduced in any form or by any electronic or mechanical means, including information storage and retrieval systems, without written permission from the author, except for the use of brief quotations in a book review.

These novels are entirely works of fiction. The names, characters and incidents portrayed in it are the work of the author's imagination. Any resemblance to actual persons, living or dead, events or localities is entirely coincidental.

Illustration © Phil Dannels
www.phildannelsdesign.com

Editing by S L Ogden
Published by Ogden Media Ltd
www.ogdenmedia.net

1

THE PIT

Finn followed Penelope Everhart through the door and into Haven, his legs moving on autopilot. General Riley followed a few paces behind, pistol pointed at his back and craggy face scrunched up into a gruff expression of deep suspicion. In that respect, it all felt very familiar. It wasn't the first time that Finn had been marched at gunpoint to the office of some official or another, yet this occasion couldn't have been more different to what he was used to. He was no longer in Zavetgrad and no longer under the yoke of the Authority, a fact that should have left him feeling euphoric, but his escape had come at a terrible cost.

Elara... Finn spoke her name only in his mind, too afraid to say it out loud in case the weight of the word finally caused his composure to buckle. *I'm so sorry, Elara...*

He wrestled with the notion that it wasn't really his fault Elara was gone, and that Juniper Jones, the special prefect who had masqueraded as his paramour and companion, already knew she was an agent of Haven. He reasoned that even if he hadn't told Juniper of his plans to escape during the test trial, they would have arrested his mentor anyway, so the outcome was already written. Then he cursed himself for trying to barter with his own feelings of guilt. It didn't matter what the Authority did or didn't know, or what they might or might not have done if Finn had made different choices. Those were hypotheticals. All that mattered was the fact he'd betrayed Elara's trust, and it was that betrayal that had gotten her killed.

Elara's words were still burning in his ears, and he could picture her in perfect clarity, bleeding out into the snow as prefect skycars descended into the test crucible in a desperate effort to stop them from escaping.

"I warned you about Juniper," Elara had said. *"I warned you and still you told her about us. So, this is on you, Finn. That's twice now you've fucked up and someone else has paid the price. Make it the last time."*

"That's twice now you've fucked up and someone else has paid the price..." Finn whispered, too quietly for General Riley to overhear. Elara had intended those words to hurt him, and she had succeeded. "...and someone else has paid the price..." he repeated, still little more than a wounded sigh.

Owen, his friend and Metalhaven brother, had been the first to die, and now Elara had joined him. These had been the only two people in the world that Finn had ever trusted, loved even, as much as he still struggled to understand what that word meant. And both were dead, because of him.

A numbness overcame him, just as it had done after Owen's death. He knew he should have felt something, but his mind blocked out the pain. A self-preservation mechanism, he realized, but he knew it wouldn't last. Anger would claim him next, then before long he would be tormenting himself with questions of what he could have done differently, and promises that he would somehow make amends, but it was all pointless because it changed nothing.

This time would be different, Finn told himself. This time, he wouldn't succumb to emotion and become maudlin and self-pitying and weak. Torturing himself was the easy option, a cop-out, but there was no punishment that fit his crime. He was beyond forgiveness and no longer naïve enough to believe he could ever make things 'right'. All Finn Brasa could do now was use the power he had as the Hero of Metalhaven – a symbol of rebellion – to crush the Authority and free the workers of Zavetgrad.

Does saving a million people absolve me for the death of two? Finn asked himself, and the simple answer was no. *But it's all I can do now, so, I'll play the role I've been handed. I'll be their hero, their redeemer, even knowing my own soul is lost. I'll tear down the walls of Zavetgrad, brick by brick, then when enough golds have died, I'll turn my rage skyward, to Nimbus, and destroy the very foundation of the Authority.*

"Finn okay-kay?" Scraps asked.

Finn's little robot pal was still clamped to his shoulder armor, and he realized the machine had been observing him closely as he wrestled with his feelings. The perceptive robot knew he was in turmoil, but Finn didn't want to burden Scraps with his worries because he was the only good thing he had left.

"I'm okay, pal, just a little overwhelmed," Finn replied, smiling at the robot.

Scraps nodded and smiled back, though his usually unflappable mechanical friend still seemed concerned.

"Elara-good is tough!" Scraps said. The name tugged at

his insides and Finn found his steps grow heavier. "She okay. Scraps knows it."

"I'm sure you're right, pal," Finn said, though it was a lie. "It'll take more than a bullet and a few regular prefects to stop The Iron Bitch of Metalhaven."

He smiled at Scraps again and this helped to put the robot's mind at ease. There was no point them both suffering, Finn reasoned. And it was not fair to burden Scraps with the truth either, because unlike him, the robot had not put a foot wrong.

Passing through the door, Finn exited the dark hangar space where his stolen special prefect skycar had been deposited and into a bright corridor with grey walls. The space was clean but rudimentary in design, not unlike the buildings in Metalhaven, but without the decades of accumulated grime and neglect. Soon the corridor had widened and branched off into other passageways and spaces where people were working at desks, chatting, and laughing while drinking from metal cups and eating snacks. Every one of them stopped to look as he walked past, their faces all adopting the same dazed expression, as if he were an extra-terrestrial being paraded before them.

Penelope finally led Finn into a teardrop-shaped office space, with desks arranged in a semi-circle around the circumference, neatly bisecting five office doors. Penelope went straight for the center door and General Riley grunted at him to follow. As with the people outside, the men and women at the desks all looked at him, with a mixture of stolen glances and side-eyed glimpses. They were all dressed in simple work clothes, like a toned-down version of the outfits that clerical staff in the Authority sector wore, with one major exception – there was not a hint of gold on anyone or anything he'd seen. In fact, it seemed that the only gold in all of Haven was the highlights on Scraps' body and the gold trim on his own prosecutor armor.

"Stand there," Riley grunted pointing to a spot in front of a simple metal desk, before closing the door and guarding it like a sentry.

Finn did as he was directed then waited as Penelope sifted through her in-tray, scowling at some of the documents and muttering at others. He used the time to look around the office, which was humble and lacking any of the extravagant accoutrements that high-ranking golds surrounded themselves with. If Penelope was the leader of Haven, as General Riley had suggested, then she didn't use that position to her advantage, or at the very least, didn't allow people to believe she was.

"Well, where to begin?" Penelope said, placing the palms of her hands onto the desk and leaning forward. The principal's emerald eyes were a painful reminder of Elara – her biological daughter – but despite the warmth of her tone and her polite half-smile, Finn sensed Penelope's unease.

"Before we begin, I want to be sure we can trust that robot," Riley grunted, wafting his pistol in the direction of Scraps. "It was built by the Authority, which means it can't be trusted."

"How rude-rude!" Scraps protested, pressing his little hands to his oil-can body. "Scraps a Metal!"

"The Authority didn't build Scraps, I did," Finn explained, as the robot and the general continued to stare each other out. "I put him together from scraps I found in the reclamation yard, hence his name. I learned about robots and coding from an illegal data device I kept hidden in my apartment."

Riley snorted. "You expect me to believe that a chrome from Metalhaven could build an advanced robot like that?"

Being labelled 'advanced' seemed to appease Scraps a little, though the robot continued his staring contest in earnest.

"Believe whatever you like, General, but Scraps stays with me," Finn said. "That's non-negotiable." Finn could sense what the general was thinking and if Riley believed he could take his robot pal away then it would be over Finn's dead body, or the general's.

"Scraps is fine to stay," Penelope said, holding up a hand to the general. "Elara fed back enough intelligence about the robot for me to be confident he is not a security threat."

Riley grunted his acceptance, though it didn't help the general's mood that Scraps was taunting the man by doing a merry victory dance on Finn's shoulder.

"Thank you, Principal Everhart," Finn said, nodding his gratitude. He also appreciated that Penelope had called Scraps 'he' rather than 'it', as General Riley had done. "I wouldn't be here without Scraps. He's saved my life on more than one occasion."

"He's a fine robot," Penelope said, winking at Scraps, "but we might have to do something about the gold. We don't use that color in Haven, for obvious reasons." She pushed herself up then sat on the edge of the desk, drumming her fingers on the metal while continuing to scrutinize him. "We'll need to remove the gold on your armor too, though I like the look. And, while we're on the subject of things that need doing, I'd ask that you please call me Pen.

Principal Everhart is too stuffy and authoritarian for my liking."

Finn nodded. "You got it, Pen," he said. The lack of formality seemed strange, considering he'd spent his entire life saying, "yes sir or yes ma'am," to every human being with a fleck of gold on them, but he figured he could get used it.

"I'm sure you have many questions, and I know that General Riley is itching to debrief you..." they both glanced at Riley, whose surly expression seemed to be chiseled out of marble, "...but to save time, why don't I just give you a whistlestop tour of everything Haven? Then if you have more questions, I can answer them at a later time."

"Honestly, my mind is such a mess right now, and I don't even know where to start," Finn replied. Then he looked around the room and shrugged. "I don't even know where we are. I guess this is your office?"

"It is," Pen said, remaining perched on the edge of her desk, instead of using her well-worn, high-back chair. "We're on level one right now, and the first two levels are given over to the administrative functions of running the Pit."

"The Pit?" Finn said. "You mean Haven?"

"We don't really call it that here," Pen said, looking embarrassed. "It sounds a little..." She reached for the word, but Finn finished the sentence for her.

"Pretentious?"

"Yes," Pen said, laughing. "Haven was actually built by the founders of the Authority, some two-hundred and sixty-plus years ago, though in truth we don't have the exact date. The project was called RADOVAULT, which stands for Radiological Defense Outpost with Advanced Underground Living Technologies." She snorted with derision. "It's the sort of techno-babble nonsense that engineers love to come up with. But, since Haven felt too ostentatious and RADOVAULT is frankly ridiculous, this underground silo became known as The Pit." She shrugged. "It's an intentionally self-deprecating title. We don't like to think of ourselves as special, like the golds do. Quite the opposite, in fact. We're just ordinary people, like the workers of Zavetgrad, except that we have the privilege of living free."

Pen's answer was everything Finn had hoped for and more. He wasn't dewy-eyed enough to believe that Haven was some sort of utopian paradise, as some people in the bars of Metalhaven had thought, and he was comforted by Pen's humility, which was a trait that simply didn't exist in the gold-lined streets of the Authority.

"You said this is a silo?" Finn said. His mind had begun to clear, and questions were now bubbling to the surface. "Just how deep does this place go and how many live here?"

"Ah, I see that you are a man who appreciates numbers," Pen said, flicking her eyes over to Scraps who was the embodiment of Finn's curiosity. "The pit is four-hundred and thirty-nine meters deep, but above us is another thirty meters of concrete and armor, as well as the garage for our skycars and vehicles. The founders who built the Pit were naturally still paranoid about the possibility of war, and so they made this place extremely hardy and defensible, lucky for us."

Finn snorted a laugh. There was a sweet irony that a facility built by Zavetgrad's founders, despots and criminals all, would become the sole refuge from their tyranny.

"There are one-hundred and forty-four floors in total, each with a radius of a hundred and seventy-two meters," Pen continued. "And at the last count, which included a certain Finn Brasa, there are twelve-thousand, six-hundred and fifty-six residents of Haven."

Finn blew out a long, low whistle. The place was huge, but it still paled in comparison to the sprawling work sectors of Zavetgrad and its carefully-regulated population of one million.

"What about Scraps?" Scraps said, hands on hips again. "Scraps resident too!"

"Quite right," Pen said, bowing apologetically to Scraps. She then turned to Riley. "Will, please update the population counter to twelve-thousand, six-hundred and fifty-seven."

General Riley let out a boisterous laugh, of the kind Finn was used to hearing from drunken workers in a recovery centre, but did nothing, clearly believing Pen's request to be a joke. However, when the principal refused to take her emerald eyes off him, he rolled his and grumbled under his breath, while tapping away at a computer on his wrist.

"Thanks-thanks!" Scraps said, bowing to the principal in return.

"Where do you get your power from?" Finn asked. The questions were coming thick and fast now.

"We have a geothermal energy source accessed from level one-four-four, though it extends deep underground," Pen explained. "I have no clue how it works, but it's a marvel to be sure. I'll show it to you if you like?"

"I would," Finn said. He wasn't being polite, the idea of seeing the Pit's power source genuinely excited the technical geek in him.

"We draw water from underground springs, but also capture surface snow, and almost everything is recycled," Pen said, continuing her whistlestop tour of the facility. "We also have a variety of farming units that produce our food, and you'll be happy to know it's not entirely algae based."

Finn laughed. "That *is* good to know."

"We also make a mighty fine ale," General Riley cut in, finally relaxing his guard enough to join in with the conversation. "Even those who came here from Metalhaven agree it puts hairs on your chest, whether you're a man or a woman."

They all laughed this time and it felt like an ice-breaker moment. Already, Finn felt more at home in the Pit than he ever had done in the Authority sector.

"I'm sure there's much more you'd like to know, but hopefully it can wait," Pen said, drawing her introductory address to a conclusion. "The esteemed general needs to debrief you and help you to understand our plans, now that you're here."

"Of course," Finn said. After his comment about ale, he felt less threatened by the gruff military man. He then yawned and it seemed to drag on for minutes before he finally shook his head and swallowed. "Though does it have to be right now?" he asked, feeling suddenly dog tired. "I slept a little on the flight over, but I can still barely keep my eyes open. I'm not sure what use I would be to the general in this state."

"I've assigned you quarters on level three in the garrison," Riley said. "It won't be quite what you were used to in the prosecutor barracks, but as a former chrome, I expect you'll find it comfortable enough."

"Thank you, General," Finn said, rubbing his eyes.

"Don't thank me just yet, the beds are harder than diamond," Riley replied, grinning.

Finn was relieved to see that the general had holstered his pistol in order to open the door. However, no sooner had it swung open than an alarm blared out from speakers in the corner of the office and the room outside. From being dead on his feet, Finn was suddenly wide-awake and alert. He knew a warning klaxon when he heard one.

"What it is, Will?" Pen asked, as Riley pressed his fingers to the comm unit in his right ear, scrunching up his eyes in an effort to hear better.

"Red alert, ma'am," Riley replied, severe but calm. "We have an incoming strike from Zavetgrad."

2
RED ALERT

Pen slid off the side of her desk and straightened her suit jacket before marching out of her office, head high. Riley waited for the principal to exit first then followed her out. It was a subtle but important nod to Pen's status and one that showed the man had more class than the self-important Head Prefects of Zavetgrad.

"We need to reach Operations," Riley said, noticing that Finn was still in the office. The alarms had caused him to freeze up and it felt like his feet were cemented to the floor. "I'll escort you to a shelter. There's one en route."

"I want to come with you," Finn said, finally compelling his body to move. "If this is an attack because of me, I need to be there."

Riley narrowed his eyes at him then glanced at Pen, who returned a gentle nod.

"Fine, follow me," Riley grunted.

Finn hurried after the general, who hadn't waited for him, and Finn noticed that the workers who had been manning the desks in the teardrop-shaped space were already hurrying into the corridor. Jogging to catch up with Pen and Riley, Finn became lost in a stream of people flooding out from other rooms and offices, all headed in the same direction. It was orderly and calm, but it was also clear from the anxious expressions and hushed voices of the massed workers that they were nervous too.

Finn caught up with Riley and Pen then a dull thump echoed through the corridor, and he felt a vibration rumble the floor. He glanced at the general, but the man's chiseled jaw remained firm. There was another thump and Finn felt this one more keenly. It not only shook his body but dislodged dust that had settled on the rafters above their heads. A third came soon after, powerful enough that he had to brace his hand against the wall to stop himself stumbling. The whisper of anxious voices grew to a concerned murmur then Finn heard crying, but the Pitch of the sound was unusually high. He was no stranger to hearing grown men and women cry, since workers would mourn the deaths of fellow chromes, whether accidental or at the hands of a sadistic prefect, but this sob was different. He tried to locate the source, but the mass of bodies was too thick, and soon he was swept away in the current.

Finn pushed ahead, trying to follow the sound, until he reached the inner ring of the Pit, a wide circular concourse with an uninhibited view to the very base of the vast silo. A detached central column ran from the top of the Pit the bottom, like a bullseye on a dartboard extruded in three dimensions. This inner silo was linked to the outer levels by bridges that spanned the gaping void, and Finn saw that it contained an array of elevator shafts, though all of them were locked down due to the alert. The sound of crying again stole his focus, and he followed the noise, easing through the crowds until he saw a woman carrying a child in her arms, while leading two more toward the closest shelter. The two on foot, a girl and boy, were perhaps seven or eight, while the child being carried was no more than three years old. Finn froze and stared at them, mouth agape. *Children...*

The last time Finn had seen a child, he had been one himself, though it was a hazy memory at best. Worker children in Zavetgrad were taken from their mothers at birth, surrogates who had been artificially impregnated against their will, then transported first to vast nurseries and then to the workhouse at age seven. From then until aged thirteen, they were 'schooled' in all of the various trades of Zavetgrad, from reclamation to farming, then bucketed according to their aptitude in each before being assigned their color. That was where Finn had first received his worker rating of five, not that he was congratulated for his efforts. There were no 'gold stars' in the workhouse of Zavetgrad, only hard lessons, and this was also where Finn had been educated in the consequences of defying the Authority. Wardens, prefects in all but name, were not averse to beating a child and Finn was on the receiving end of a stick far more often than most. His buddies in the workhouse, the closest of those being Owen, would ask him why? *Because fuck them, that's why...*

"Finn, are you okay?"

It was Pen and it wasn't until she'd spoken to him that he realized she had taken hold of his arm, perhaps afraid that he might collapse on the spot.

"Yes, sorry," Finn said, shaking himself out of his daze, though he still couldn't take his eyes off the family, who were now waiting in line to enter a shelter. "I'm just not used to seeing children, that's all. The Authority inject us with something after we leave the workhouse for our individual districts, and it clouds our memories." He laughed, darkly. "They didn't want us burdened by the trauma of our youth in case it affected productivity."

Pen nodded. She was also now watching the family and Finn noticed that she had tightened her grip on his arm, perhaps subconsciously.

"They take so much, and give nothing in return," Pen said, her tone flat. "And they won't stop, until we make them."

Another shockwave rumbled through the Pit, and if it weren't for Pen's hold on him, Finn would have stumbled.

"Come, we must reach Operations," Pen said, guiding Finn through the crowd, though progress continued to be slow. "From there, we can gauge the threat and determine what sort of response is needed."

"Does this happen often?" Finn asked, blinking some of the falling dust from his eyes. "The attacks, I mean?"

"They have been increasing, of late," Pen replied, still guiding him. Despite her position and the urgency of her task, she did not call out for people to step aside. It was as if she was just another worker in the Pit. "We have been increasing the rate at which we liberate workers from Zavetgrad over a period of several years, and the Authority has ramped up its response in kind. They launch rocket attacks like this every week now, like clockwork, to remind us they know we're here. This attack, I suspect, is more to do with your arrival."

Finn nodded. He'd already figured that much out himself.

The swell of the crowds took them close to the barrier

fence that separated the inner circle from the elevator silo in the center. A gust of hot air rose past Finn's face as he butted up against the trellis, and the heat was stifling. Even in the prosecutor barracks, the temperature was maintained at a steady seventy degrees Fahrenheit, which itself was already ten degrees warmer than his tenement building in Metalhaven, but the air blowing through the chasm felt hotter than laser light.

"It's the primary air circulation system," Pen said, noticing that Finn was perspiring. "It helps to circulate warm air around the Pit and prevent pockets of carbon dioxide from forming, but I agree it can feel a little toasty sometimes."

Two more rockets thudded in the ground above their heads and this time Finn was shaken off his feet. Cries and screams erupted around the Pit but were soon drowned out by the screech of metal. Finn looked up and saw a section of the roof collapse. Concrete and metal fell and crashed through the barrier fence ahead of where Finn and Pen were huddled together for safety. Another rocket hit and the shockwave cracked open the floor, like a fissure opening in the ground during an earthquake. There were more desperate screams, then a section of the inner walkway dropped, and people began to slide toward the void. Amongst them was the woman and her three children.

"Scraps, go high and let me know what you see!" Finn said, pushing away from Pen and running toward danger.

Rotors sprang from the robot's head, and he zoomed over the trellis while Finn hurried through the crowd, helping people to their feet, and shepherding them toward others, who were also trying to get people to safety. The pit shook and debris rained down, thudding into bodies, and knocking people off their feet. Finn reached an older man who had been hit on the head and helped him up. Another worker pushed forward to help and Finn saw that it was Pen.

"You should go back, this floor could collapse at any moment," Finn said, as Pen threw the injured man's arm over her shoulder and helped him toward a uniformed soldier, also aiding in the effort.

"I could say the same to you," Pen replied. He recognized the look in her eyes from Elara and saw the same dogged determination. "This is my pit, Finn. I'm not going anywhere."

Finn knew it was pointless to argue and pressed on, using the added grip provided by his prosecutor boots and gloves to ease himself down the slope. Ropes were thrown toward him by other uniformed soldiers, and he tied them around the waists of the those who were trapped, clinging to the fractured floor with blood-stained fingers.

"Pull!" Pen yelled, taking the strain herself, her once pristine grey suit already blackened and torn.

The injured citizens were heaved clear, but Finn could see more workers below, bodies pressed to the floor, which was now hanging above the five-hundred-meter chasm that separated the inner circle and elevator silo. He looked for Scraps and saw that the robot had wedged his oil-can body into the cracked concrete and was using himself as a foothold for a citizen who was desperately close to falling. Finn inched closer and to his horror realized it was the mother he'd seen earlier. She was hanging on by the tips of her fingers, her three children clinging to her body for safety.

"Pen, I need more rope!" Finn yelled, sliding deeper toward the woman and the chasm.

The Principal of the Pit sprang into action, leading the soldiers and other citizens in the rescue effort. Ropes were slid toward him and given slack, and Finn was finally able to reach the woman's side. He glanced over the edge of the fractured walkway and wished he hadn't. The brief few minutes he'd spent on top of the apartment block with Elara in the test crucible, when she had first shown him the venue, had taught Finn that he was no fan of heights. The aching void below him only confirmed this.

"You're going to be okay," Finn said to the woman, who was shaking from the superhuman effort of supporting her own weight and the weight of her three children. "I'm going to get you out of here, okay?"

The woman nodded but he'd never seen someone look so afraid. The prospect of dying was the most primal of all fears, and Finn had seen it all too many times before, but this was different. The mother wasn't afraid for her own life, but for the lives of her children. It was terror on another level and it spurned Finn on to save her.

"Take this," Finn said, removing his prosecutor webbing and slipping it over the woman's head. "Slide your arms through, like this..." he added, shuffling closer and grabbing the waistband of her pants to support her weight. "Don't worry, I've got you."

The woman fought her fear and began threading her arms through the webbing, one by one. Rockets continued to slam into the rocky ground above the silo, but they were coming less frequently, which Finn hoped was a sign the attack was waning. With the webbing finally in place, Finn fastened the clasps before tying one of the ropes to the harness. He tugged on it, and it was secure. The he took another rope and wove it under the arms of the three-year-old, and through the belt-loops of the other children, to secure them to their mother.

"Pen, pull her up!" Finn called out.

The principal took up the strain and slowly the woman and her family began to climb. Pen was at the head of the group of rescue workers, leading from the front in a way that Finn could never have imaged a regent or head prefect to have done. In the Authority, you looked after number one. In the Pit, you looked after each other.

"You okay, pal?" Finn said, looking down at Scraps. The robot was trying to extricate himself from the crack in the floor where he'd embedded himself to provide a foothold for the mother.

"Stuck-stuck!" Scraps cried, bashing the concrete with his hands, but the robot's forte was brains not brawn and he barely scuffed the surface.

"Hang on, I'm coming," Finn said.

Letting out some rope, he slid to the very edge of the collapsed walkway then made the mistake of looking down again. Cursing, he pressed his eyes shut tightly.

"Deep-deep!" Scraps said. "Finn not fall!"

"I don't intend to, pal, but I can't leave you here, can I?" Finn said, smiling at his robot.

Pulling his knife out of the stow in his armor, Finn began chipping away at the concrete, using the sharp blade to nibble the material until Scraps was finally able to pull himself free. Climbing out of the crack, Scraps perched himself on the edge of the precipice and dusted himself down. His oil-can body was dented and much of the gold had been scraped off his paintwork.

"Make yourself look beautiful later, pal, I'm sort of

hanging here," Finn said, amused that his robot's first concern was his appearance. "Some of us don't have rotors, remember?"

Scraps nodded then sprang the blades from the top of his head and spun them up, blowing dust into Finn's face. Suddenly, another rocket slammed into the ground above them, and it felt like a direct hit to the core of the silo. Rocks and debris bounced off Finn's armor and vanished into the chasm, then the fractured walkway dropped, and Finn's feet slipped over the edge. He cursed and tensed his muscles, gripping his rope tighter and scrambling to regain a footing, but it felt like his stomach was still falling. Then there was a scream, high pitched and shrill like a whistle, and Finn saw the young girl hurtling toward him. Her belt loops had snapped, and the impact of the rocket had shaken her loose from her mother's desperate grasp. He reached out on instinct and caught the girl, pulling her close to his chrome armor. Then the walkway collapsed from underneath them and for a single, gut-wrenching second, they were in free fall, before the rope became taut, and they were snapped back and left hanging above the chasm. Finn cried out as the jolt almost pulled his arm out of its socket, but his armor helped to brace against the shock, and he clung on. He could hear shouts and screams from above him but the rush of blood pounding in his ears muffled the words. Then he saw Scraps, hovering in front of him, a rope clutched between his little metal hands.

"Be quick, Scraps, I can't hold on for long," Finn hissed through gritted teeth.

His prosecutor training had enhanced his strength beyond the already amplified levels that years of toil in Metalhaven had given him, but his iron grip was still faltering.

Scraps rushed into action looping the rope around the girl and fashioning a makeshift harness.

"Done-done!" Scraps yelled. "Finn let go!"

"Are you sure?" Finn said. The burn in his muscles was almost too much to bear, but he clung on for fear that if he released the girl, she would vanish in the darkness below him.

"Sure-sure!" Scraps said, waving his hands above his ahead. "Let go!"

Finn trusted his robot and released the girl, who swayed gently away from him, screaming at the top of her lungs. He watched anxiously as the girl was rapidly hauled to safety, then wrapped his legs around the rope to anchor himself and began to slowly hitch himself up. The daily assault courses he'd endured at the prosecutor barracks had been grueling, but the climb was even more arduous, and by the time he reached the top, Pen and others grabbing his arms and pulling him the rest of the way, he felt like his body was ready to explode from agony. Scraps landed by his side, metal fingers steepled together in worry, and Finn smiled at the robot – it might have been a grimace, it was hard to tell – then hugged him close.

"Thanks, pal," he said, gasping the words between gulps of humid air. "I don't know how many times you saved my ass now, but don't stop doing it, okay?"

Scraps giggled, changing from concern to happiness at the flip of a switch.

"Okay-kay!" the little robot replied.

"Are you alright?" Pen asked, crouching by his side and helping to support his aching body. "Both of you, I mean," she added, winking at Scraps.

"I'm fine but how's the girl?" Finn said. he couldn't see her and not knowing if she was safe was killing him.

"Don't worry, everyone is out of danger," Pen answered, resting a hand on his armored shoulder to comfort him. "No-one died today, thanks to you."

Finn shook his head. "I think it was more than just me," he replied, accepting Pen's help to stand. "I also have you to thank for not being a splat at the bottom of the silo," he added, highlighting the principal's own heroism.

"Perhaps," Pen said, graciously accepting his argument. "But they only see you…"

Pen nodded toward the throng of workers who had been caught by debris or rescued from the fallen walkway and were now being tended to by medics. The woman and her children were amongst them, and all four were looking at Finn. Then he realized it wasn't just the family but everyone, not only in the group of injured people, but across the entire inner circle of the Pit.

"Perhaps 'Hero' might be the appropriate name for you after all," Pen said.

"But I didn't do this on my own," Finn felt like he was taking credit other people's bravery, and it didn't sit right with him.

"No, but when you ran toward danger instead of away from it, you showed us who you are," Pen replied. "Now, do you understand? Do you see what you represent, not only to the people of Metalhaven, but the people here too?"

Finn sighed and shook his head. Elara's last words to him were clear in his mind, as if she were right in front of him, saying them to his face.

"This isn't about you, Finn, it never was. It's about what

you represent. It's about the change you can bring. Whether you like it or not, you're the spark that will light the fuse that will bring down the Authority and even Nimbus itself. I know you don't want it. You probably don't even deserve it. But it's on you, Finn."

"Elara made me understand what I can be," Finn said, half-answering Pen's question. "She also said I don't deserve it, and she was right about that too."

Pen shrugged and cocked her head to one side. "I know at least four people who might disagree with that," she said, looking at the family, who were hugging each other in a tight huddle.

A chirruping sound emanated from Pen's suit jacket, and she reached into an inside pocket and removed a slim communicator device. Finn could see the name *Gen. Riley* glowing on the device's screen.

"What's the situation, Will?" Pen asked, sounding remarkably calm considering everything that had just happened.

"I launched the QRA skycars and that seems to have chased them off," came the gruff reply from Riley. He sounded irritated. "Between them and our perimeter defenses we shot down five of the bastards, but eight still got away."

"What about casualties?" This question was asked with more trepidation.

"Forty-two injuries reported so far, but the worst of it is broken bones," Riley replied. "All considered, we got off lightly. This was a much heavier attack than we're used to, but I sense a bigger one is coming. We might have less time than we thought."

"Understood, Will, I'll join you shortly," Pen said.

She closed the channel the slid the device back into her pocket before noticing Finn's concerned expression.

"You were probably expecting a nice quiet life in Haven," she said, still managing a smile. "I'm sorry to disappoint."

"Nothing about Haven has disappointed me yet, I just didn't expect you to be under threat like this," Finn answered. "Maybe it was the name, but I thought people would be safe from the Authority here. I guess I was wrong."

Pen hooked her arm through his and began leading him away, as she had done before the attack had hit in full force. People made way as they approached, many still stealing furtive glances at Finn.

"Haven has always existed on borrowed time," Pen said, nodding and waving to people as they walked past, always presenting a smiling face. "From the moment the first workers from Metalhaven set foot in this place, the clock started ticking. We've had a hundred and twenty-six years to build and prepare, and to grow our numbers. That's time enough. Now, it's time we fought back."

3

OTHER WAYS TO FIGHT

The operations center was a hive of activity with men and women in military and civilian clothes bustling from station to station to conduct their urgent business. The chatter was louder than a Metalhaven recovery center on a trial night, but the atmosphere was the opposite; calm, coordinated and in control.

Finn hovered by the door as Pen went inside to speak to General Riley. The general was in the center of the operations room, a raised circular dais with banks of screens and work consoles arcing around the circumference. Other uniformed officers were with him, all of whom saluted as Pen arrived and stepped onto the platform with them. Computer devices were thrust in front of the principal's eyes, while Riley and the other officers directed Pen's attention to the contents of several screens, all in the same professional but hurried manner as the other workers in the room.

Finn felt that he was intruding on important matters that he couldn't contribute to, so he stepped outside to watch the repair crews and emergency workers who were busy repairing the damage sustained in the attack. The section of outer circle walkway that had collapsed was cordoned off but already there were a dozen workers toiling to fix the damage. He noticed that the crew was assisted by automated tools similar to ones he'd seen in Zavetgrad's construction sector, Stonehaven. He crept closer, trying to keep out of sight and out of the way as much as possible, and observed that the repair crew all wore orange patches on their shoulders, the same color as Stonehaven.

"Why do you think they still wear their old color, pal?" Finn asked Scraps, who was perched on his shoulder. "It must be by choice. I can't image that Pen would force them to do it."

Scraps shrugged. "Others wear old colors too. Look-look!"

Scraps pointed to a group of three women who were headed toward one of the bridges that spanned the void between the inner circle walkway and the elevator silo. They all wore plain grey suits, and at first Finn failed to notice any other color until he spotted that the cuffs and lapels of the jackets were trimmed in white.

"Spacehaven?" Finn said and Scraps nodded.

"And there, look-look!" Scraps added.

Finn scoured the sea of faces on the busy walkway, which had already returned to normal after the attack, and saw another group of workers in overalls, fixing a damaged power relay. Their hard hats were colored red for Volthaven.

"I wonder why they do it?" Finn said, thinking out loud. "You'd have thought they'd want to forget everything about Zavetgrad."

Scraps shrugged again. "Finn wears chrome," the robot

pointed out, tapping his armored shoulder pauldrons. "And Scraps chrome too!" He frowned and dusted down his scratched and dented body. "Scraps need fixing!"

"We'll get you sorted, pal, don't worry," Finn said, patting his robot on the head. "And you're right, I guess I have stayed faithful to my old color."

He recalled how his brief return to Metalhaven during his prosecutor training had stirred up feelings of nostalgia. He missed the ale, and the tradition of a 'pint and a fight', and he especially missed the people. Owen's face invaded his thoughts, but he pushed the memory away, reminding himself that he'd vowed not to succumb to emotion and self-pity.

"Ha-ha!" Scraps laughed.

Finn frowned at the robot. "What's so funny?"

"Look-look!" Scraps said, pointing back in the direction of the cordoned off area where the collapsed walkway was being repaired. "Foremen!"

Finn redirected his scowl to the work area then also found himself laughing. Scraps was right. In amongst the former Stonehaven workers and their various construction automatons were three Foreman-class robots. In Metalhaven, these autocratic machines were the unsleeping middle managers of the reclamation yards, always watching over his shoulder and dishing out additional shift hours for misdemeanors as minor as cussing at them. Finn hated the machines but on this occasion, he couldn't be happier to see them.

"Come on, let's say hello," Finn said, keen to discover how turning their coats had affected the personalities of the slave-driving robots.

Finn crossed the inner walkway to the edge of the safety barricade, garnering dozens more stolen glances from Haven citizens enroute. Some members of the work crew nodded or saluted by tapping their safety helmets, but in true Stonehaven fashion, they were too pragmatic and stoical to recognize Finn's newfound celebrity status.

"What's up chief?" one of the workers said, resting on a sledgehammer like it was a crutch. "Can we help you?"

"I was just curious about them," Finn said, pointing to one of the foremen robots. To his surprise the machine noticed him and waved, which left him feeling uneasy. He'd never seen a foreman wave before and everything about the gesture seemed wrong. "It must be nice to have them working for you, for a change."

"Oh, don't mind Bob," the worker said, nodding in the direction of the robot who had waved at Finn. "He's just one of the guys, aren't you Bob?"

"Yes, it is gratifying to be productive," the foreman replied. "A good day's work is good for the soul!"

Finn scowled at the machine, which sounded exactly like the robot middle managers Finn remembered, except it was cheerful, like Scraps, which also didn't sit right with him. He was too used to foremen being assholes.

"But doesn't it feel strange working with them?" Finn asked the man. "I've gone entire days without sleep because of the extra shift hours one of these bastards gave me."

The worker and the robot both laughed, and Finn's anxiety rocketed to newfound heights. No matter how wholesome the two seemed, it felt like a waking nightmare.

"Yeah, I remember those robots too, but Bob is different,"

the man said. "Robots in Haven are equals. We couldn't function without them."

"Bob is right, we play an important role," the machine added.

Finn's frown was now so intense that his eyes had narrowed to barely more than a slit.

"Which Bob are you talking about?" he asked.

"That Bob," said Bob the foreman, pointing to the worker.

"You're both called Bob?"

The worker laughed. "Yeah, it started as a joke, but then it stuck."

Finn shook his head, wondering if he'd perhaps suffered a concussion at some point during the test trial or during his efforts rescuing the girl and her mother.

"So, what are the other foremen called?" Finn said, almost afraid to ask.

"That's Bob Two, and the other is Bob Three," the man replied, deadly serious. "They're all offshoots of the same base code, you see." Bob Two and Bob Three then downed tools and waved at Finn in perfect synchronization. It sent a shiver of fear racing down his spine. "You have no idea how hard it is to crack a Foreman Logic Processor, so when we do manage to hack one, we just duplicate the code into blanked chips."

"Actually, I do have some experience cracking FLPs," Finn said, hooking a thumb toward Scraps, who waved at the workers. "Maybe we could help out? It would make a nice change from fighting prefects and other prosecutors."

The quartet of Bobs all laughed then human Bob suddenly looked past Finn and stood up, swinging his sledgehammer over his shoulder.

"Something tells me you might not quite be done with that yet," Bob said.

Finn heard the thump of boots approaching and turned to see a soldier in camo fatigues walking toward him from the direction of the operations center.

"Sir, Principal Everhart and General Riley have requested your presence," the soldier said. "If you'd please follow me."

"Duty calls," Bob added, casually.

Finn nodded to the man. "Keep up the good work." He looked at the three robots but, despite knowing they were benevolent, he couldn't help but feel his gut tighten. "That goes for you three as well."

"We Bobs are pleased you find our work satisfactory!" the three ex-foremen said as one.

Finn shook his head then set off in the direction of operations, but he hadn't gone far before the workman called out to him.

"We're all rooting for you, by the way," Bob said, hammer still rested over his shoulder. "And not just the old Stonehaven crew. The greens, reds, whites... all of us. We know what you did back there."

The man sighed and the weight of the hammer seemed to press down on him more greatly. Then Bob the robot surprised him again by resting a consoling hand on the worker's shoulder. It was an unexpected and touching gesture that seemed genuinely heartfelt, especially coming from a machine that until that moment Finn had considered incapable of emotion.

"Tomorrow, I'll have been out of Zavetgrad for nine years, but there isn't a day goes by that I don't wish I could free my buddies too," Bob continued. "The truth is most of them are probably dead by now."

Finn nodded. He recognized the guilt because he'd experienced it himself, intensely.

"I'll do what I can," Finn replied, careful not to overpromise. "I don't know how yet, but I won't stop until everyone is free."

Bob smiled then saluted by tapping his hardhat before returning to work. Finn watched the mixed human-robot crew for a few more seconds, a combination of man and machine that would have been impossible in Zavetgrad, then turned and walked in lockstep with the soldier. To his credit, the officer had waited patiently, without trying to hurry him. It was another example of the natural empathy that the people of Haven possessed; a trait entirely alien to Zavetgrad and the Authority.

More heads turned as Finn traversed the inner circle and this time, he held his head high and returned the nods and smiles of those brave enough to hold his gaze for more than a microsecond. He'd gone to the work crew with the intention of teasing the robot foreman, to get back at the machine race for the years of backbreaking work they had driven him to perform. Instead, he'd come away even more certain of the need to protect Haven at all costs. It was a place where even the machines were free.

"Ah, there you are," Pen said, as Finn was guided through the security barrier protecting the entrance to operations. "I thought you'd gotten lost."

"I didn't want to get in the way of whatever you were doing," Finn replied. "I guess I still feel a little out of place here."

"Everyone who arrives here from Zavetgrad feels the same way, at least for a time," Pen replied, "It's only natural."

"To be honest, it's the foremen that weird me out the most," Finn said, glancing back through the open door. "I'm not sure I'll ever get used to those things being nice."

Pen seemed to find this amusing. "If you think that a friendly foreman is strange then wait until you meet the reprogrammed evaluator robots. They get turned into a trauma councilors. I thought that was a nice touch."

Finn shook his head fiercely. "No thank you. I'd be perfectly happy never seeing one of those shithead machines for the rest of my life."

Finn noticed that the mood in the operations center had changed and that the hustle and bustle of the workers and soldiers had eased from a rolling boil to a gentle simmer.

"I take it that everything is back to normal?" Finn asked.

"For now," General Riley grunted. "But the Authority's attacks are becoming more frequent and sustained. We're getting better at shooting down their skycars but if they continue to hit us, the Pit will sustain a serious breach in a matter of weeks. We may be required to relocate operations to a lower level."

Pen nodded. "Make those arrangements now, general. We need to be ready."

"Weeks?" Finn cut in. The general's bleak assessment had shocked him. "I had no idea the situation was so…"

"Grave…" the general cut in. Finn had struggled to find the right word, but he was going to opt for something less bleak. "That's why we need you and why we can't wait."

"Wait for what?" Finn asked. "What can I do?" The urge

to act was compelling, but he continued to feel useless and frustrated.

"We've been infiltrating Zavetgrad for years," Pen said. "We've planted operatives in all the work sectors and even managed to get some agents inside the Authority, but the Special Prefecture has become adept at rooting out our Metals." She paused biting back anger. "As you know, the golds are skilled at extracting information from those they capture."

Riley grunted under his breath and Finn sensed that the general had some experience with interrogations. He suddenly realized he knew nothing of the man's background, and this made him wary.

"We've been patient, but the simple fact is that we're running out of time," Riley said, unaware of Finn's probing thoughts. "We need a way to rally the workers and get them to rise up against the Authority, and for that we need a catalyst."

"You mean me," Finn said, and Riley nodded.

"Thanks to our operatives, we heard about what happened in Metalhaven's most recent yard one trial," Riley continued, arms now folded across his broad chest. "The one where you decided to go for a 'pint and a fight' with your old worker pals."

"It wasn't exactly like that..." Finn protested, but Riley ignored him.

"That stunt, as reckless as it was, gave us some assurances," Riley continued. "It showed that the people are truly behind you, and ready to fight."

"What Will is trying to say, in his own unique manner, is that you're the first person to stand against the Authority and live since the uprising that founded Haven," Pen added. "The incident in the Recovery Center was only small, but the broadcast you transmitted from the skycar as you escaped Zavetgrad had a much more profound impact. It showed that the Authority couldn't break you and turn you into a gold. It showed the people that you're still one of them, out here fighting for their freedom. You have no idea how powerful that message was."

Finn felt slightly set upon, as if the principal and general had prepared their speeches a long time in advance. What bothered him was why. Since he'd already committed to helping them, a rousing sales pitch was hardly necessary.

"Thankfully, you urged caution," Riley said. He and the principal made for a surprisingly effective tag-team, given their wildly different outlooks and personalities. "Had you not done so then we might have already seen a spate of riots and a brutal response from the Authority that would have extinguished this flame before it had chance to spread."

"Look, I appreciate the background, but this isn't necessary," Finn said. "I'm here and I'm all in. As soon as your medics have patched me up, we can plan an assault and force our way into Zavetgrad. With your soldiers and the people fighting with us, those gold bastards don't stand a chance."

Pen and General Riley exchanged nervous glances and Finn realized that their speech hadn't been designed as a rallying cry to war. They wanted him for something else.

"What is it?" Finn asked. "We are going back, right?"

"When the time is right, my forces will move in," General Riley replied. "But you will not be going with them."

Finn felt like the general had just punched him in the face.

"But that's crazy, you need me!" Finn said. "I'm the Hero

of Metalhaven, if I don't go back and fight then why would any of the workers risk their necks?"

"You're too valuable to risk," Pen said. "All it would take is one lucky bullet and the symbol of our rebellion dies. Without you, we can't unite the sectors against the Authority."

Finn drew in a deep breath and let it puff out of his mouth like smoke from the exhaust of a laboring engine. "Then what the hell am I supposed to do?" he asked.

Riley looked to Pen, and it was clear that he was passing the buck to the principal to give him the bad news.

"Propaganda is a powerful tool," Pen said. Her tone had become more urgent and for once she wasn't smiling. "We need to prepare the sectors for what's to come. We need to make it clear what will be required of them and what awaits them should they succeed."

Finn shook his head. Thanks to the data device he'd stolen from yard seven, he'd read all about the use of propaganda in war and he knew what Pen was asking of him.

"You want me to the be the face of your 'campaign'?" Finn said, making no effort to hide his disgust at the idea. "You want to make a bunch of videos that you can beam into the recovery centers to convince the people to fight."

"You've already proven how powerful your voice can be," Pen said. The reason for highlighting his earlier broadcast was suddenly apparent. "We've spent decades training soldiers for this very moment, Finn. Another body on the front line won't make a damned bit of difference, but in front of a lens you can be more powerful than an entire company of the general's best fighters."

Finn shook his head again, not because he didn't

understand Pen's argument, or even disagree with it, but because it felt cowardly.

"I owe it to the workers to fight at their side," Finn said. "Too many people have already died because of me, and I'm only here because of their sacrifice. I can't hide away in a studio, wearing this armor like a costume and pretending to be something I'm not, like a fucking actor. I have to be out there! They have to see me for real, not on a screen."

"Clear your head, there's too much at stake to risk you on the front line," Riley cut in, abruptly. "Do you think I don't want to be out there, fighting with my troops, instead of being a fucking armchair general in the Pit?" This was the first time Finn had heard Riley swear, and the man was venting anger like a bull snorting. "We all have a role, and your part cannot be played by anyone else. You don't have to like it, but if you want this rebellion to succeed, you have to do what's required of you, not what you want."

Clearly, the plan had been for Pen to deliver the news in the hope that her natural charm won Finn over, but now that the principal had failed, it was the general's turn to try. And what the general lacked in charm he made up for in hard-hitting bluntness.

"The danger is more present than you realize, Finn," Pen said, playing good cop to Riley's bad. "While we've managed to infiltrate Zavetgrad, we recently learned that the Authority may have compromised Haven too."

The principal's latest revelation stopped Finn in his tracks. "How many have gotten inside?"

"The honest answer is that we don't know," Pen admitted. "We captured an agent a few weeks ago, but they died before we could extract any information from them.

"Suicide," Riley grunted. "We don't know how they did it."

"I understand your feelings, Finn, I really do, but I promise this is the best way to help us," Pen continued. "You are the face of our rebellion. It can only be you."

Finn took another deep breath and rubbed his eyes. He understood Pen's rationale, but she was wrong to say that she understood his feelings. The idea of others fighting and dying in his name, while he remained safely cocooned beneath thousands of tons of concrete and stone made him sick to the stomach.

"I know this is a lot, on top of what has already been a lot," Pen added, her familiar smile finally returning. "Get some rest, Finn. We'll talk more tomorrow."

Despite the size of the operations room, Finn felt closed in and claustrophobic and welcomed the chance to escape. The soldier who had come to find him on the inner circle walkway escorted him out, and Finn again found the eyes of Haven's population falling upon him. The weight of expectation was unbearable. He didn't want to be their symbol, just as he never wanted to be a prosecutor, or the Hero of Metalhaven. All he wanted was to fight, and now even that was being taken away from him.

4

OLD FRIENDS

Finn woke up on his front, face smashed into the pillow, which was stuck there by dried-on drool, and with his arm dangling over the side of the rock-hard cot bed. He'd been shown to his quarters by one of Riley's officers, a name he couldn't remember, and had gotten as far as the bedroom before collapsing onto the mattress still in full prosecutor armor. That last part had been a mistake, he realized, as he pulled his still-weary body off the bed and flexed his aching muscles. Armor was great at protecting a person from harm, but it was apparent that wearing it in bed did not aid a restful night's sleep.

"What time is it, pal?" Finn asked Scraps, who was sitting on the simple bedside table, dangling his legs over the side.

"Oh-six-fourteen!" Scraps said. "Finn sleep well?"

Finn rubbed the sleep from his eyes and massaged his jaw, which was aching because of his awkward sleeping position.

"Well, I slept, so I guess that's something," he replied, still not sure whether the rest had done him any good. He certainly didn't feel refreshed. Then his stomach growled liked one of General Riley's complaints, causing Scraps to giggle. "I'm pretty sure I'm hungry though."

"Finn stinks!"

"What?" Finn scowled at his little robot pal then sniffed his armpits and almost fell unconscious again. "Okay, fair point. Perhaps I should shower first."

Finn pushed himself off the bed and took a look around his new room, which didn't take long, because it was even smaller than his apartment in Metalhaven had been. There was a bedroom, which was really just part of the main space, cordoned off by a flimsy screen door, a kitchenette that was only good for making drinks, a cramped WC, and a living space big enough for a desk and a chair.

"Quite a difference from my apartment in the barracks, huh, pal?" Finn said, smiling at Scraps.

"Scraps like-like," the robot said. "This real."

Finn nodded, understanding the sentiment Scraps was trying to convey. His quarters in the Authority sector may have been luxurious but they were never really his and he didn't belong there. This room, for all its spartan austerity, was honest, and after nine weeks of living a lie, Finn was ready for a little honesty.

"Well, there's no shower, so I'm going to need to find a shower block," Finn said, hands on hips. "And I'll need something fresh to wear too."

"Look-look!" Scraps said.

The robot hovered over to the desk, which was little more than a rotor-assisted leap considering the short distance, and pointed to a pile of clothes that lay neatly folded on the chair.

It was a set of the same uniform as worn by Riley and the other officers, except without any rank insignia or a name tag. Finn pulled the chair back and saw that there was also a pair of polished military boots underneath the desk. He checked the sizing by pressing the sole of the boot to his foot and it was spot on.

"It seems that they've thought of everything," Finn said. He picked up the jacket from the bundle of clothes and shook it out. "I'm not sure I agree with their choice of fashion, though," he added, looking at the digital camouflage pattern of the uniform.

"At least it clean," Scraps said, shrugging. "Unlike Finn!"

Finn scowled at the robot, who appeared particularly pleased with his quick-witted responses.

"I don't suppose you've already hacked the Haven computer system and figured out where the washrooms are on this floor?" Finn asked. "Hell, I'm not even sure which floor we're on."

Scraps didn't answer and Finn saw that the robot's eyes were closed and that his arms were hanging limply by his side.

"Buddy, are you okay?" Finn asked, resting a hand on Scraps, and shaking him gently. The robot jolted awake, but the glow behind his mechanical eyes remained dull. "When was the last time you recharged?"

Scraps shrugged. "Long-time." Then he pointed toward the ceiling. "No sun-sun."

"Why didn't you charge up overnight, while I was out cold?" Finn asked.

Scraps looked embarrassed. "Scraps watch Finn. Scraps make sure Finn okay."

Finn felt his heart swell and he could have kissed the robot, despite being scuffed and dirty from his heroics during the attack, but he was far too self-conscious to do such a thing.

"Thank, pal, you're my guardian angel," Finn said, patting the machine on the head like a dog instead. "Thanks for always having my back."

Someone has to...

The memory of Owen speaking to him in yard seven snuck up and attacked without warning like an assassin. Finn's gut twisted, forcing him to grab his stomach and bend forward to steel himself against the wave of pain and nausea that had suddenly gripped him.

"Finn okay?" Scraps asked, concerned.

"Yeah, pal, just a few lingering injuries," he lied. "I'll be fine before you know it."

Scraps nodded, though the machine didn't look entirely convinced, and Finn spent a few moments breathing in through his mouth and out through his nose until the discomfort eased. There were times he thought he'd gotten over the trauma of Owen's death then his mind and body would remind him that he was wrong. In a way, he was glad of this, because it didn't let him forget what he was fighting for. Besides, he didn't deserve to be free of the pain, anyway.

"Let me try to find a power cord somewhere," Finn said, changing the subject back to the pressing issue of Scraps' low battery.

The repairs Finn had made to Scraps after his trial had included an upgraded power core and solar-recharging panels, but deep underground in the Pit, these were useless. He searched through the desk drawer and single small closet before checking the kitchenette and unplugging the electric kettle that had been provided.

"Will this do?" Finn asked, holding up the cord so Scraps could see it.

"Yep-yep!" Scraps said, holding his hand outstretched, like a baby reaching for a rattle.

Finn found an outlet next to the desk and plugged in the cord before handing the other end to his robot. A panel popped open in Scraps' dented and scuffed body and he connected the plug to his core. There was a soft thrum as current began to flow into his friend.

"There you go, pal," Finn said, patting Scraps on the head again. "How long until you're fully charged?"

Scraps shrugged. "Low output," he said, pointing to the socket in the wall. "Maybe two hours."

"Plenty of time for me to get cleaned up and find some breakfast," Finn said. "Will you be okay here by yourself?"

"Scraps okay!" Scraps said. The influx of power had energized him in more ways than one. "Scraps also need fix," the robot added, pointing to his dents and scrapes.

"I'll be back soon," Finn said, removing the armor panels from the base layer and laying them out on the bed. He then grabbed the bundle of clothes and the new boots. "That's assuming I don't get lost," he added, turning the manual handle, and pulling open the door.

Scraps giggled and waved at him, and he waved back before stepping outside and closing the door. He took a moment to get his bearings, noting his door and corridor numbers so that he'd be able to find his way back, then picked a direction and walked. It wasn't long before it became painfully evident that he'd chosen the wrong way to go.

"Shit, there must be a shower block around here somewhere," Finn muttered, stopping at the intersection of another corridor that looked exactly the same as the last.

"Straight down there, second right."

Finn hadn't noticed that one of the doors on the corridor was open. Peering through it, he saw a woman in military fatigues working at her desk.

"Sorry, which way?" Finn asked, leaning on the frame.

"North, on Corridor E, then second right," the woman said, pointing the way. "You can't miss it."

"Got it, I think," Finn said. "Thanks."

Finn had been about to head off when the woman called out, "Hey, aren't you Finn Brasa?"

"Who's asking?" Finn replied, cagily. His time in Metalhaven had taught him to answer such questions with caution. Usually, if anyone came asking for you, it wasn't to give you good news.

"The name's Hannity," the woman said, getting up from her desk. Finn immediately spotted the chrome patch on the arm of her military jacket. "Corporal Jane Hannity."

The woman offered Finn her hand and he took it. Her grip was strong, and her hands were rough and calloused.

"Which yard were you in?" Finn asked.

"Three," Hannity replied.

"Tough yard," Finn said, with genuine respect.

Metalhaven reclamation yards were numbered according to their hazard level from one to thirteen. Three contained freight vessels and large naval support ships, which were extremely dangerous to work on. People would often fall through rusted and cracked-open decks and disappear into the bowels of the vessels, never to be seen again.

"I'm looking forward to the fight," Hannity said. "I'll be right there with you, on the front lines. I can't wait to see the look on the faces of those bastard prefects when we come smashing through their fence."

"Me too," Finn said. He didn't have the heart, or the guts, to tell Hannity that he wasn't going to be fighting alongside her, and instead filming a bunch of propaganda videos from inside the Pit. "We'll give them hell, and then some."

"Metal and Blood," the soldier said, saluting Finn.

"Metal and Blood," Finn answered, returning the salute, or his imitation of it.

Hannity returned to her desk and Finn walked away, feeling like a coward. He almost forgot the soldier's directions then saw the sign for Corridor E and headed along it, desperate to find the shower block in the hope that hot, running water might wash away the stink of his shame as well as his sweat.

Hannity's directions proved correct, and Finn found the shower block to be clean and also mercifully empty. He set down his clean clothes on a bench then plucked a towel from a rack and stripped off his training uniform. He folded it neatly alongside his clean clothes, making a mental note to find a laundry facility to get it processed, then headed into the showers. The water flowed fast and hot and for several minutes he just stood under the head, allowing the needles of water to massage his face and neck. Then he grabbed the block of soap and smiled as he examined its deep red color. It was the same carbolic soap that they used in the prosecutor barracks to not only wash their bodies but help to clean the dozens of cuts and grazes that had been acquired during the day's training.

Wetting the soap, he buffed it into a thick lather then applied it to his body. The slightly sweet odor of Phenol invaded his senses and all he could think about was Elara and how it smelled of her. He pressed his forehead to the cool tiles and let the water flow across his back but despite the soothing heat, he still felt cold. Owen's death he could at least blame partly on Corbin Radcliffe, but Elara was all his fault. It was his choice to leave her, and he desperately wished he could have that time again, so he could go back to the test crucible and drag his mentor to the skycar, kicking and screaming if he had to. He hated himself for running out on her. The reasons behind that decision no longer mattered. Even if trying to save her had gotten him killed too, he would rather that than the living hell he was enduring.

"Stop it!" Finn said, bashing his head against the wall to knock the sentimentality out of him. "This is your life, now deal with it!" he snarled, aggressively rubbing his hair and body to rinse the soap away, yet the smell of her remained.

Stepping out of the shower block, he dressed quickly then found a laundry processor and bagged his training uniform, remembering to add his name and room number to the label. The fatigues fit well, and the combination of clean clothes and body made him feel vaguely human again. Exiting the washroom, he suddenly picked up the smell of food and was drawn to it, like a moth to a flame. He let his nose guide him until the sound of chinking crockery led him to a canteen. Unlike the washroom, it was bustling with activity, and at first, he was reluctant to enter, but the sheer volume of bodies meant that he could easily escape into the crowd and blend in.

The food was buffet style and Finn grabbed a plate and a tray and joined the queue, ogling the selection on offer. It was a far cry from the restaurants of the Authority sector, and he was glad of it, because he hankered for real food, not the fancy cuisine that golds gorged on. There were engineered proteins and algae breads, but also fresh vegetables prepared in a variety of sauces that were rich and fulfilling, the exact opposite to the delicate and refined cuisine of the golds. He loaded up his plate like a glutton, but he didn't care. He wanted to drink it all in and remind himself of who he really was.

The time spent queueing had given other diners ample opportunity to see his face and recognize him. There were nods and polite, deferential greetings from everyone he passed by, but the people in the room respected his space and he found a small bistro table in the corner, away from the bustle of the main hall. The stolen glances in his direction didn't bother him because he only had eyes for his food, and he demolished the plate with the same gusto he used to carve up tanks and APCs with a laser cutter. Satisfied, he wiped his mouth with a napkin and tossed it onto the plate, before resting back in his chair and closing his eyes, allowing the drone of chatter to clear his mind, like white noise.

"Mind if I join you?"

Finn peeked one eye open and saw a woman standing next to the vacant chair opposite, smiling at him as if they knew one another. He was about to politely decline the offer when he noticed the white patch on the shoulder of her casual work clothes, and he sat bolt upright.

"Cora?"

Her hair had been cut shorter and her clothes were

naturally different to the offender's trial jumpsuit she'd be wearing when they'd parted, but it was her happy expression that had kept him from recognizing her. The Cora who had escaped their trial had not been a joyful woman.

"I'd heard that you got out," Cora said.

Finn almost jumped out of his chair and before he knew it, their arms were wrapped around one another in a tight embrace. Finn was not a hugger, and he barely knew the woman, but their shared ordeal had created a unique bond, a connection that no-one else could understand. He'd never expected to see Cora again and, until that moment, he hadn't even known she'd made it to Haven alive. With everything that had happened since his own arrival, it hadn't even crossed his mind to look for her. Thankfully, she had found him first.

"How do you like the food?" Cora said, sitting opposite Finn. "I suppose it's nothing like what you were used to in the Authority sector."

"Honestly, what I just ate was better than anything I had in the prosecutor barracks," Finn said, resting his hands on his full belly. "Apart from maybe croissants. I do miss croissants. And macarons."

Cora frowned. "I'm afraid I don't know what either of those are, so I'm fairly sure we don't have them here."

"I'm happy to do without," Finn said. "No amount of pastries could take away the bitter aftertaste of all the lies I was forced to tell, every single day."

Cora nodded them became more reflective. "I heard about The Shadow, Elara Cage," she said, rocking a fork back and forth on the table. "Operations kept me updated about your progress, whenever they could. I found out that she was a Metal not long after I arrived here."

It wouldn't have taken much to push Finn back into a maudlin state-of-mind, but he'd already decided that he was done with self-pity and regret.

"It was my fault she got shot and left behind," Finn said, choosing not to varnish the facts. "I got tricked by someone posing as my friend and she paid the price. That's twice someone has died because of mistakes I've made."

"Pen told me what happened," Cora said. She reached across the table and squeezed Finn's hand. "Don't be so hard on yourself. You couldn't have known."

Finn nodded and smiled then patted Cora's hand before slipping his out from beneath hers. He didn't want to be comforted. If anything, he'd rather Cora had agreed with him and even blamed him. He deserved to have his failures laid bare and to be tried and convicted in a real courthouse, but none of that was going to happen. His only penance was to have his crimes go unpunished and know that he would never be held to account in the way he believed he should be.

"So, what about you?" Finn said, forcing a smile while trying to coax Cora into talking about herself, rather than him. "A brilliant worker from Spacehaven must be in demand in the Pit?"

"I must admit, I have enjoyed my time here," Cora said, and Finn breathed a quiet sigh of relief that his gambit had worked. "They assigned me to the mid-levels, science and engineering, where I can use my skills for the betterment of the Pit and the entire human race, not just for the golds and the privileged few who go to Nimbus."

"How are your living quarters?" Finn asked. "They've got

me up in the barracks on level three. It's not quite the silk sheets and fluffy-pillows experience of my apartment in the gold sector."

"I'll bet!" Cora laughed. "They've given me an apartment on fifty-fifty, which isn't much bigger than my room in Spacehaven, but it feels like home here. I like my work and I like the people I work with." She shrugged. "It's been hard to adjust, especially when you're used to being told what to do and when to do it, every hour of the day. Here, there's more freedom. You're allowed to have ideas and even to disagree with your superiors, without being threatened with extra shift hours or a nightstick to the back of the knee. There's trust. It's an incredible feeling to be trusted."

Finn nodded and smiled along. He also knew how it felt to have trust, but unlike Cora, he also understood the consequences of breaking someone's confidence. Then a dark thought crept up on him from out of nowhere and he felt his blood run cold. If Cora had made it to Haven, then it meant Soren Driscoll had too. He sat straighter in his chair, wet his lips with the soya-based milk drink he'd selected to accompany his meal, then met Cora's eyes.

"What about Soren?" Finn asked. "I'm assuming he made it too?"

The mention of the man's name caused Cora's muscles to tense up and she wrapped her arms around her body, hugging it as if she were suddenly cold, despite the canteen being maintained at a steady seventy Fahrenheit.

"Yes, he made it," Cora said, and it didn't take a genius in reading emotions to know she wasn't happy about the fact. "The Metal who rescued us was debriefed after our landing, so they know all about him. I argued he was dangerous but was told that 'everyone gets a fresh start in the Pit', so he was admitted like everyone else, with a clean slate."

Finn sighed and rubbed the back of his neck. On the one hand, he could understand the sentiment behind Haven's policy. After all, life in Zavetgrad was hard and didn't exactly bring out the best in people. Yet he couldn't escape the fact that if it hadn't been for Soren, he wouldn't have accidentally injured Captain Victor Roth, and he wouldn't have ended up on trial. His temper had played a part, he didn't deny it, but everything traced back to Soren and he couldn't forgive the man for that.

"Where is he now?" Finn asked, hoping that he'd been assigned shit-shoveling duty, or something equally unpleasant.

"He works on fifteen, which is the communications level, where they route mail and messages to everyone in the Pit, and control radio comms too," Cora explained. "Honestly, I try my best to avoid him but sometimes I'm sent to fix things up on fifteen and he tries to be nice. It freaks me out but he's like a changed man."

"Bullshit!" Finn snort-laughed so hard he almost fell off his chair. "I don't care how sweetly he smiles at you; Soren Driscoll is not a changed man. His die was cast a long time ago and there's no changing him now."

Cora shrugged. "You might not think so, if you met him."

"I'm not meeting him," Finn hit back, without a millisecond of delay. "If I ever see that fucker again, I'll toss him into the void and find out how well he flies."

The PA system blared into life and Finn was surprised to discover that his name was being called.

"Finn Brasa, please contact your nearest communications

kiosk..." the nasally voice of the comms operator said. *"I repeat, Finn Brasa to the nearest comms kiosk. Thank you..."*

The speaker clicked off and everyone in the canteen was suddenly looking in his direction, but Finn tried to ignore their stares.

"How do I find a comms kiosk?"

"I'll show you," Cora said. She stood and offered Finn her hand, which he accepted. The former Spacehaven worker then led him out of the canteen, to another barrage of nods and hushed acknowledgments from the other diners, then guided him to a ten-by-ten-foot cabin situated on the inner walkway. An emblem of a paper envelope was embossed on the wall above the serving window.

"Finn Brasa, reporting as ordered," Finn said to the man behind the counter.

He expected to be greeted like a celebrity, but the kiosk worker simply eyed him over the top of thick-rimmed spectacles and huffed as if he were already bored of his custom.

"Look into the camera," the man said, in one long monotone drawl.

Cora pointed to the lens and Finn stared into it. There was a flash of light, which briefly blinded him.

"Place your hand here..." the man said, in the same sleepy drawl.

Finn did as he was instructed, and his palm print was scanned. The kiosk worker then switched up a gear and began tapping away at a computer, which projected lurid green symbols onto his face. A few seconds later a machine to the man's left spat out a rectangular card that looked remarkably similar to his Metalhaven ident.

"Take this," the worker said, thrusting the card at Finn. "Your presence has been requested on level one-four-four."

Finn was about to ask the man who had requested his presence and how he was supposed to reach one-four-four, but the worker had already begun serving another customer.

"All kiosk workers are like that, you'll get used to it," Cora said. It was clear that the exchange had amused her.

"It's actually nice not to be treated like a messiah for a change," Finn replied. "On the other hand, I do feel like putting my fist through his teeth."

Cora laughed then tapped the freshly printed card in his hand, which was still warm from the machine.

"To reach one-four-four, cross the bridge and enter any one of the elevators," Cora said. "Tap the number then scan your ident and the elevator will do the rest. It'll take a few minutes to get all the way down there, but it's worth it to see the core."

Cora turned to leave, but Finn grabbed her sleeve. "Hey, how do I find you again?"

Cora pointed to the comms kiosk. "You can use the kiosk to send a message or route a call but don't worry, I'll check in on you again soon."

Finn nodded then they embraced again, this time less urgently, and Cora stepped away. Finn was about to head off when this time it was Cora who delayed their parting.

"Hey, you've made mistakes, sure, but look at the good you've done too," Cora said. "Look at the hope you've sprung. You're a good man, Finn. Don't ever forget that."

Cora smiled then headed away leaving Finn lost for words and more than a little emotional. He collected his thoughts then turned toward the central pillar and began weaving himself through the traffic toward the elevators. He got as far as the bridge before discovering that someone was already there waiting for him.

"Hello Finn," said Soren Driscoll. "I was hoping to find you."

5
LIFE IS FRAGILE

"What do you want, Soren?" Finn said, resisting the urge to run at the man and knock him off his feet. "I have nothing to say to you."

Soren held up his hands and tilted his wide head down. "I'm not here for a fight, Finn, I just want to talk."

"About what?" Finn said.

Soren stepped forward and Finn clenched his fists, which made his former Metalhaven co-worker think twice about coming any closer.

"I just wanted to say that I'm glad you got out," Soren said. His amenable tone of voice was disturbingly unfamiliar. "And I wanted to show you that I'm different now."

"Is that supposed to be some kind of apology?" Finn said. "Because I didn't hear the words, 'I'm sorry', in any of that."

Soren thought for a moment, and Finn could practically hear the rusted cogs whirring in the man's brain as his old enemy struggled with the concept of humbling himself.

"I'm sorry for how things went down," Soren eventually replied, and Finn snorted a laugh and shook his head. It was exactly the sort of non-apology he'd expected from Soren. "I've made a fresh start here. I got a new job, in communications."

Soren gestured to the drab-looking work clothes he was wearing, which didn't suit his burly frame and square head. He looked like a prefect thug pretending to be a clerical worker.

"It's different to what I'm used to, but it beats manual labor, and the hours are better too." The man laughed and attempted to smile but it was crooked and unnatural, like everything else about this new Soren Driscoll.

"Bully for you, Soren," Finn said, in a mocking tone. "Now, I have somewhere else to be."

Finn started walking, taking a wide arc so that he could pass by without coming within arm's reach of the man for fear he might still lash out, but Soren shuffled back and blocked his path. Finn felt his pulse quicken and his eyes flashed with anger.

"I thought you'd be glad I was different," Soren grunted. There was more of the old bully in his manner now. "It took a lot for me to come here. The least you could do is acknowledge that."

"I know why you're here, Soren, and you can forget it," Finn said. His blood was pumping, and his patience was already worn threadbare. "You want me to forgive you and pat you on the back for your new job and new life but that's never going to happen." He aimed a finger toward the side of the bridge. "Now get the fuck out of my way."

Soren ground his teeth together and for a moment Finn thought they were going to come to blows, then the man stepped aside.

"I'm sorry it has to be this way," Soren said, waving Finn on like he was directing traffic. "But whatever you think of me, *I am* different here. I'm not the same person I was in Metalhaven."

"You can keep your excuses," Finn said, drawing level with the man. He knew he should have kept on walking, but Soren had gotten his hooks into him, and he couldn't pull himself away. "Life in Metalhaven was the same for everyone but the difference is that you chose to be an insufferable prick."

Anger flared in Soren's eyes and the man bristled but while he flexed the stubby fingers of each hand, he resisted clenching them into fists.

"I came here to say my piece, and I've said it," Soren said, showing impressive restraint. The man then offered Finn his hand. "No hard feelings?"

The invitation to shake hands was insulting enough but the added offer of no hard feelings was too much for Finn to take.

"No hard feelings?" Finn said. Without realizing it, he was advancing on Soren. "*No hard feelings?!*" Finn grabbed Soren and slammed him into barrier separating the bridge from the chasm below, using his strength to bend the man's thick back over the metal railing. "What about Khloe and Melody?" Finn yelled. "What about your own buddy, Corbin? Do you think he has no hard feelings?"

"That wasn't my fault!" Soren cried. He was struggling to free himself, but Finn's prosecutor training had made him stronger than Soren by far and the man was powerless to stop him.

"What about Owen, you fuck!" Finn roared, pushing

Soren so far over the railings that gravity was threatening to tug the man free of his grasp. "I had to watch him die! I had to taste his blood in my mouth!"

Suddenly, hands grabbed his shoulders and waist and three Haven soldiers dragged Finn away from Soren, who collapsed to the deck, trembling with fear. Finn shook off the soldiers, then stole a knife from one of the corporals, a trick he'd learned in combat training at the prosecutor barracks. He was about to switch the blade into a reverse grip and plunge it into Soren's neck, when he heard the sound of pistols being drawn and loaded, and he swiftly concealed the weapon up his sleeve.

"It's okay!" Soren said, holding up his hands to the armed soldiers. "It's just a little misunderstanding, that's all."

The soldiers lowered their weapons, but continued to watch Finn closely for his next move. If it had just been the soldiers, he might still have acted, but they weren't the only people watching. Traffic on the bridge had ground to a halt and dozens of citizens had stopped to watch the affray.

"I did what I had to do to survive," Soren said, pulling his shirt over his round belly and tucking it into the waistband of his pants. "That's all any of us can do and I won't apologize for that!" Finn still had the knife and the idea of burying it into Soren's flesh remained at the forefront of his mind, then what the man said next stopped him dead. "But if it makes a difference, then I'm sorry about Owen, and I'm sorry for my part in it."

"Violence against another person is a crime in Haven," another voice said. Finn saw that a fourth soldier had arrived; a lieutenant. The officer then turned to Soren. "Sir, do you wish to press charges?"

Soren shook his head. The old bully Finn knew from Metalhaven would have sneered and jumped at the chance to get Finn into trouble, but this Soren didn't twist the knife.

"Like I said, it's just a misunderstanding," Soren said to the officer, smiling his crooked smile at the man. "Thanks anyway, but you can go now."

The lieutenant nodded and the other soldiers holstered their weapons and stood by as Finn stormed toward the bank of elevators, adrenaline still coursing through his veins. The people on the bridge parted like iron filings repelled by a powerful magnet and Finn jumped inside the first available elevator car, causing the few other occupants who were inside to flee like rats from a sinking ship. He hammered the number one-four-four into the panel and scanned his ident while staring at the floor. He didn't want to look up in case Soren was still on the bridge, watching him, but curiosity compelled him to do so, and he was relieved to discover that his old adversary was gone.

The doors closed and the car began to descend, and with each level that slipped by, his anger began to ebb, like water draining down a plughole. On level fifteen the car stopped, and the doors opened with a tuneful ping to reveal a host of waiting travelers. Finn smiled and stepped aside to let them in, his rage no longer burning so hot it deterred others from entering. The car filled quickly, and the elevator resumed its descent only to stop again ten floors later, then after another fifteen floors, and another twenty after that. At each stop, people got out and others got in, punching new numbers into the panel, and adding more time to the journey. The delay at least gave him chance to recover his composure, and soon thoughts of Soren were pushed to the back of his mind, where they belonged.

Cora wasn't kidding when she said this would take a few minutes... Finn thought, smiling at the latest batch of embarkees, who were looking at him with a mixture of awe and reverie, like everyone else that had entered and exited the car since his journey began.

A woman and a young boy got on at floor one-ten and punched the number for the habitat level on one-three-one, which was the lowest floor anyone else had entered, besides Finn. He nodded and smiled at the woman, who had clearly recognized him and was smiling back with anxious eyes, but like everyone else she didn't speak a word. The young boy, on the other hand, was regarding him with deep curiosity and even a touch of suspicion, and the child's probing scowl was making Finn nervous.

"Are you the superhero from the bad city?" the boy asked, still scowling.

"Tobias, shush..." the woman said, but the boy ignored her.

"You look like him, mister," the boy continued, to another reprimand from his mother. "I think you are."

"I'm no superhero, kid," Finn replied. It was still a novelty to see a child, let alone speak to one. "But I am from the bad city. It's called Zavetgrad."

"I think you are a superhero," Tobias said, focusing on the aspect of Finn that most interested him. "Mom says you beat the bad people in the city and that no-one has done that for more than a million years."

"Tobias, shush!" the mother said again, smiling

apologetically at Finn. "And I said a hundred years, not a million…" she added, under her breath.

"What's your superpower?" Tobias continued, undeterred by his mother's attempts to silence him. "You must have one."

"I do," Finn said, mimicking the voice of what he imagined a superhero to sound like. "I can eat ten protein sausages in under a minute…"

The boy laughed and it was so sharp and shrill it made everyone in the elevator car jump.

"That's no superpower, even I can do that!" Tobias boasted.

"Oh yeah?" Finn said, narrowing his eyes at the child. "Then we should have a contest, and the loser has to wash the other's dirty socks for a week."

The boy chuckled and the mother also choked down a laugh.

"Are you going to stop the bad people from bombing us?" Tobias said, suddenly turning contemplative. His mother was paying very close attention now, as was everyone else in the car.

"Yes, I am," Finn said. He didn't know how he was going to do it, but he was determined to make that happen. "I'm going to do everything I can to stop the bad city from bothering us ever again."

The boy beamed a smile at him then the elevator jerked to a stop and the doors opened on one-three-one. This time, everyone got out.

"Bye!" Tobias said, waving at Finn as his mother hurried him away.

"Bye Tobias," Finn said, waving back. "I'll let you know about that eating contest."

The sound of the boy's laughter lingered even after the door had closed and the car began its final descent to level one-four-four. He found that the sound had wiped away any trace of anger and bitterness that remained after his encounter with Soren. *If anyone has a superpower, it's Tobias...* Finn thought.

More than six minutes after entering it, the elevator finally arrived at its destination, and Finn was more than ready to leave its claustrophobic four walls behind. The doors opened and he was hit by a wall of sound that physically knocked him backward a step. It was the sound of raw power, like a Nimbus rocket launching itself through the atmosphere and into space. He stepped outside and into an enormous rock cavern that looked to be a natural feature that had been further hollowed out by heavy machinery. There was a circular walkway, like the one on level three but without any kiosks and offices leading off from it, and a long bridge that led to a titanic power generator that filled over half of the space.

The generator was roughly spherical and it glowed orange like an old incandescent light bulb. A bank of turbines surrounded it, encased inside obelisk-like columns that reached from the ground of the cave to the ceiling a hundred meters above him. Steam hissed from dozens of vents, while an intricate web of conduits snaked off from the machine and disappeared into the walls. Finally, he saw Pen, standing beneath the monstrous machine on the other side of the bridge, and looking tiny in comparison. She waved and he crossed the bridge to join her, feeling the searing heat of the place seep into his bones and make him sweat from every pore.

"I don't how you can stand it," Finn said, unfastening the top three buttons of his jacket. "Even after three months in the Authority sector, I'm still more used to the cold."

"I came from Seedhaven, so heat is my natural habitat," Pen said, looking up at the vast generator. "Hundreds of farming units stacked side-by-side and one atop the other puts out almost as much heat as this majestic contraption does."

"I hadn't even thought to ask about your history," Finn said, feeling embarrassed to admit it. "For some reason, I assumed you were born in Haven."

Pen shook her head gently. "No, but I have been here for a very long time. More than twenty-five years, in fact."

"How did you get out?" Finn asked.

"The same way as most people; rescued during a trial," Pen replied. "I had been reassigned to the birthing center to act as a surrogate mother, on account of my ability to carry a child to term, but I refused. Then, when the Authority tried to force me there anyway, I fought the prefects and killed one of them. Stabbed him in the neck with a fork, as it happens." She sighed and looked distant as if reliving that moment of her past. "There was a surprising amount of blood."

"There always is," Finn said, recalling the all-too-many occasions when he'd been forced to bleed someone or deal with his own injuries. He was about to ask Pen if she'd given birth to Elara in the center when he realized that she never made it that far. "So, how do you know that Elara is your daughter?" he asked.

Pen turned away from the machine and rested against the

railings, elbows hooked over the balustrade in a casual pose that didn't match her formal suit.

"A predecessor of mine directed a Metal to infiltrate the records office in the Authority sector and transmit the genetic makeup of all workers who were born and assigned a color," Pen explained. "We've had an operative in that office ever since. The idea was that if people knew who they were connected to, at least on a DNA-level, it might help to foster a sense of community inside Haven, and the notion that we're not just a group of individuals but a family."

Finn nodded. "From what I've seen so far, it seems to have worked."

Pen half-nodded. "Yes, though it's not always good news. For many people, their biological relatives are long-dead."

Finn's head dropped and he felt another wave of sickening guilt come upon him, exacerbated by the stifling heat in the reactor room.

"And now your blood-daughter is dead too, thanks to me," Finn said. "I'm surprised you let me stay in Haven after learning that." He desperately wanted Pen to be angry at him, and throw him over the railings, like he'd almost done to Soren, but she barely batted an eyelid.

"This cavern may be as deep as the Pits of hell but if you've come looking for my condemnation, then I'm sorry to disappoint you," Pen replied. "In truth, I barely knew Elara. We've conversed only four or five times, and for no more than a few minutes. I had hoped to meet her one day, but we were little more than strangers to one another."

Despite what she'd said, Pen's sadness and regret at never meeting her daughter was obvious. This should have been reason enough for her to blame Finn for leaving Elara behind, but the principal either hid her bitterness well, or had learned not to succumb to such dark emotions.

"I also doubt that giving you my forgiveness will stop you from hating yourself, but you have it all the same," Pen added, squeezing Finn's hand. He wanted to pull it away, but he didn't for fear of insulting her.

"I'm not looking for forgiveness, from you or from anyone else," Finn said, gently coaxing his hand from underneath Pen's. "I just want to help, so that others don't have to lose people, like we have."

Pen nodded and smiled, then gestured to the generator, which continued to beat like a giant heart, filling the cavern with light and heat.

"It took the founder Metals years to figure out how this generator worked," Pen said, placing the palm of her hand onto a part of the machine's base, like she was trying to soothe an anxious stallion. "It wasn't until the first people from Spacehaven arrived here that its function was truly understood, and the Pit could be brought back to life. Without this, everyone dies."

"You want me to understand how fragile Haven is," Finn said, guessing the reason why Pen wanted him to see the cavern. "You're trying to show me how easily things could collapse, if we don't all play our chosen part, my part being that of the heroic star of Haven's propaganda material."

Pen shrugged and cocked her head to one side, looking like a thief caught in the act.

"It's true what they say about you double-fives," Pen said, playfully. "You are smart."

"I also don't need to be reminded of how fragile life is," Finn said. He understood Pen's motives but didn't appreciate the attempt to manipulate him. "Like I told you, I'm here to help, and I'll help in whatever way will speed the downfall of the Authority, even if that means the gun in my hand is a prop instead of the real thing."

Pen bowed her head to him, a gracious gesture that highlighted her regret for playing mind games with him, instead of just speaking plainly. Then the elevator car pinged, and the doors began to grind open.

"That's strange," Pen said, pushing away from the banister. "No-one besides you and I are cleared to be down here today."

Finn's senses shot to high-alert, and he allowed the knife he still had concealed in his sleeve to slide down into his hand. A man walked out of the elevator, dressed in combat fatigues like Finn, and marched toward them. Instinctively, Finn positioned himself between the intruder and the principal and hid the knife behind his body.

"Who are you?" Finn shouted the demand to the new arrival. "You're not supposed to be down here. Explain yourself!"

The soldier raised a pistol and Finn twisted his body and pulled Pen to the ground as shots rang out and ricocheted off the metal barrier lining each side of the bridge. A bullet grazed past his shoulder, drawing blood, but Pen was safe and soon the attacker's weapon had clicked empty. Finn heard the tell-tale sound of the magazine being released but he wasn't going to allow the soldier to load another. Springing up, he threw the knife at the man with the precision of a sharpshooter and buried the blade deep into his left eye socket. The soldier went down, pistol skidding across the stone floor, and Finn raced to the body. Despite the horrific injury, the man was still alive.

"Who are you?" Finn barked, grabbing the handle of the knife and threatening to push it into the man's brain. "Answer me!"

"Traitor scum!" the soldier hissed. "Juniper sends her regards."

Electricity crackled through the blade of the knife and Finn was jolted clear. Then the smell of burned flesh filled his nostrils and when he looked back at the soldier, the man's face and head was burned blacker than the inky stone in the cave.

6
INFILTRATORS

General Riley bustled into the primary medical center on level seven and drew the curtain around the bay containing the body of the dead insurgent, yanking it so hard he almost pulled it off its fixings. Pen was standing over the body, peering into the infiltrator's burned-out eyes, while Finn watched from the corner, his breath still labored from the effort of hauling the corpse from level one-four-four to the medical center.

"How the hell did this man get inside the reactor level?" Pen said, showing an uncharacteristic flash of anger. "And who is he? I need answers, General."

Another man might have reacted defensively to the implication that the infiltrator's presence on the station was his fault, but General Riley didn't make excuses for himself or pass the buck.

"I have my team working on it, ma'am, but the honest answer is we don't know," Riley said. "We've suspected that agents from Zavetgrad had infiltrated the Pit for some time, but this is the first direct evidence."

"Why now?" Finn asked. "If this agent and others have been here for weeks or months already, then why haven't they tried to kill Pen sooner?"

"I don't believe that the principal was the intended target of this attack," Riley grunted, ominously.

It took a moment for Finn to realize the implication of the general's words.

"Will is right, it makes more sense for them to kill you," Pen said, concurring with her general. "While assassinating me or even the general might inconvenience operations in the Pit for a time, the truth is that neither of us is irreplaceable." She looked at Finn with her intense green eyes, so reminiscent of Elara. "You, however, are a direct threat to the Authority and it makes sense that they would try to eliminate that threat as soon as possible."

"This could be a prelude to something bigger," Riley added. "I already have the Pit on full security alert, but we should be prepared for a large-scale assault."

Pen nodded. "In the meantime, we need to find out everything we can about our dead assassin, especially how we might recognize others like him."

A man wearing a traditional white lab coat pulled back the curtain and bustled inside. His entrance was so sudden that Riley's instinct was to draw his weapon, and Finn figured the doctor was lucky not to have been shot.

"Doctor Jensen, I need to understand how this man died, and I need to know now," Pen said, as the physician began a hurried physical examination of the body.

"Who is he?" the doctor asked, while pulling a scanner over the top of the dead operative's head and activating it. Energy surged through the device, which hummed like a laser powering up. "These burns appear to have originated on the inside."

"Just tell us what we need to know, doctor," Riley cut in. The general wasn't keen to divulge any more information than he considered absolutely necessary. "This is a matter of Haven security and requires the utmost discretion."

The doctor scowled at Riley then pulled a pair of rimless spectacles from his coat pocket, flipping open the arms and sliding them onto his face in a single fluid motion. Pen backed away from the bed to allow the doctor to work, though General Riley remained by Jenson's side, arms folded, scrutinizing every aspect of the man's work.

"Where did you get a doctor from?" Finn asked as Pen drew by his side. "The only doctors I've ever met were golds."

"Doctor Jenson is a defector," Pen explained. "He was assigned to a gene bank in Volthaven but began refusing orders to force seed and egg extractions from workers. Had he been a regular red he would have been sent to trial; instead, he was placed under house arrest and threatened with execution if his disobedience continued. We got to him first."

"I guess that makes him pretty valuable around here," Finn said, figuring that looking after the health of more than twelve-thousand residents would present a serious challenge.

"He is, though we've also trained our own doctors, including robot medics," Pen replied. "The Pit's archives contained a treasure-trove of information from the old world, including a virtual reality medical school, run by an algorithm that adapts to the skills of each student and the needs of the Pit." Pen smiled at him. "You can think of it as an advanced version of the illegal data device that you kept in your Metalhaven apartment."

As if to reinforce her point, a modified foreman-class robot swept past the curtain and began assisting Doctor Jenson, still under the watchful gaze of General Riley.

"I still can't get used to seeing those things working for us, rather than against us," Finn said. The mere sight of a foreman put him on the defensive.

"I have found the cause of death," Doctor Jenson announced, and Finn and Pen instinctively moved to the bedside. The doctor activated a screen on the wall, which showed a scan of the dead man's head and brain. Finn didn't need to be a doctor to understand there was a lot of damage. "A device was implanted into this man's temporal lobe that triggered a massive electrical shock."

"It's a kill switch," Riley grunted. "Was it self-activated?"

Jenson shook his head. "I believe the trigger mechanism was automatic. The temporal lobe is responsible for processing sensory input, amongst other things, and I believe the device was monitoring this man's visual and auditory senses. It could have perhaps detected that the operative had been compromised, and triggered the 'kill switch', as the general so eloquently put it."

"Life and death, decided by an algorithm," Riley commented. "That makes perfect sense for the Authority. The Regents trust no-one, not even their own special prefects."

An officer wearing combat fatigues appeared at the edge of the curtain. Finn recognized the man as the Lieutenant who had shown him to his quarters the night before. His name was Alex Thornfield.

"Sir, we have incoming skycars from Zavetgrad," Thornfield said in the calm and professional manner of a soldier. "We're detecting eight vehicles, already over Disko Island and approaching fast."

"Why didn't we detect them sooner?" Riley answered. He was irritated, but that irritation was not directed at Lieutenant Riley specifically, as the bearer of the bad news.

"They approached low, practically skimming the surface," Thornfield said. "They are special prefect skycars, matching a troop-transport configuration."

"An invasion force," Riley said, tightening his grip around the handle of his sidearm. "Launch our quick reaction alert skycars and arm all air defenses. I will join you in operations momentarily."

The lieutenant acknowledged the order and hurried away, then Riley directed his intimidating gaze toward Doctor Jenson.

"I need a way to detect these enemy agents, doctor," Riley said, and his insistent tone made Jenson stand straighter. "The very survival of the Pit depends on us rooting out these traitors before they can do any more damage."

"I will get right to work, General," the doctor replied.

To his credit, Finn thought that Jenson didn't appear intimidated by the task, though as a former gene bank physician, he would have been used to dealing with prefects. And prefects were not subtle in their methods of getting what they wanted.

"Ma'am, if you'll follow me," Riley grunted. He then looked at Finn. "And you too, hero. We might be able to use your help."

The general threw back the curtain and marched toward the exit, making everyone in the medical center jump with fright as he stormed through the facility like a hurricane on course to make landfall. Finn and Pen had to jog to catch up, by which point Riley was already inside an elevator, holding open the doors for them. There were others waiting outside, their expressions a mixture of caution and respect, well aware that the general's focused determination demanded an unobstructed path.

Finn waited for Pen to enter first then slid through the door, which closed so fast it almost trapped his jacket. Riley used his identification card to override the controls and send the car to level one without stopping, at a rate of speed that felt frankly reckless. The doors pinged open, and Riley led the way again, sweeping through the doors of the operation center like a force of nature.

"Report!" Riley called out, and the powerful command snapped everyone in the room to attention, whether they were military or civilian.

"Sir, the hangar doors are jammed, and we have been unable to launch our QRA skycars," Lieutenant Thornfield said. "It appears that someone has manually blocked the doors."

"Well, get them open!" Riley barked.

"I have a team on it, sir, but they estimate thirty minutes at the very least to clear the obstruction," Thornfield replied. The general looked ready to erupt but the officer wasn't finished with his report. "And we have another problem, sir. The anti-aircraft batteries are not responding."

Riley turned toward the AA operator's station, chested puffed out and face flushed with anger.

"Sergeant, explain yourself!" Riley barked. "Bring the air defenses online at once!"

The sergeant, a man in his late twenties with an angular

face and blue eyes stood up and faced the general. "I have disabled the air defenses, and they will remain offline." The man spoke to Riley sharply and without the respect his rank demanded.

"What do you mean by that, man?" Riley said, stepping toward the operator's station. "I gave you a command and you will obey it!"

The sergeant pulled open his jacket to reveal a belt lined with explosive charges. Finn recognized them at once because similar charges were used in Metalhaven and Stonehaven to clear unsalvageable wreckage and demolish old structures that were on the verge of collapse.

"Zavetgrad eternal!" the sergeant cried, shouting the resounding declaration at the top of his lungs.

Riley's face twisted with rage, and the general aimed his pistol at the infiltrator, but the belt exploded before a shot could be fired. At the same time, Lieutenant Thornfield had thrown himself at his superior officer and tackled him to the ground, while Finn had ducked and protected Pen, using his own body as a shield. The operations room filled with choking, black smoke but Finn forced his eyes open and looked toward the AA operator's station. It had been utterly destroyed, taking six surrounding stations with it. General Riley was on the ground, alongside Thornfield, who had shrapnel embedded into his arms and back, though the man was conscious and struggling to his feet.

"Report!" Riley cried, though Finn barely made out the word through the ringing in his ears. "All stations, report!"

Slowly, the accounts were relayed, one by one. Six people lay dead, not including the infiltrator who had detonated the suicide bomb, and the AA control station, along with a number of secondary consoles, were wrecked. There were a dozen more casualties, including Thornfield, the general and Finn himself, who had also taken shrapnel wounds, but Finn had suffered far worse, and his determination was not diminished.

"Medical teams to operations at once," Pen called out, directing the order to the civilian crews on the far side of the room, away from the epicenter of the blast. "Emergency lockdown. As of this moment, the Pit is on a disaster footing."

"Sir, pressure sensors on the surface suggest that the enemy skycars have landed," Thornfield called out. Despite his injuries and the fact that he was bleeding heavily from cuts to his back and head, the man had refused medical attention. "Emergency exit hatch one alpha has been blown. Special prefects will be entering the Pit."

If Riley had looked furious before, he was now on the verge of going thermonuclear.

"Lieutenant, order all defense forces to the garage, and get the principal to safety," Riley boomed. "I will lead the defense of the Pit, personally."

Thornfield acknowledged the order and began speaking into a microphone at one of the control stations. Finn could hear the officer's voice echoing around the Pit, then all of a sudden his words fell silent.

"General, all internal communications just went offline," a corporal at another station announced. "We are unable to contact any other level."

Communications... Finn thought, his stomach knotting at the thought of what might have just happened. *Soren works in communications...*

"Are our security cameras still online?" Pen said, hustling to the general's side, despite Thornfield's attempts to usher her away.

"Yes, ma'am," the operator replied.

"Show me level fifteen," Pen ordered.

The operator worked his station and the communications center was displayed on the surviving monitors. Workers were on their knees with their hands on their heads, held at gunpoint by others also wearing civilian clothing.

"Soren..." Finn said out loud, the words tasting bitter on his tongue.

"Lieutenant, send a runner to fifteen and inform the corporal in command of the situation,"

Riley said. Despite the enormous setbacks, the man had kept his head. "Then get the principal to a safe house."

"General, let me deal with the invaders in the comms room," Finn said, stepping forward. If Soren was involved, then he would deal with his rival once and for all. "I have more combat training and experience than any of your soldiers. It makes sense for me to go."

Riley considered refuting Finn's assertion, but it would have been mere bravado, and in the end the general agreed.

"Report to Corporal Pela Casteel on level fifteen," Riley said. Finn glanced at Pen, and it was clear she disagreed with the order, but she also knew there was no time for debate. "Tell her I sent you and take this."

Riley tossed his identification card to Finn, and he caught it cleanly with his off hand. Finn turned to leave but the general was not done.

"And hero..." Riley said. Finn met the man's eyes. "Don't die or the principal will have my balls on the block."

Finn nodded and ran outside, heading directly for the bank of elevators in the central column. However, he wasn't going to level fifteen just yet. First, he needed to stop by his quarters on level three. If he was going to fight, then he needed his prosecutor armor and weapons.

7
ZAVETGRAD ETERNAL

Finn raced to his quarters, adrenaline helping to focus his mind and remember the directions without getting lost in the Pit's maze of corridors. He slammed his ident to the lock panel then turned the handle and burst inside, scaring Scraps, and causing the little robot to fall off the desk, where he'd been recharging.

"What wrong?!" Scraps cried, using his rotors to climb off the floor and hover in front of Finn. "Bad men back?"

"Yes, pal, we've got special prefects trying to fight their way inside," Finn said, rushing to his bedroom compartment and finding his armor neatly laid-out on the blankets, alongside his freshly laundered prosecutor training uniform. "I need to get suited-up, can you help me?"

Scraps nodded and the robot began collecting sections of his armor, while Finn stripped off his combat fatigues and pulled his old uniform back on. The prosecutor base-layer had been specifically designed so that his armor panels would attach via magnetism. He recalled how little time it had taken

Elara to secure the panels during his confirmation ceremony, prior to the test-trial, and hoped it would be as simple the second time.

"Okay, I'm ready," Finn said, standing with his arms out to his side and his legs shoulder-width apart.

Scraps began buzzing around him and in less than a minute, armored panels had snapped into place on his legs and shoulders. Finn grabbed the chest plate and pressed it into place, before helping scraps with the back armor, which was almost too heavy for the little robot to lift.

"I wish my laser cannon still worked," Finn said, finding his ink-black baseball bat resting next to the bed and attaching it to his back scabbard, also using magnets. "The special prefect I fought on level one-four-four was armed with a pistol and I don't fancy bringing a club to a gunfight."

"Scraps already fixed!" the robot said, pointing to the desk. In addition to recharging his battery, the robot had been busy repairing Finn's laser. "Scraps got bored," he added, apologetically, as if he'd done something wrong.

"Well done, pal," Finn said, patting the robot. "What would I do without you, eh?"

Scraps giggled then flew over to the laser cannon and made some final adjustments. The weapon's power meter then flashed into life and the bars lit up in sequence until it showed one-hundred-percent charge.

"I never thought I'd be using this again so soon," Finn said, taking the weapon and fixing it to the magnetic holster on his hip.

He headed toward the door but caught his reflection in the mirror, which made him stop and do a double take. The sight of Finn dressed in full prosecutor armor and equipped with an advanced laser cannon was enough even to scare himself. The design of his gear had been styled loosely on samurai armor, but Finn had likened himself more to a Ronin, a warrior who served no lord or master. This time, it was different. This time, Finn was fighting for Haven as one of those who had been freed from the Authority's oppressive regime. Now, the prefects of Zavetgrad were invading the Pit in force, with the goal of destroying everything the Metals had built over the last hundred and twenty years. He wasn't going to allow that to happen, not while he drew breath.

Finn pulled open the door, which had rebounded shut after he'd burst through it, then discovered that Scraps was hovering just behind his shoulder.

"No, pal, I need you to stay here, where it's safe," Finn said, turning around and barring the robot's exit. "It's too dangerous out there. I don't want you to get hurt."

Scraps pressed his little metal hands to his hips and scowled at Finn.

"Scraps no want Finn hurt. But Finn go anyway!" the robot said, sternly. Scraps then held up a finger in anticipation of making another astute point. "Also, Scraps can fix comms. Scraps clever!"

Finn wanted to argue but he couldn't deny the robot's logic, or the fact that he wouldn't even be alive without his help.

"Fine, but stay out of harm's way," Finn said, wagging a finger right back at his mechanical buddy. "I don't want to have to bang you back together and re-do your paint job again."

Scraps nodded. "Okay-kay!" the robot replied, switching from obstinate to cheerful in the blink of an eye. "Oh, wait-wait!"

"Wait for what?" Finn said, as Scraps zoomed back into the room. "We don't have much time, pal." Scraps returned a moment later and dropped a device into Finn's hand, but he had no idea what it was.

"Here, use-use!" Scraps said, pointing to his ear hole. "Earpiece... Scraps and Finn can talk-talk!"

Finn nodded then pressed the communications device into his ear and wiggled it until it fit snugly. "Can you hear me?" he said, turning the earpiece toward Scraps.

"Yes-yes! Finn right in front of me," Scraps said, throwing his arms out wide.

"No, I mean can you hear me through this thing," Finn said, shaking his head at the robot.

"Oh! Yes-yes!" Scraps answered then giggled. "Sorry-sorry." The robot zoomed over Finn's shoulder and into the corridor outside, stopping about ten meters away. "Testing-testing, one-two-three!"

Scraps' voice in his ear was so loud it made Finn jump and he ended up banging his head on the frame of the door. "You might need to turn the volume down a touch," he said, wincing and rubbing his temples. His eyes were watering.

"Okay now?" Scraps said, and the voice was clear in Finn's head.

"Perfect," Finn said, rubbing the wetness from his eyes. "Now, let's go. We need to reach the primary comms room on level fifteen."

Scraps nodded. "Follow! Scraps knows the way," the

robot said, swiveling in mid-air then speeding away along the corridor.

Finn chased after the robot and caught up with him on the bridge leading to the central pillar. The Pit was on alert status so the walkway and bridge were clear, allowing him to race toward the nearest elevator without having to push through the crowds that would normally be gathered outside. The rattle of gunfire was reverberating around the void and Finn glanced over the railings, just about able to make out the outlines of soldiers advancing along the inner walkway on level fifteen.

"Quick-quick!" Scraps called out, waving Finn over from inside an empty car.

Finn jumped through the doors, pressed General Riley's ident card to the pad and punched in the number for level fifteen. Without the need to stop every two or three floors, the journey was swift and soon Finn was running toward the primary comms room, this time following the sound of gunfire rather than his robot buddy.

Could this really all be down to Soren? Finn thought, as his armored body cut through the humid air circulating from the reactor cave far below them. *It can't be a coincidence that comms was taken over just after he started working there...*

Cylindrical pillars wide enough to hide a body behind were dotted around the walkway, holding up the level above them, and Finn used the structures to work his way toward the comms room, wary of catching a stray bullet. The entirety of level fifteen was dedicated to communications, either radio, digital or physical, but the primary comms room was the control center that coordinated it all, and Finn could see it was under siege. A group of men and women in Haven military uniforms and civilian clothes were guarding the entrance, all armed with pistols, while a squad of soldiers in combat fatigues were pinned down behind kiosks and pillars twenty meters away.

"Scraps, go high and be my eyes in the sky," Finn said, spotting a cluster of four soldiers behind a kiosk a short dash away.

"Roger-roger!" Scraps said, saluting then zooming over the barrier surrounding the walkway and hovering over the void space, where he could get a clear look at the infiltrators.

"Scraps sees ten," the robot reported through Finn's earpiece. "And one soldier on knees. Corporal stripes."

Finn cursed under his breath. Riley had told him to find Corporal Casteel, who was in charge of the level, but if Scraps was right then it was likely she'd already been captured.

"Got it, pal, keep me updated, but stay out of the line of fire," Finn replied.

The robot acknowledged him then Finn darted to the kiosk, startling the four soldiers who were huddled behind it, as bullets pinged off the metal panels and ricocheted off the nearby pillars like pinballs. For a moment, Finn thought that the soldier's weapons were going to be turned on him when they saw his armor then recognized his face.

"Am I glad to see you," said one of the soldiers, who appeared to be in charge. "They have us pinned down. We can't even poke a finger out of cover without it being shot off."

"I'm looking for Corporal Casteel," Finn said.

"They have her as a hostage," the soldier replied,

confirming Finn's suspicions. "I'm Private Benson, and unfortunately, I'm in charge."

"I see ten guarding the door to the comms room, but do you know how many others are inside?" Finn asked. Riley would have probably given the private an earbashing for his lackluster attitude to command, but Finn wasn't a soldier, and the man wasn't his responsibility.

"I'm not sure, maybe another dozen, who knows?" Benson said, shrugging. "I was in the comms room when some guy pulled a gun and shot four workers dead. The bastard didn't even blink."

"A soldier shot these people?" Finn asked.

"Nah, it was just some regular dude, working at a comms station," Benson replied, and Finn cursed Soren's name again. "After that, it all went to shit. Our guys turned on us and shot a bunch more dead, and I barely got out before they sealed the door." Benson cursed and shook his head. "Half of our damned security detail turned against us; men and women I'd known for years in some cases. We tried to fight our way back in, but they kicked our asses, and I've already lost six of the people we had left."

"Scraps, how many soldiers are left fighting for us?" Finn said, pressing his finger to the comms device to tighten the seal around the earpiece.

"Six-six," Scraps replied. "Four with Finn. Two behind pillars."

"Who the hell are you talking to?" Benson said but Finn ignored him.

"Look, private, an army of special prefects are fighting their way into the Pit as we speak, so we have to retake that control room and let other squads know what's coming,"

Finn said. The mere mention of special prefects made the soldier shudder as if someone had walked over his grave. "I'll handle those assholes guarding the door, but I need to know you have my back."

Benson scowled at him. "You, by yourself?"

"With you backing me up, yes," Finn said, annoyed that Benson had missed out his part. "I can hit them hard and take down three, maybe four, but if you're not following me, guns firing, then I'm dead."

Benson nodded. "You got it, Redeemer, we're with you."

If Finn had been uncertain of the power his name held then the look on Benson's face, and the faces of the other three soldiers, wiped any such doubts away. From being pinned down and rudderless in the face of an overwhelming force, the soldiers of Haven were now prepared to charge into combat at his side. It was a stark reminder of his importance as a figurehead of the rebellion.

"Buddy, I'm going in," Finn said, speaking to his robotic observer. "I'm counting on you to help me avoid a bullet."

"Roger-roger!" Scraps said. "Scraps guide Finn!"

"Ready?" Finn said, turning to Benson.

"Yes, sir," the soldier replied.

Finn almost corrected him since he wasn't an officer any more than he was a gold but let it slide. Drawing the laser cannon from its magnetic holster, Finn looked toward Scraps, hovering in the distance, and the robot gave him the signal to move. Nine-weeks of intense combat training had furnished Finn with the skills, speed, and fitness to move like the wind, and he reached the next pillar before the infiltrators had even seen him coming. Gunfire filled the walkway, but Finn waited behind cover, knowing that the pistols only had maybe seventeen rounds before they would need reloading.

"Go-go!" Scraps called.

Finn moved out, running directly at the comms room and aiming his cannon at the agents of the Authority, who were scrambling to reload. He opened fire, burning neat and perfectly aimed holes into the chests of three infiltrators before ducking behind another pillar. To his rear, Benson and the other soldiers were also advancing, blanketing the enemy with shots.

"Go-go!" Scraps said again, and Finn moved out without hesitation, trusting his robot with his life without even a second thought.

His laser fizzed again and again, and two more spies fell. Then Benson took a hit and went down but his squad stayed true to their word and didn't slow their attack, killing two more spies and leaving only three standing. Finn hesitated, considering running to Benson's aid, but the man shook his head and waved him on.

"I'm okay!" Benson called out, clutching the wound to his shoulder. "Kick their asses!"

Finn didn't need telling twice. He holstered his laser cannon and drew the baseball bat from its magnetic back scabbard, gripping it tightly and waiting for the word to move.

"Go-go!" Scraps yelled, his little voice urgent but not afraid.

Finn darted out of cover and charged into the enemy position like a storm cloud rolling across mountains and bringing with it the full force of nature's fury. He swung the bat and the sound of metal on bone rang out louder than any gunshot. One of the spies drew a bead on him but he smacked the pistol out of the spy's hand, breaking knuckles and fingers and leaving the man screeching in pain. Then a shot was fired, and Finn felt the thump of speeding metal strike his chest, but his prosecutor armor was equal to the task. He jabbed the bat into the infiltrator's gut, bending him double, then brought it down sharply across the back of the spy's neck, like an executioner's axe, knocking the man out cold.

"Clear!" Finn yelled and the other soldiers roared their appreciation, like they were part of the crowd at a trial, cheering for their favorite prosecutors as they made a kill inside the crucible.

"Who are you?" the woman with corporal stripes asked. She was still on her knees, hands bound behind her back.

"General Riley sent me," Finn said, skirting the topic of his celebrity identity. "Are you Corporal Casteel?" he added, using his knife to cut the woman's bonds.

"Yes," Casteel replied, still shellshocked.

"We need to get in there," Finn said. He held up Riley's identification card. "This should override the door. Then we can storm the comms room and get back control. Special prefects are already inside the Pit, so we don't have time to waste."

Casteel nodded then took the card from Finn's hand. The other soldiers arrived, including Benson, who was being helped by his squadmates.

"Redeemer and I will move in first then the rest of you follow," Casteel said, taking charge of the situation. Finn was impressed with how easily she'd shrugged off her ordeal. "Benson, you're hurt, so stay back."

"I can still fight," Benson said, brandishing his pistol as if to make that point. "I want to finish this."

"Shouldn't we all storm the room at once?" Finn asked, uncertain as to why Casteel was suggesting only the two of them enter. "We'd have a better chance of taking them by surprise."

Casteel shook her head. "We don't know how many infiltrators are inside, or how many hostages they've taken. If we storm in all guns blazing, we risk killing innocents and causing too much collateral damage."

Finn scowled at the corporal but nodded his ascent. He didn't agree but he deferred to her judgement. Despite Benson calling him, 'sir', as if he were the officer in charge, it was actually Casteel who was in command. The corporal picked up a weapon from the floor, checked the magazine then moved to the left side of the door, Riley's ident card in hand. Finn moved to the other side and the rest of the soldiers took cover a few meters back, waiting for the order to begin the assault.

"On three..." Casteel said.

She counted down but the "one" was silent then she pressed the ident to the door and it juddered open just enough for her and Finn to enter. Casteel ran in first, weapon raised, and Finn followed, cannon charged and ready.

"Zavetgrad Eternal!"

Finn slid to a stop, heart thumping in his chest. The Authority's rallying cry hadn't been shouted by one of the infiltrators inside the comms room but by Corporal Casteel herself. The woman slammed Riley's ident against the inner lock panel and the doors thudded shut again, trapping Benson and the others outside. Finn pointed his laser cannon at the corporal then a dozen pistols were aimed at him, and he knew it was futile to resist.

"Stand down, I have him!" Casteel ordered as Finn lowered his weapon. The turncoat then smiled at Finn and waved General Riley's identification card at him. "Thank you for this, Traitor of Zavetgrad," the woman sneered. "It will make infiltrating the rest of the Pit so much easier."

8

CORPORAL CASTEEL

Finn scanned his eyes around the comms room, spotting four soldiers in Haven military fatigues that were holding the room hostage at gunpoint, and a man in regular clothes who also appeared to be with them. To Finn's surprise, that man wasn't Soren Driscoll. Instead, the spy was a thin and severe-looking man who wore a Spacehaven patch on the left shoulder of his suit jacket, though the look of disdain on the man's face gave him away as a gold from the Authority sector. Finn had seen that same look all too many times before and could recognize it a mile off.

"Sir, communications have been contained, as planned," the thin-faced man said. He was addressing Casteel, who now appeared to be the most senior Authority agent in the room.

"Good, keep everything locked down," Casteel said. "The traitor of Metalhaven forced me to reveal myself, and we need to adapt our plan."

Casteel's attention switched to one of the workers and Finn suddenly realized that the spy was looking at Soren Driscoll. His old enemy was on his knees in front of his console, hands on his head, the same as the twenty other comms workers in the room. Soren glanced at him, and Finn saw dried blood streaked down the man's face from an ugly cut above his right eye. Soren looked madder than a bottle of wasps but for once the man's ire was not directed at Finn but at the infiltrators who had detained and injured him.

"Toss that away," Casteel said to Finn, using the barrel of her pistol to point at his laser cannon. "And don't try anything foolish, or I'll start killing hostages."

"Don't pretend that you're not going to kill them, anyway," Finn said, tossing his laser weapon behind one of the comms consoles. "That's why you're here, isn't it? To wipe us all out?"

Casteel's smile reminded him of the sadistic prefects from Metalhaven and he wanted to laser the smug expression right off her face.

"Our job here is simply to ensure communications stay offline, but I had hoped to remain under cover," Casteel said, refusing to directly answer Finn's question about the fate of the Pit, though her silence on the topic spoke volumes. "My plan was to fight and free myself so that I could join General Riley's little band of rebels." She shrugged. "I'd have loved to put a bullet in the head of that pompous oaf, but the traitor of Metalhaven will have to do instead."

"You'd fight and even kill your own people, just to get a shot at the general?" Finn asked.

"Of course," Casteel said, with contempt. "Unlike you, I'm a patriot, *Prosecutor Brasa*, and I'm willing to sacrifice anything for the one, true nation of Zavetgrad!"

Finn remembered the attacker in the reactor room and how his brain-bomb had detonated the moment the man was compromised, and he realized something about the infiltrators. They had all come to Haven accepting it was a one-way trip. They were zealots and fanatics who were willing to lay down their lives for the Authority, which meant Finn had to tread carefully. People who weren't afraid to die couldn't be bargained with, which meant the only way out was to kill them first.

Finn then caught movement in the corner of his eye and spotted Scraps lurking behind one of the comms consoles. *He must have flown in while the door was open, and no-one saw him...* Finn thought. Then to his horror he realized that Soren had seen Scraps too and fear gripped him. He was terrified that the former Metalhaven worker would act like his old self, and sell Finn out to the Authority to save his own skin.

"What are you looking at, traitor?" Casteel said. Finn's eyes snapped back to the corporal, and he worried that he'd given Scraps away. Casteel ducked and weaved her head, searching the area where Scraps had been hiding, but the robot had slipped out of sight. "I warned you, no tricks, or people will start dying."

Casteel took a step toward his robot's hiding place and Finn knew his chance to act was slipping away. He braced himself, ready to charge Casteel in the hope he could subdue the corporal and the other soldiers before people started dying, when Soren spoke up.

"He was looking at me, you dumb gold bitch," Soren grunted.

Casteel's hand flew and Soren was knocked to the floor by a savage pistol whip that opened the wound above his eye and caused fresh blood to pour down the man's face.

"How dare you speak to me like that?" Casteel snarled,

dropping her knee onto Soren's neck, and restricting the blood supply to his brain. She forced the barrel of her pistol into Soren's mouth and for a heart-stopping moment, Finn thought she was going to pull the trigger. "Wait, you two know each other?" Casteel added.

"Me and Finn go way back, don't we, pussy?" Soren said, mumbling because of the cold steel in his mouth.

Casteel looked first at Finn then back at Soren and her eyes widened with surprise. "You two were in the same trial," the corporal said, beaming at them both. "I thought I recognized you."

"Do you want an autograph or something?" Soren grunted. "Fucking golds..."

Casteel struck him again with the frame of her pistol and Soren was barely able to cling onto consciousness. Standing up, Casteel wiped the drool from the barrel of her weapon onto Soren's shirt then lazily aimed it at Finn instead.

"Maybe, I'll bring you both back to Zavetgrad," Casteel said, standing over Soren. "Two traitors from Metalhaven, united again to face the Authority's righteous judgement."

Soren used his sleeve to mop blood from the fresh cut to his head then glowered at Casteel with resentful eyes. It was the sort of look that invited another beating, but the spy was still too preoccupied with Finn to bother with Soren. Finn then grasped what Soren had done, and the thought was as unsettling as the notion of being paraded through Zavetgrad like a Roman triumph. Soren's distraction had prevented Scraps from being seen, and as wild as it seemed, Finn wondered whether Soren had helped him on purpose.

"So, what happens now, Casteel?" Finn asked. Soren's distraction, intentional or otherwise, had allowed Scraps to reach his laser cannon, and he needed to give the robot time to develop whatever plan his Foreman Logic Processor had hatched. "You've obviously been inside Haven for some time, so why attack now?"

"Don't play coy, traitor, you know why," Casteel said, marching around the room and causing each worker she passed to flinch and recoil from her. "Your little broadcast caused an almighty stink, but the civil unrest will end once we drag you naked through every work sector in Zavetgrad. Then everyone will see what happens when you defy the Authority."

Finn chanced another look toward Scraps and the robot had picked up the laser weapon but was struggling to aim it; it was almost as big as he was. Soren had seen Scraps too, but the man made no effort to sound the alarm.

"There will be mass publics hangings, of course," Casteel continued, still parading around the comms room, regaling her captive audience with gory details of the Authority's planned reprisals. "And the regents of each sector will put on a series of special trials to execute the collaborators and give back to those who refused to take up arms against their own nation." Casteel stopped in front of a worker and grabbed the woman's chin, forcing the terrified captive to look into her eyes. "And we'll be giving away some of the most generous prize packages ever, including the fabled 'week off work'," Casteel added, before laughing. "We give with one hand and take with the other. It's a strategy that's worked for more than two centuries and it will continue to work for centuries to come. Your rebellion will die, just as the first rebellion died, and everyone in this pit will burn."

Soren was looking at Finn, trying to draw his attention to

Scraps. Casteel was still distracted tormenting the female worker, and Finn took a chance to look. Scraps was sitting down, laser cannon propped up on the floor and supported by his little legs, but while the robot's finger was on the trigger, the weapon was aimed into empty space. Scraps didn't have the strength to lift it, which meant Finn had to bring Casteel into its line of fire instead.

"From what I saw in operations, your invasion force won't get far," Finn said, walking toward Casteel and into what he hoped was the projected path of the laser cannon. "You may as well trigger that little bomb in your brain now, because it will be more merciful than what I'll do to you, once your plan falls apart."

Casteel's muscles tensed up as Finn continued to walk toward her. Then the four infiltrator soldiers turned their weapons on him instead of the hostages, but the corporal stood them down, harshly. Finn had offered a challenge and, as a proud gold, Casteel wouldn't stand for being disrespected by a lowly chrome.

"If you weren't more valuable alive then I would do what the prosecutors in your trial failed to achieve, and cut you down to size," Casteel said.

"Try it," Finn replied, casually. "I'll even give you the first punch."

Casteel and the soldiers laughed but Finn knew the corporal had taken the bait.

"We only need you alive, not undamaged," Casteel said, marching toward Finn wearing a hard expression that foretold of violence. "And maybe a broken jaw and a few missing teeth will finally shut you up," the corporal added, bitterly.

The civilian infiltrator wearing the Spacehaven patch seemed anxious and the man blocked Casteel's path.

"Sir, he's trying to rile you," the thin man said. "Our orders are to contain this facility, nothing more."

"I know our orders!" Casteel snarled, shoving her co-conspirator aside. "But this false gold needs to be taught a lesson."

Finn stood his ground and didn't try to block when Casteel lashed him around the side of the head with the frame of her pistol. He staggered back and dropped to one knee, glancing to where Scraps was hidden, but Casteel still wasn't in the line of fire, so he fought the pain and pushed himself up.

"Is that all you've got?" Finn said, dabbing blood from his split lip while shuffling to his right, pretending to still be reeling from Casteel's blow. "I thought you 'special prefects' were supposed to be tough?"

Casteel gritted her teeth and pulled back her arm, ready to strike again. The thin man continued to complain, and urge restraint, but she shut him down then hammered Finn across the side of the face again. He fell to his knees, still play-acting; Casteel was almost in range.

"When I'm done with you, there won't be anything left to parade through the streets," Casteel hissed. She grabbed a fistful of Finn's hair, then slid a knife from her belt and pressed it to his neck. "Now, which body part shall I remove first?"

Finn saw his chance and grabbed Casteel then spun her around to face Scraps. The laser cannon fired, and the robot was sent barreling across the floor from the kickback, but the shot landed true, burning a hole deep into the spy's chest.

Stripping the pistol from Casteel's limp hand, Finn pivoted again and shot two of the soldiers in the head before the corporal's quivering body had even hit the ground.

The other two soldiers returned fire and he felt a bullet graze his leg, carving a groove into his armor, but he held his nerve and continued firing, forcing the infiltrators to dive for cover. Then Soren jumped up and charged at the civilian infiltrator, crashing into the thin man like a runaway ground car. The soldiers ran to their comrade's aid and Finn moved out, weapon raised, but he didn't need to pull the trigger, because every worker in the room had sprung into action too, following Soren's lead. The soldiers were dragged to the ground and their weapons were stripped from their hands before the mob set upon them like a pack of wolves.

Finn returned to Corporal Casteel then knelt by her side and pressed his fingers to her neck. The faint thump of a pulse pushed back. He searched her pockets and retrieved General Riley's ident card before opening the door and allowing Private Benson inside, along with the rest of his squad, but the siege was already over. Casteel aside, the other infiltrators lay dead, their faces and heads burned by the explosive devices implanted into their brains.

"What the hell happened here?" Benson said, lowering his weapon.

"Corporal Casteel was an enemy agent, that's what happened," Finn said.

"What? No!" Benson said. "Not Pela, come on!"

The soldier reacted as if Finn had told him his wife was having an affair. It spoke of how thorough and insidious Casteel's deception and betrayal had been.

"She's still alive and we need to keep her that way," Finn

continued, not wanting to dwell on Benson's shock. "Their brain bombs already killed the other infiltrators but maybe getting lasered in the chest disrupted Casteel's trigger mechanism, I don't know. But whatever the reason, we need her alive so we can make her talk."

"Don't worry, she ain't dying on us, at least not today," Benson said, nodding to a field medic who hurried to the corporal's body and set to work.

Finn retrieved his laser cannon then saw Scraps in the corner of the room, looking dizzy but functional. The robot gave him an unsteady wave to indicate he was okay, and Finn waved back.

"Contact General Riley," Finn said, turning again to Private Benson. "Let him know that the comms room is secure, then get as many fighters as you can to the garage level."

"Yes, sir," Benson replied. The man winced and staggered back against the wall; hand pressed over the wound to his shoulder.

"And get that seen to, before you bleed out," Finn added, resting a hand on the private's good shoulder. "We don't know how many of Riley's soldiers are working for the Authority, so we need all the good ones to stay alive."

Benson laughed weakly. "Now, that's an order I can get behind."

Finn was about to remind Benson that he couldn't give the man an order any more than Scraps could, but he figured that if it meant the soldier would do as he said, there was no harm in allowing the pretense to continue.

Finn then heard the sound of rotors whirring and Scraps came hurtling toward him, weaving a chaotic course through the room. The robot botched the attempted landing on his shoulder, but Finn was quick enough to catch him and make sure Scraps didn't fall.

"Are you okay, pal?" Finn said. Then he saw a bullet hole in Scraps oil-can body and his gut knotted. "You're hit."

"Scraps okay!" the robot replied, cheerfully. "Circuits just scrambled."

"Are you sure?" Finn asked, inspecting the hole but he could see all the way through Scraps from one side of his scuffed body to the other.

"Nothing broken," Scraps said. He poked his finger into the hole then shrugged. "But Scraps could use a patch-up!"

Finn laughed then he saw Soren watching him and the smile fell off his face. Soren dusted himself down and moved a few paces closer, staying out of striking range, perhaps worried Finn would attack him again.

"It's nice to see you fighting for the right side for a change," Finn said.

There was the hint of a smile, but Soren got rid of it before it could take root. "Fuck you, Finn, I still don't like you," Soren grunted. Then the man nodded to Casteel. "But I liked her less."

Soren spat a globule of phlegm onto Casteel's jacket, then he walked away to receive the congratulations and thanks of his co-workers, who were looking at Soren like he was a hero.

"Soren asshole!" Scraps said.

"Hey!" Finn scowled at his robot. "You swore..." Scraps shrugged and smiled sweetly at him, and Finn couldn't stay angry. "Don't make it a habit, okay?"

"Okay-kay!" Scraps chirruped.

The communications systems all switched back on and

the room was suddenly filled with the chatter of dozens of voices from dozens of floors, but rising above them all were the gruff tones of General Riley.

"This is General Riley to all available forces. Proceed at once to the garage level. Enemy soldiers have entered the Pit. Repeat, enemy soldiers have entered the Pit!"

9
PROTECT THE PIT

Finn left Private Benson in charge of the comm rooms, and under the care and attention of a medical robot who had arrived to pick up the pieces after the fight. He rushed toward the central elevator pillar with Scraps flying by his side and saw dozens more soldiers in Haven military fatigues also making their way to the garage level. Some were cramming themselves into elevators while others were charging up the emergency access stairwells. General Riley's call to arms had worked, Finn realized, but they still had to repel the invasion force, or the Pit would fall.

"We'll take the elevator, it will be quicker," Finn said to Scraps, joining other soldiers who were also running across the bridge.

"Scraps hold door!" the robot replied, then he zoomed ahead and sped into a waiting elevator car, causing the soldiers inside to jump back in surprise. "Wait-wait!" Scraps called out to the soldiers.

The men and women in the elevator were torn between doing as the curious little robot said and blasting him to pieces with their sidearms. Then the soldiers saw Finn charging toward them, cutting an imposing figure in his chrome prosecutor armor, and there was no further disharmony. A corporal slammed his hand against the edge of the door as it began to close, while a private on the other side did the same.

"Thanks," Finn said, squeezing inside.

He was winded from the sprint, but he didn't allow himself to show it and stood tall, towering over most of the soldiers in the car. This was a trick he'd learned from Elara during his prosecutor training. *Always look strong....* His mentor had told him. *If they see that you're tired or hurt they'll see you as weak, so it doesn't matter if you feel like dying... always look strong.*

The car began to ascend, and Scraps landed on Finn's shoulder, his circuits no longer scrambled from being shot across the comms room like a missile. He heard his name, or variations of it, being whispered behind him. *Redeemer... the prosecutor... the rebel from Metalhaven...* There was everything but his actual name, and Finn knew that he'd already become the symbol Elara said he could be.

The elevator doors opened on the garage and Finn was met with the sound of gunfire crackling through the cavernous space. The garage level was a giant underground parking lot for the skycars that Haven used to fight off attacks from Zavetgrad, except this time Authority spies had prevented them from launching. Some of the skycars, along with their support vehicles, ranging from fuel trucks and rescue cars to maintenance vans, had been destroyed, likely as a result of grenades or explosives. Some fires had been extinguished while other vehicles were still smoldering, pumping acrid smoke into the air and clouding Finn's view ahead.

He ran outside, spotting a squad of soldiers huddled behind a burned-out rescue vehicle that was acting as a shield, and he quickly joined them. Every other soldier who'd been inside the elevator with him piled in at his rear, crouched low with weapons held ready.

"What are you orders, sir?" the corporal who'd held the door for him said. It took Finn a second to realize that the soldier was talking to him. "Our officer is dead, and we've never had to fight like this."

Finn read the man's name tag and it said, *Chang*. Then he noticed that the twenty other soldiers huddled behind the vehicle were also looking to him for direction. Finn considered telling them that he wasn't their officer, but he chose to accept the mantle of leadership, in his own way.

"Look, I'm not a soldier but I know how to fight, and I know how to win," Finn said, addressing the group as a whole, who were hanging off his every word. "I'm guessing that you've all been trained for this, so I don't need to tell you what to do, but I also know that fighting for real is a lot different to training. If you're afraid then good, because fear will keep you alive, but don't for one second think these fuckers will stop coming. The only way we save the Pit is to fight and kill them first, and that's exactly what we're going to do."

"Metal and blood!" a soldier called out from behind him, then the rallying cry was repeated in force by all twenty soldiers, so loud it hurt Finn's ears, but it also sent a shiver racing down his spine. It was like a drug and Finn drank it in and allowed the buzz of adrenaline to fill him up.

"Follow me!" Finn roared, raising his laser cannon. "Follow me and let's kick these Authority fuckers out of the Pit!"

Finn ran out and Scraps leapt off his shoulder and went high, again acting as Finn's eyes and ears in the sky. Through the smoke he spotted General Riley, pinned down behind a burning skycar with the remnants of his squad, a meagre five soldiers. The two acknowledged each other with quick nods of their heads, but Riley was on his own, at least until Finn could thin the numbers of the opposing force. A unit of special prefects was trying to work its way around the damaged skycar and catch Riley's squad in a crossfire, but they hadn't yet seen Finn coming.

"Metal and blood!" Finn yelled and the cry was repeated again. All twenty soldiers were hot on his heels, stirred into action by a shared hatred of the Authority that was powerful enough to overcome mortal fear.

"Take cover!" the lead prefect yelled but Finn had caught them in the open and there was no escape.

Finn's laser cannon flashed, and the lead prefect was hit in the neck, the heat from the beam cauterizing his arteries and cutting off the blood supply to his brain. The other prefects scrambled for cover, but Finn fired again and again, slicing through flesh with the same ease that his laser cutter used to carve up tanks and APCs. Gunfire erupted behind him, and the remainder of the prefect squad was caught in a hailstorm of bullets and cut down before they could reach safety. A cheer rang out, but Authority reinforcements were close behind and as they returned fire, two of Finn's squad were hit and killed instantly.

"With me!" Finn shouted, waving the soldiers on, then

racing toward General Riley, who gave them covering fire as they pushed on through the smoke-blackened space.

"We need to close and seal the top hatch in section seven!" Riley shouted, wasting no time on greetings, and getting straight to business. "A dozen more skycars are inbound and if those prefects get inside then we won't have the numbers to hold them off."

Finn nodded then checked on Scraps. The robot was lurking near another burning skycar, hiding in the rafters of the industrial space to avoid being seen.

"I can move down the left, and try to cut them off," Finn said, noting that another force of special prefects was gathering, ready to assault the general's position.

"The bastards are dug in behind that wrecked skycar," Riley replied, casting his eyes in the direction Finn intended to go. "I've tried to get down there, but they cut down a quarter of my squad before we could get close."

"Don't worry, I have eyes in the sky," Finn said, smiling as Scraps waved at him from his hiding spot. "I'll distract them and overrun their position."

Riley narrowed his eyes, clearly curious to learn how Finn intended to accomplish this feat, but another barrage of gunfire from the advancing prefects cleared any questions that were on his mind.

"Then take your squad and give them hell," Riley said. "Once you're through, attack the enemy forces barricaded inside the skycar hangar in section five, and my squad will assault from the right flank."

Finn didn't know the location of section five, or even what a 'flank' was, but he figured he'd work it out as he went along. He turned to Corporal Chang, ready to relay the general's orders, but the corporal had heard everything.

"Give the word, sir, we're with you," Chang said, and the rest of the squad murmured their agreement.

Finn blew out a heavy sigh then checked on his target, ducking and flinching instinctively as bullets pinballed off the floors and walls, striking up the discordant melody of war.

"Scraps, I'm coming your way," Finn said, pressing the communicator device deeper into his ear. "See if you can distract the prefects underneath you, but don't put yourself in danger. I don't know how many space parts they have lying around in the Pit to fix you up."

"Scraps be safe!" the robot replied, coming through loud and clear in his earpiece. "Wait for signal!"

"What signal?" Finn asked, scowling.

"Finn will know!" Scraps replied, cheerfully.

Finn could have pressed the robot for more detail but, as with General Riley, the constant chime and ping of bullets skipping off metal nearby persuaded him that expedience was the more prudent strategy.

"What's the command, sir?" Chang, said.

The initial hit of adrenaline was waning and, in its place, came a creeping uncertainty. Fear was an insidious assassin that targeted the courage of all men and women, and Finn wasn't immune to its powers, but his training had taught him to hide it well.

"We go on my order," Finn said, ensuring that his voice was strong and confident. "I've arranged a little surprise for the special prefects, and when it hits, they'll be too preoccupied to see us coming."

"Yes, sir," Chang replied, though Finn could still sense the man's doubt. He glanced back at the other seventeen soldiers that had become his squad and saw the same fear in their eyes too.

"If we stick together, we'll get through this," Finn said, trying to lean into his role and give the soldiers the confidence they needed. "Trust me, I've been in worse fights than this."

"But these special prefects are like machines," Chang said, trying to stop his hands trembling. "Even as kids, they're trained to hate and kill us. They're unstoppable."

"No, they're not," Finn said. He grabbed Chang's shoulder, and the weight of his grip almost bowled the man over. "I trained with these people, I lived as one of them for months, and I promise you that they're just flesh and blood."

"Sir, I heard that apprentice prosecutors fight one another, like in a trial," another soldier said, a woman about Finn's age.

"We do," Finn replied, recalling the contests all too vividly.

"Did you beat them?" the woman asked. Her eyes flicked across to where the squad of special prefects were waiting. "The other apprentices, I mean. The ones like the prefects out there."

Finn chanced a look at the special prefects facing them. Encased in their black carapace armor and impenetrable visors, he could understand why the soldiers saw them as something unnatural, to be feared.

"I beat them as often as I could," Finn said. He could have embellished the truth, but he'd spent enough time pretending to be something he wasn't, and he was done lying. "They're tough bastards, but they're only human. If we stick together, I promise we can win."

The soldier nodded then Chang turned to the others. "You heard him, they're only human!"

The soldiers cheered in reply then the docking garage was suddenly lit up from the inside as a huge fireball swept across the space. Finn squinted against the intense flare of light then he heard screams of pain and terror. By the time his eyes had adjusted, special prefects were charging out of cover, flames clinging to their carapace armor like they were burning cannonballs. Then Finn saw Scraps, still hiding in the rafters, but now holding an upturned can of aviation fuel in his hands.

"That's our signal, go!" Finn cried.

Finn led the charge, and he could feel Chang and the others close behind as if their breath was on his neck. He aimed and fired, focusing his laser light onto the prefects who had evaded the firestorm, and bodies fell at his feet like dominos toppling. Gunfire overtook him then his squad stormed the enemy position, ignoring the flames that had engulfed the skycar and bludgeoning the remaining prefects unconscious with fists and feet, elbows and gun butts, until none were left standing.

"Secure the area," Chang said, and the squad obeyed, taking the surviving prefects prisoner, and defending the position.

With his squad behind him, Finn turned toward the hatch in section seven that Riley had told him needed to be closed. The general's soldiers had advanced and gained ground, but their numbers were growing thin.

"Prefects coming!" Scraps yelled, flying down from above. "Outside hatch. Two hundred or more!"

"How close are they?" Finn asked. After the euphoric

high of taking the prefect position, Scraps' news had sunk him to a new low.

"One minute," Scraps replied, rubbing his metal knuckles together. "Some already coming through!"

Finn cursed under his breath. They didn't have the forces to hold back that many. He checked the power level on his laser, and he only had enough charge for a few more shots, five or six at most, but he had no choice. They either sealed the hatch or lost the Pit.

"Corporal Chang, you're with me," Finn said. "Bring as many others as we can spare. We have to close the hatch, or we'll be overrun in seconds."

Chang nodded then called out the names of ten other soldiers. A firefight had already begun on the outer wall of the docking garage, with Riley's forces fighting in close quarters with prefect reinforcements that were pouring inside like water from a leaking roof.

"Metal and blood!" Finn yelled and he drew his baseball bat and held it high. He didn't have quite the same stature as King Arthur holding Excalibur aloft, but it had the same effect of galvanizing his troops into action.

Finn ran at the enemy as fast and as hard as he could, facing them on open ground with barely a stone pillar or upturned maintenance cart for cover, but the time for strategy was done. *Sometimes, a good bar brawl is what it takes to sort shit out,* Finn thought as the rush of air streaming past his face pressed back his hair and squeezed water from his eyes. He aimed his cannon at the prefects who were clambering down the rickety, snow-covered staircase leading to the outside, and squeezed the trigger, spitting burning light at his enemies and thinning the field. Some prefects jumped down, breaking ankles and legs in the fall, but others simply climbed over them and charged.

Finn's laser gave out and he tossed it aside, gripping the baseball bat with both hands. Bullets flashed toward him and deflected off his armor, each shot causing a spark of light like a match being struck. He reached the closest prefect and swung the bat so hard he smashed the man's visor and flattened his perfect nose. A second swing broke the ribs of another prefect and a third crushed a man's neck and sent him quivering to the floor. Chang and the others piled into the fight like rabid animals and soon the forces of the Authority were falling back, but Finn didn't let up his pursuit. He chased the bastards all the way back out into the freezing cold, smashing bone and bruising muscle with relentless fury. Soon, the prefects were fleeing from him, as if he were a demon coming to claim their souls. Then he saw the dozens of black skycars descending toward the Pit and he slid to a stop. It was an invasion force big enough to take the entire silo.

"Finn, get back in here!" Riley was at the top of the staircase, waving to him. "We have to shut the hatch!"

Finn ran and machine gun fire chased him but by some miracle the bullets missed him. Riley grabbed his arm and pulled him through, almost causing Finn to fall the ten meter drop into the docking garage, but the general's grip on him was strong.

"Close it!" Riley yelled, and his soldiers began to turn a massive wheel, which began to slowly grind the hatch shut.

The prefect skycars touched down and Finn saw dozens... hundreds of the Authority's most elite and sadistic warriors jump out and run toward him but it was too late. The hatch ground shut and locking bolts thumped into place. Finn climbed down and Riley followed. The man had taken three bullets to the chest, but his vest had kept them out. Even so, the general looked like he'd fought the battle all by himself. There was more blood on his face than there was in his veins.

"Emergency seals!" Riley grunted and the soldiers obeyed, turning another huge wheel, and sliding a slab of metal thick enough to repel a nuclear blast over the hatch, forming a second barrier that no amount of force could penetrate. The general then turned to his troops and held his pistol aloft. "The pit is secured. Haven endures!"

"Haven endures!" was shouted back at him, then the chant changed and became something more familiar. "Metal and Blood! Metal and Blood!"

Finn could hardly believe how so few voices could fill the cavernous docking garage with sound, and a tear welled in his eye. He considered brushing it away but didn't. He allowed himself to feel the moment, every bit of it, and it felt good. They'd repelled the Authority and forced them back to Zavetgrad with their tails between their legs, but Finn knew that the fight was far from over. Haven was saved but it was also compromised and that meant he had to make a difficult choice, once that he knew Riley and Pen wouldn't agree with. But that was for another time. Now, it was time to celebrate.

10

SPIES IN OUR MIDST

If the battle to save the Pit had been brutal then the aftermath was no less unpleasant. The bodies of the dead littered the docking garage and whether a special prefect of the Authority or a soldier of Haven, the stench of blood was the same. Corporal Chang had been put in charge of the cleanup operation, a foul duty that was no reward for the man's bravery and heroism in the face of a terrifying enemy. Even so, it had to be done.

The bodies were separated into individual lines, one for Haven soldiers and the other for special prefects. Any serviceable weapons and equipment were recovered then the enemy dead were carted away to be incinerated without ceremony. Finn figured he should have felt some sympathy for the friends and perhaps loved ones of the dead, but he didn't. His life growing up in Zavetgrad had left him as cold as the frozen junk that filled the yards of Metalhaven.

Haven's dead were to be transported back into the Pit, first to the morgue, where they would remain until Pen and General Riley had time to conduct a memorial service. Then they too would be cremated and smoke from the incinerators would billow from vents on the surface and deposit the ashen remains of the fallen all across Disko Island. Yet, thanks to the grit and determination of those who had defended the Pit, they would be remembered.

Finn left the docking garage with Riley and an escort of three soldiers from the general's own unit. Scraps was clamped to his shoulder armor, though the robot was in repair mode, so his sensory inputs were numbed. He looked like a wooden parrot on a waxwork dummy of a pirate captain but as amusing as this was, Finn was simply glad his friend was still in one piece. Haven remained on alert status since the special prefect skycars were still loitering on the outside, probing for ways to get in, but without their operatives to aid them, the Pit was once again an impenetrable stronghold.

"You did good today," Riley grunted, as the group walked across the bridge to the central bank of elevators on level one. "You make a good soldier, a good officer."

"I'm just a chrome from Metalhaven who happens to have a bit of training," Finn replied. He couldn't explain why he was so reluctant to accept praise, but it simply felt more honest to rebuff it. "To me, slicing up asshole prefects is no different to cutting up tanks."

Riley scrutinized him out of the corner of his eye as they walked. The general had a brooding intensity, but he was more than just a blunt instrument of war and there was intelligence behind his eyes too.

"Still holding on to the role of reluctant hero, I see," Riley said. "You'd do well to drop that façade and embrace what you are."

"I'm not *holding on* to anything," Finn replied. He

resented the implication that his humility was an act. "And it's not a façade. I *am* just a guy from Metalhaven who's here by accident, not by some grand design. I'm a consequence of events I had no control over."

Riley gave a contemplative grunt in reply, though it was obvious to Finn that the general didn't accept his answer. Riley then stopped at the elevator and hammered the button with his blood-stained fist. The car was currently on level twenty-nine, which gave the man ample time to continue his interrogation.

"I can understand why you're reluctant to embrace your role," Riley said, and Finn rolled his eyes. He was a captive audience and had little choice but to listen. "You fucked up and people died, people you cared about, but you've also saved more lives than you've lost."

"I know what I've lost, General," Finn said, willing the elevator car to arrive faster.

"I'm no psychiatrist, but I understand grief," Riley said. "Since I became general of the Pit, I've lost more people than I care to remember. It makes you question everything you do, accepting that your next decision could lead to more deaths. It would be easier to defer these responsibilities to others but to do so, knowing that withdrawing your influence could lead to an even greater loss of life, would be cowardly."

The accusation of cowardice, whether implied or meant directly, enraged Finn and he turned to Riley, fists clenched at his sides. The general faced him without fear or regret for what he'd said.

"I know you're not a coward, Finn," Riley added, quick to make that point and diffuse the tension between them.

"But I also know that we have more chance of winning this fight with you than without you."

"I am with you," Finn said. "I'm here, aren't I?"

Riley's climbdown had abated his anger but he was still offended at the suggestion he wasn't committed, especially after helping to defend the Pit.

"You're here, but you're not all in, not yet," Riley said, turning back to the elevator car, which was now on level six and approaching fast. "You might hate the Authority for what they've done to you, and I don't blame you, but being a leader doesn't mean you have to become like them."

The elevator door pinged open, and Finn breathed a sigh of relief, hoping that Riley would break off his little pep talk. But the general didn't step inside and instead pressed his hand to the door to stop it from closing again.

"What I'm trying to say is that you're doing the right thing, Finn," Riley said, as the three other soldiers entered the car behind him. "You're on the right side. In case you needed someone to tell you that."

Riley didn't wait for Finn to answer and instead stepped into the elevator and removed his ident card. Finn sighed heavily then stepped in beside him and the doors closed. As much as the conversation had been uncomfortable, he appreciated what Riley was trying to say and even accepted it. Even so, no amount of logical analysis would change how he felt.

Riley hit the button for level seven and the elevator car sped to its target floor without delay. Finn realized that he didn't actually know where they were headed, but their destination quickly became clear as Riley bustled out in the lead, heading toward Medical Seven, the Pit's primary hospital facility. Pen was already waiting for them when they arrived, with Lieutenant Alex Thornfield standing dutifully by her side. The lieutenant saluted Riley who returned the acknowledgement stiffly on account of the man's extensive injuries, the effects of which the general continued to shrug off. Finn recognized the technique, since learning how to disregard pain was something he'd been taught during prosecutor training.

"Well done, to the both of you," Pen said, acknowledging the efforts of Finn and General Riley in the defense of the Pit.

"I think you mean the three of us," Finn said, tapping Scraps, and the robot hummed back to life. "If it wasn't for Scraps, Casteel would still be in control of the comms room, and special prefects would be running riot throughout the Pit."

Pen nodded the Scraps. "It seems we owe you our gratitude, Scraps. Thanks to you and the others, Haven endures."

Riley and Lieutenant Thornfield both repeated, "Haven endures", and Finn was reminded of how much both the Authority and the rebel faction enjoyed their slogans. Scraps then jumped off Finn's shoulder and trotted over to the table beside Casteel's bed, using one of the power-outlets to top up his charge.

"Alex took good care of me," Pen added, also acknowledging the role that Thornfield had played, though the man looked oddly ashamed considering the praise he'd received.

"I regret I could not fight alongside you, sir," Thornfield said, revealing the source of his shame.

"Keeping the principal safe was a critical duty and I would

not have entrusted it to anyone else," Riley replied, and Thornfield's chin lifted a fraction. "Well done, Lieutenant."

Despite his gruff and surly nature, Riley could be inspiring, and it was clear that the admiration of his commanding officer meant a lot to the lieutenant.

"Now that the special prefects have been sent packing, let's see what we can find out from Corporal Casteel," Pen said.

The principal led them into a private medical bay and Finn saw the enemy agent lying on one of the diagnostic beds, either sedated or unconscious from her injuries.

"Doctor Jenson believes the laser blast that Miss Casteel sustained to her spine disrupted the electrical triggers that would have normally caused her 'brain bomb' to detonate," Pen explained. "However, the effect may not be permanent, and she could 'blow' at any moment."

"Then we need to wake her up and interrogate her now," Riley said, showing no compassion for the injured woman's condition. The general turned to one of his soldiers. "Find Jenson and bring him here."

The soldier nodded and departed the medical bay while Riley moved to Casteel's bedside and looked down at the woman with resentful eyes.

"Pela was one of my own," Riley grunted, bitterly. "I had her marked for sergeant and even a commission." The man shook his head. "This is my fault, ma'am. I accept full responsibility and offer my resignation."

"Resignation not accepted," Pen replied, barely a heartbeat later. "Now is not the time to assign blame, Will," she added, choosing to use the general's given name, as she almost always did. "But we should accept the possibility there may still be other enemy agents posing as Haven soldiers, and in other areas of the Pit. We need to root them out quickly before they can do any more damage."

"How did Casteel go undetected?" Finn asked. "In the comms room, the other infiltrators spoke to her with deference, as if she was someone senior within the special prefecture."

"We have our own version of the Authority's loyalty evaluation, and I can assure you that our vetting processes are rigorous," Riley said. "Pela and all the others passed this test, which means the test is worthless."

Finn realized that the general had taken his comment to heart and viewed it as an attack on his competence. Nevertheless, he wasn't going to apologize because there had been failings. And as wounded as the general's pride was, Finn respected that he'd accepted responsibility for his failure to detect the spies in their midst.

"Where is that damned doctor?" Riley growled, pushing away from the bed. "If he's not here soon, I'll wake her myself and beat the answers out of her."

"That's not how we operate here, as you well know," Pen said, speaking sternly to the general.

"I know," Riley replied, folding his arms to stop himself strangling the soldier who had betrayed him. "But old habits die hard."

It was a curious response and it made Finn realize that he still knew practically nothing about General Riley, including how he had come to be 'General of the Pit'."

"What do you mean by that?" Finn asked, frowning at Riley. "What old habits are you trying to let go of?"

Riley looked to Pen, who now had the appearance of a woman with a secret, and the general nodded his assent.

"Will came to us from Zavetgrad many years ago but he wasn't a worker, he was the Head Prefect of Stonehaven," Pen said.

Finn tensed up and his finger instinctively slipped onto the trigger of his laser cannon, which had recovered enough charge for one or two shots. The soldiers behind Riley saw the shift in his posture and reached for their weapons but Riley raised his hand and stood them down.

"There was a time when I deserved a blast from that laser cannon, but I saw the error of my ways," Riley said.

"The error of your ways?" Finn snorted, then laughed harshly. "You talk as if being the leader of a sadistic mob of authoritarian thugs was just a little blip in your career."

"I can assure you that's not the case," Riley hit back. "You're not the only one with regrets, Finn. I saw things I'll never forget, and I did things I can never be forgiven for."

Finn tilted his head to one side and studied the general's gruff expression. Riley was hiding his pain well, but not well enough that Finn couldn't see through the cracks in the man's armor.

"If you're expecting sympathy, you won't get any from me," Finn said. "As a Head Prefect, you would have been responsible for thousands of workers living and dying in pain and misery. Whatever horrors keep you awake at night is nothing compared to the suffering you've caused."

His cold-hearted response visibly shocked Pen but Riley wasn't surprised or angered by the venomous outburst.

"I'm not asking for sympathy or forgiveness, and I deserve none," Riley said, standing tall and accepting Finn's condemnation. "But unlike you, I've at least tried to put that past behind me."

Finn and the general continued to stare at one another, neither blinking, until Doctor Jenson was bustled through the door by the soldier Riley had sent to fetch him. The doctor looked harried and set upon, and clearly didn't appreciate being summoned.

"Doctor, I need to know how this soldier defeated our vetting process," Riley said, turning away from Finn and returning to the matter at hand, as if their exchange hadn't happened. "Scan her brain and figure it out, now."

"Ma'am, I must protest," Jenson said, appealing to the coolest head in the room. "It could take me days or even weeks to uncover how this was possible. I can't be expected to just magic the answer out of thin air!"

Pen tried to mediate between Jenson and the general, but Riley's dislike of the doctor was plain and the atmosphere in the room became acerbic. Finn considered trying to intervene, but he was more on Riley's side than the doctor's. They had to find the answer, even if doing so required the scientific equivalent of pulling a rabbit out of hat. Then he had a thought and he kicked himself for not suggesting it sooner.

"I may have an answer," Finn said, interrupting what was quickly becoming a slanging match between Riley and Jenson. "At the start of my prosecutor training, Elara asked me to swallow some kind of inhibitor device. She said that it attached to my nervous system and masked the physiological indicators of when I was lying." He shrugged. "I managed to fool the loyalty evaluator robot for nine weeks straight, so the thing must have worked."

"Will you submit to a medical examination?" Pen asked, seizing on the opportunity to move things forward.

Finn laughed. "It's actually nice to be asked for a change, but sure. So long as it doesn't involve sticking a needle in my balls."

Pen and the others all frowned at him but thankfully none of them asked him to elaborate. Doctor Jenson directed Finn to the medical bed beside Casteel and Finn winked at Scraps to set the anxious-looking bot's electronic mind at ease. Jenson got to work, and a scan image of Finn's central nervous system was projected above his body as a hologram. Within seconds the doctor had identified the inhibitor chip, and an analysis of the device was scrolling across a monitor above Finn's head.

"That was quick," Finn commented, craning his neck to look at the scan. "I thought you used to work in a Gene Bank, stealing people's DNA, not in medical research."

"Actually, I performed many functions in Zavetgrad," Jenson replied, snootily. The doctor appeared offended that Finn had thought so little of his abilities. "I did whatever the Authority told me to do, until I could no longer stomach the undertakings that were asked of me."

Jenson was rubbing his knuckles together in an attempt to disguise that his hands were shaking, and Finn chose to quit his line of questioning. He understood better than most how traumatic reliving past events could be.

"Now scan me," Pen said, shooing Finn off the bed like he was a dog that had been caught lounging on the sofa. It amused Finn and also Scraps, who giggled his appreciation. "We need to be certain that we can trust one another, before we widen our search for other infiltrators."

Jenson ran the scan and the analysis proceeded exactly as it had done with Finn, but revealed no inhibitor device present in the principal's body.

"You are clear, ma'am," Jenson confirmed.

"Well, that's a relief..." Pen said to a ripple of muted laughter.

"Now scan me," Riley grunted, offering his hand to Pen, and helping her off the bed, like a gentleman helping a countess step down from her coach. The general replaced Pen on the bed and glowered at Jenson. "Make it quick."

Jenson huffed his disapproval of the general's disrespectful tone but proceeded with the analysis. The scan ran for several seconds longer than it had done for Pen and even for Finn, then the readings began to fluctuate.

"What is taking so long?" Riley grumbled. The man did not like being still.

Jenson ignored the general then the readings finally stabilized, and the doctor took a step back. The holographic image of General Riley was displaying an inhibitor chip attached to his nervous system in the same location as the one in Finn's body.

"The general is an enemy agent!" Jenson said, aiming a finger at Riley. "His inhibitor device was stealthed, but I found it. Restrain him, quickly!"

"What?" Riley roared, jumping off the bed but the three soldiers who'd arrived with him drew their pistols and aimed them at their commander, before looking to Pen for instructions. "This is insane, I'm not an infiltrator!"

Finn's mind was a jumble of thoughts. His gut told him that the general was being honest, but the scan reading revealed otherwise, and he was painfully aware of how

Juniper Jones, another agent of the special prefecture, had so easily deceived him in the past. He looked at Pen, but the principal appeared unfeasibly cool.

"Stand down your weapons," Pen said, holding up a hand to the soldiers, who obeyed. The principal then looked Jenson in the eyes. "But arrest him."

Finn wondered how Pen knew when he saw that another medical scan had appeared as a hologram above the head of Doctor Jenson, also showing an inhibitor chip in the man's nervous system. Then he saw Scraps, interfaced with a second medical scanner. The robot smiled at Finn and waved with his free hand.

"Doctor bad man!" Scraps said, wagging his finger at Jenson. "General-good!"

Riley surged toward Jenson and hit the man with a straight right that could have knocked down a wall. The doctor was floored in an instant and Riley stood over the spy, shaking the stinging pain out of his fist.

"That was only to make sure his brain bomb doesn't go off," Riley said, noticing that Pen was giving him the side-eye. The principal continued to look at him suspiciously and the general fessed up. "Okay, so maybe it wasn't *just* because of that…"

11
SP175K

Finn and General Riley hauled Doctor Jenson's unconscious body onto a trolley then Lieutenant Thornfield was recruited to wheel the infiltrator into a secure room, though only after Scraps confirmed that the young officer wasn't a spy. Thornfield finished strapping Jenson to the trolley then turned to General Riley to receive his orders.

"Once you've locked up this piece of trash, see if you can find another doctor and send them to me," Riley said. "Then begin a program to scan everyone in the Pit for these inhibitor devices, starting with those in the most senior positions."

The officer nodded and began pushing the trolley out of the room, but Riley caught the man's arm and held him back.

"And stay alert, Lieutenant," Riley added, in a more somber tone that hinted at a human side to the gruff general. "Until we know who we can trust, keep close."

Thornfield nodded then hastened his exit, wary of providing an opportunity for the other staff and patients of Medical Seven to get a look at who was on the trolley. Meanwhile, Finn had returned his attention to Corporal Pela

Casteel, the soldier who had revealed herself as an infiltrator from the Authority. The woman was still sedated on a bed in the room, for fear that waking her might trigger the 'brain bomb' in her head and prevent General Riley from interrogating her.

"Where's that new doctor?" Riley grunted, arms folded and foot tapping impatiently on the polished tile floor. "I want answers, and Corporal Casteel, if that's even her name, is the only one who can give them to us."

No sooner had Riley spoken than a Foreman-class robot stomped into the room. It was an older Gen III design that looked identical to the robot yard managers that Finn had spent his entire life in Metalhaven sparring with, and its arrival immediately set him on edge.

"What the fuck do you want?" Finn snapped, drawing a look of surprise not only from the robot but from Riley and Pen too.

"I do not want anything," the machine replied, politely. "I was summoned. I am your new doctor."

"No way," Finn said, shaking his head. "We can barely trust the human staff in this place so there's not a chance in hell I'm trusting an old foreman from Zavetgrad."

"I can assure you that my circuits have been reprogrammed," the robot replied, still cheerful and polite. "I no longer serve the Authority. I work for the people of Haven."

"Isn't there anyone else?" Finn asked. "Anyone human, I mean."

The robot manipulated its crude mechanical muscles to mimic a facial expression that approximated outrage. "Sir, there is no-one else," the machine replied, huffily. "All the other doctors are tending to the wounded. If you would prefer, I can request that a *human* physician be reassigned from life-saving surgical duties to attend to your whims."

The robot's brazen response did nothing to endear it to Finn, nor did Riley or Pen look particularly impressed.

"I agree with Finn," Riley grunted, arms still folded. "We're low on trust around here and a machine that used to do the Authority's bidding would not be my first choice either."

The robot huffed indignantly then Finn and Riley both looked to Pen, as did the foreman doctor. It was their way of saying, "It's your call, ma'am..." to the principal of the Pit.

"I understand your concerns but don't see that we have much of a choice," Pen said. She then looked at Scraps who, as ever, was quietly observing everything that was going on. "Unless Scraps can perform the procedure to disable Casteel's brain bomb?"

Scraps held up his little hands. "Scraps no surgeon," the robot said, sorrowfully. Then it turned its clever eyes to the foreman, who stared back at Scraps, warily. "But Scraps can fix robot. Make robot less sassy."

Finn smiled. "Now, that sounds like a very good idea."

"Er, I must protest!" the robot said. "I am not sassy!"

"Do it," Riley said, in his usual gruff manner. "And while you're poking around in its electronic brain, make sure it doesn't have any traitorous intentions too."

"I beg your pardon!" the foreman protested, pressing its hands to its hips, ironically reinforcing how sassy it was.

At the same time the foreman was complaining, Scraps had already taken flight and was hovering above the robot's head. He then deactivated his rotors and dropped on the larger machine like a bomb, before sticking his little metal fingers into the foreman's auditory holes.

"Oh, my..." the foreman said. The machine had suddenly become as stiff as a board and was staring into space. "I feel a little tingly..." the robot added, before abruptly shutting down.

"You were supposed to fix it, not break it," Riley grumbled, as Scraps jumped off the foreman's head and landed back on the bedside table.

"Foreman not broken," Scraps said, confidently. "Not now, anyway!"

"What did you do, pal?" Finn asked.

"Foreman's base code all skew-whiff. Scraps fix!" the little robot explained. "Also reprogram surgical subroutines."

"It doesn't look like much of surgeon right now," Riley said, moving in front of the foreman and staring at it, eye to eye.

Suddenly, a deep, energetic thrum vibrated the robot's frame and the foreman powered up. Riley jumped back, his hand going to his sidearm, but Pen moved to the general's side and rested her hand on his.

"Not yet, general," Pen said. "Let's find out if Scraps really did fix this robot before you blow its brains out."

Riley remained on-edge, but he nodded and allowed the re-programmed foreman to complete its boot up sequence. Scraps looked entirely unconcerned, which was all the evidence Finn needed to know that everything was fine.

"Hello, I am Doctor Doctor, your new Senior Consultant Surgeon," the foreman said in a classier version of its old voice, and without the sass. "I understand that you require me to remove a nervous system inhibitor device and a neural shock device from this patient," the robot added, pointing to Casteel on the bed. "This will be a simple procedure."

"Are you sure its fixed?" Riley said, scowling at the reprogrammed machine. "It called itself Doctor Doctor, which must be a glitch."

Scraps giggled. "No glitch! Doctor Doctor funny!"

"You called it Doctor Doctor on purpose?" Riley said and Scraps nodded. "For a joke?" Riley added, just to be certain he understood, and Scraps nodded again. The general let out an elaborate sigh to highlight his disapproval then turned to Pen. "I say we proceed."

"I agree," Pen replied. "Doctor Doctor, please carry out the procedure."

"Yes, ma'am," the robot said, bowing respectfully to Pen before approaching the bed where Casteel was lying. "If Scraps could assist me?" the machine added, looking to the principal for her assent.

"Of course," Pen said, shrugging.

A sterile field was established around Casteel's bed then the surgical robot quickly got to work, ably assisted by Scraps, who had decided to wear a surgical mask over his little mouth. Finn guessed that this was most likely for comedic effect but since it didn't interfere with the procedure, he didn't complain and neither did Riley or Pen. Less than thirty minutes after the surgery had begun the robot was finished and both the inhibitor chip and brain bomb sat in a kidney tray to the side of the bed.

"All done," Doctor Doctor said, cheerfully, and without arrogance. "Do you require anything else?"

"Yes, I need you to wake her up," Riley said.

The doctor tilted its robotic head to one side. "That

would be dangerous so soon after surgery. I recommend a period of convalescence."

"No, wake her up, now" Riley said again, more forcefully. "Once she's answered my questions, she can rest."

The robot doctor nodded and administered the stimulant without further protest, before turning back to Riley. "If that is all then my services are urgently required elsewhere," Doctor Doctor said. "There are still many wounded."

Riley nodded. "Go, save some lives."

The modified foreman nodded then swept out of the room. Finn realized that Scraps had not only provided a way for them to interrogate Casteel, but inadvertently also provided the Pit with a life-saving master surgeon too. He idly wondered how many people his little robot pal would save that day, without knowing it.

Casteel began to stir, and Finn moved to the side of her bed, with Riley and Pen surrounding the spy from other angles. Casteel's eyes fluttered then opened. She scowled at Finn first then at Riley and Pen, before her survival instincts kicked in. She thrashed and kicked but the restraints held firm and she was unable to free herself.

"Why aren't I dead?" Casteel demanded, perversely annoyed by that fact. "I should be dead."

"You mean because of this?" Riley said, holding the brain bomb between thumb and forefinger. It was no bigger than a matchhead. "I'm afraid we disabled your suicide device and also the chip that allowed you to fool my loyalty checks."

Casteel scowled at the tiny explosive then at Riley before lying still on the bed, eyes staring blankly up at the clinical white ceiling.

"You will get nothing from me, traitor," Casteel said. "You may as well execute me now."

"That it not our way," Pen cut in. "You are our prisoner, and you will never leave the Pit, but how you choose to spend your days here depends entirely on the answers to our questions."

Casteel snorted a laugh at the principal. "So, if I sell myself out, you'll give me a nice cozy room, with some fresh-cut flowers, is that it?" She shook her head. "You underestimate me, Principal. I will never betray the Authority, no matter what you threaten me with." Casteel nodded toward Riley. "Ask Riley. He knows that I would endure any manner of torture and degradation before betraying my Regent. Unlike your general, I am not a traitor."

Finn glanced at Riley out of the corner of his eye, expecting the man to be bristling from the insult but to his credit, Riley's craggy face betrayed no hint of anger. The general was calm and unflustered.

"Nevertheless, I will ask my questions," Riley said, standing tall with his hands pressed to the small of his back.

"Ask away, traitor," Casteel replied, refusing to look Riley in the eyes. "Then we can proceed to my execution."

"As you wish," Riley said. "What is your real name? You can answer that, at least."

Finn wasn't sure why the general was proceeding with an interrogation he knew would fail but stood witness anyway, curious as to what the spy might reveal under pressure.

"My name is Special Prefect Evelina Rostova, service ID, SP175K. That is all I will tell you."

"Are you willing to cooperate to secure your own safety?" Riley continued.

"No." The answer was emphatic.

"What do you believe will happen to you if you refuse to answer my questions?"

Rostova laughed. "Nothing will happen. You don't have the stomach to do what is necessary." The special prefect finally looked at Riley but only to show her contempt for him. "If I were conducting this interrogation, I would have already attached live wires to your genitalia and had you writhing in agony."

Riley ignored Rostova's attempt to intimidate him and continued his questions in a methodical, objective manner.

"Give me the names of other Authority operatives currently in Haven."

The special prefect spat onto Riley's boots then returned to staring at the ceiling. "There is you answer, traitor."

"How are you communicating with the Authority?" Riley continued.

"Fuck you."

"Tell me about your hidden communications channels." Riley's tone was sterner.

"Tell me how it feels to betray your nation," Rostov said in reply. "Does it make you feel proud?"

"Who ordered the attack on the Pit?" Riley said, sterner still.

"The Authority ordered it, of course."

"Give me a name."

"No."

Riley's hand was now loitering beside his holstered sidearm.

"What is the backup plan in the event the invasion fails?"

Riley said. Finn could sense a change in the man's temperament.

"There is no backup plan, fool," Rostova said. "I should be dead, but thanks to your meddling, I have to sit here and endure your inane questions."

"What do you believe your superiors will do once they learn you are Haven's prisoner?" This question was asked with considerable bite. Riley wanted to provoke a reaction from the special prefect, but she seemed not to care about anything, even her own life.

"You already know the answer, Head Prefect Riley," Rostova said. She was smiling at him, trying to provoke Riley right back. "You saw what the Authority did to you and the one you loved. My fate will be no different. I am marked for death because I failed my mission, and I deserve to die. I am not important. Only Nimbus matters."

"The lives of more than ten thousand free citizens of Haven matter more to me than the whole of the Authority combined," Riley said, leaning in closer to Rostova. His hand was now on the grip of his pistol. "Principal Everhart may not subscribe to my preferred methods of extracting information, but in time you will talk. I don't care if it takes months or even years, but you will talk."

"You don't have months or years to wait," Rostova said, and Finn felt his heart leap. The spy had finally revealed something, but he held his nerve so as not to show he'd noticed. "You are all traitors, or sons and daughters of traitors, and one day soon, this silo will burn, and the embers of your blackened bodies will darken the sky over this godforsaken island."

Riley lost his cool and before Finn knew it, the general's hands were around Rostova's throat, strangling her.

"General Riley, stand down!" Pen said, stepping beside Riley, but the man continued to choke the life out of Rostova. "General, I have given you an order. Stand down or I will have you arrested and removed!"

Riley growled then finally unfurled his hands from around Rostova's neck. The special prefect gasped air into her lungs, but with her hands restrained she was unable to massage her throat. For several seconds she hacked and gagged, then finally began to laugh. The sound made Finn's blood run cold.

"See how toothless you are," Rostova croaked. She then looked at Finn and it felt like a dark spell had been cast on him. "And you are the worst of them all, worker scum," she spat. "You were given a second chance, a chance to become gold, and you repaid the Authority's generosity and benevolence with lies and deceit." The prefect's rage suddenly abated, and she was smiling again. "Juniper Jones gave us all a message should we find you..."

Finn felt his throat tighten and his mouth went dry. "What message?"

"She told us to inform you that your precious mentor, Elara Cage, is still alive..."

Finn suddenly felt lightheaded, and he had to grab the steel bars at the foot of the bed to stop himself from falling. Then he was in the grip of anger.

"Where is she?" Finn growled.

"In a cold interrogation cell, of course, and I promise you that she is not being treated as softly as I am." Rostova laughed and it sickened Finn how she was able to derive amusement from his suffering. "Your co-conspirator is scheduled for trial tomorrow night," the spy continued to a stunned silence. Only the gentle ticking of the clock on the wall punctuated the deathly stillness that had enveloped the room. "It is a special trial for a very special offender that will take place across all the yards in Metalhaven, from one to thirteen. One offender, hunted by a squad of special prefects, led by two prosecutors. It will be a spectacular event. I hope The Shadow gives everyone a good show."

"A good show?" Finn snarled. He grabbed a scalpel from a side-table and was suddenly at Rostova's bedside, the blade pressed to the woman's throat.

"Finn, no!" Pen said, but the principal's words didn't reach him.

"Who are the two prosecutors?" Finn said, drawing blood. "Tell me!"

"I'll tell you because your agony amuses me," Rostova said, pushing the blade deeper into her own flesh, as if she enjoyed the pain. "The prosecutor's names are Herald and Inferno, who you know better as Ivan Volkov and Tonya Duke."

Finn staggered away from the bed, shaking his head. "You're lying..."

"You know I'm not," Rostova sneered. "Your old classmates will hunt down Elara Cage and ensure that she dies a slow, painful death, her final moments filled will terror and crushing loneliness." She laughed again, and Finn's gut twisted as if the blade in his hand were buried into his own flesh. "And it's all your fault, Hero of Metalhaven," Rostova added, suddenly impassioned. "It's all your fault because you betrayed her and left her to die!"

For several seconds, Finn simply stood in shock, staring at the grinning face of Special Prefect Evelina Rostova. The he raised his laser cannon, aimed it at the women's heart and fired.

"Finn!"

Pen rushed to the bedside, but Finn's shot had landed true and smoke rose from the charred cavity in Rostova's chest. It was a quick death. Quick and clean. More than she deserved.

"That was not your decision to make," Pen said, spinning around and facing Finn. He'd never seen the principal angry and it made her even more formidable. "We do not execute prisoners in Haven, and if you are to stay here then you will abide by our laws!"

"I'm not staying here," Finn said, coolly. He looked to General Riley, who had made no effort to condemn his actions. "I'm not staying here because I'm going back to Zavetgrad," Finn added, evenly. "I'm going back for Elara."

12

OUT OF THE SHADOWS

Finn waited for Pen and General Riley to enter the principal's office on level one for what he expected to be the second interrogation of the day. The interrogation of Corporal Casteel, or Special Prefect Rostova as they now knew her, had failed, and Finn intended to be equally defiant, though for very different reasons.

Finn was about to follow Riley though the door when he spotted Lieutenant Thornfield, handheld scanner at the ready, checking the principal's staff for inhibitor chips. The officer was backed up by two armed soldiers, vigilantly standing by should they be required to subdue and arrest another Authority agent. The atmosphere was palpably tense. Everyone was looking at one other, fearful of who might be revealed to be a spy, or perhaps fearful of being revealed themselves.

"Are you coming?" Riley grunted with his usual lack of charm.

Finn smiled at Scraps on his shoulder then patted his pal on the stomach, causing the robot to giggle, before stepping inside the office and closing the door behind him. Pen stood behind her desk, framed by an oil painting of Disko Island that was hung on the far wall. The image perfectly captured the stark, unforgiving wilderness above them, yet there was something hopeful about the painting too. He studied it for a moment longer and realized that the sun rising above a crooked brook had given birth to flecks of green and amber that he hadn't noticed at first, but which hinted at the possibility of life recovering in what had seemed a barren, lifeless world. The look on Pen's face painted a very different picture, however, and her expression contained no ambiguity. She was furious and a ticking time-bomb, waiting to explode. He decided to get in first and pre-empt the verbal onslaught he knew was awaiting him.

"I've made my decision and there's nothing either of you can say to change my mind," Finn said, immediately going on a war footing. "As hard as it might be to admit, the truth is we came desperately close to losing the Pit today. Casteel or Rostova, or whatever we're calling that dead prefect, let slip that we may only have weeks before the Authority moves again. We don't have time to debate this."

"Time is exactly what we need," Pen replied. Finn had gotten so used to the principal's gregarious nature that seeing her riled up came as a shock. "Right now, you're angry and emotional and not thinking straight. We all need time to clear our heads, especially you."

"I am thinking clearly," Finn said, holding his ground. "This is the first time I've been certain about anything since I was arrested in Metalhaven and sent to trial. Ever since then, I've been so caught up with just staying alive that I never had time to consider what I wanted. Now, I know what needs to be done. I know what *I* need to do."

"What you need to do is take a step back and think," Pen said, unmoved by his impassioned speech. "If you charge off back to Zavetgrad now and get killed or captured, the Regents win. They'll parade you through the streets of every work sector as a warning to others of what happens when you defy the Authority."

Pen's analysis of his potential fate was chillingly similar to what Casteel had told him in the comms room before the infiltrator was revealed to be a spy. Yet, even knowing this he was undeterred.

"I know you want me to stay here and pose for videos and flyers in the hope of stirring up a city-wide revolt, but we're past that now," Finn said. "By the time we drop those leaflets into Zavetgrad and beam those messages to the TV screens inside every recovery center, the Authority will have already brutally crushed any thoughts of rebellion and the momentum we have right now will be gone."

"You don't know that," Pen argued but Finn was certain. While Pen had grown up in the Pit, he'd lived his entire life under the heel of the Authority, and he knew how swiftly and decisively they could act.

"I *do* know," Finn insisted. "People are still buzzing after my broadcast so now is the time to strike, not in weeks or even days. By then the prefects will have broken the will of the workers and our chance will be lost."

He took a step toward the principal. She had intentionally placed her desk as a barrier between them to make it clear she was speaking as the Principal of the Pit and not his friend, but he wanted to reach out to Pen the human being, not the figurehead.

"We need to do this now," Finn said, driving his message home. "But with or without your help, I'm going. I'll find a way."

Pen sighed then glanced at General Riley, shooting him the same frustrated look that had adorned her normally smiling face since Finn had first entered the office.

"You've been unusually quiet, Will," Pen said, drawing the general into the conversation whether he wanted to participate or not. "I'm surprised you have nothing to say on the matter."

"I'm listening," Riley answered, somewhat cagily. "To both sides of the argument."

Pen narrowed her eyes at him. "Come now, Will, we've known each other too long. You've already made up your mind whose side you're on."

"I'm on the side of Haven," General Riley said. "I'm on the side of life."

It was pompous reply from the usually straight-talking general, but Finn could sense that Riley was having difficulty standing apart from Pen. He was the quintessential soldier, used to following orders and defending his nation and its leader with his life if so required but in this matter, it was clear he sided with Finn, whether he admitted it or not. The principal's intense green eyes scrutinized Riley for a few seconds longer and Finn felt uncomfortable watching the man squirm, before Pen finally released the general and focused back on him.

"This isn't about taking the correct course of action, it's about Elara Cage," Pen said. The gloves had come off. "This is about your guilt, Finn. Special Prefect Rostova told you about Elara precisely because she knew you'd want to save her. She was trying to lure you into a trap, you must see that?"

Finn had walked into the office expecting Elara to be Pen's first line of attack. And while he appreciated that the principal had tried to reason with him without dragging his personal feelings for his mentor into the discussion, he was prepared for it.

"I know it's trap," Finn admitted, being honest with Pen as well as himself. "I know their ways and how their minds work, but I don't just want to save her out of guilt, though I admit, that is part of it."

"Then make me understand, Finn," Pen said leaning forward with the palms of her hands pressed to the desk. "Make me understand why we should take such an awful risk, after so much has already been sacrificed to bring you here."

"Elara is the Iron Bitch of Metalhaven," Finn said, moving closer. By leaning in, Pen had taken the first step in removing the divide between them, and he knew he was close to reaching her. "By putting her on trial, the Authority has let all the workers of Zavetgrad know that Elara fought for them. Rescuing her will rally the people, especially if I lead the fight to save her. If we let Elara die, then we send the message that Haven doesn't care about the workers of Zavetgrad. If we're not prepared to fight for one of our own, a Metal, then why would we fight for them?"

Pen considered his answer, her stare becoming so intense that he feared it might blind him, like a laser blast to the eyes. His argument had been convincing, and he could see that Pen was wavering. The fact that the general had already made his position clear, even though he'd not said so outright, was the tipping factor.

"So, General Riley, how do we make this happen?" Pen said, employing the officer's official title to reinforce the fact she was pissed off with him.

"Getting into Zavetgrad remains a challenge and we don't have the forces to mount a direct assault, not until we have the support of the people," Riley began. "My recommendation would be to send a single infiltration team into the city with the objective of disrupting this special trial. If we can rescue Elara Cage right from under their noses, when every worker in every city is watching, Zavetgrad will erupt like a volcano."

Finn felt electricity race down his spine. While he'd been talking and trying to convince the principal, it appeared that General Riley had been quietly formulating a plan.

"I recommended five soldiers, including Finn, but because of the likelihood it will be a one-way mission, this has to be volunteer only," Riley continued. The general then turned to Finn. "In short, I can get you in but getting you out again may not be possible. Everything else is down to you."

Finn nodded. "I accept those terms." He then rapped his knuckles on his chest armor. "And so far, we have a team of one, which is a start."

"Two-two!" Scraps called out. "Scraps on team!"

Finn laughed but he also shook his head. "Not a chance, pal, I need you here in the Pit, feeding me intel and coordinating with General Riley."

Scraps scowled at him. "Scraps not stay..." the robot said, huffily.

"Buddy, given how many times you've saved my ass, I'd

love you to come along, but inside Zavetgrad, you can hardly blend in," Finn said. "You can help me more from here."

Scraps folded his arms and turned his head away in a sulk. Yet while the robot had succeeded in making him feel like a shit-bag, he wasn't going to change his mind. Scraps was the smartest computer in the entire pit, and he was convinced Pen and Riley would need his skills if a future invasion of Zavetgrad was ever to succeed.

"I'll put the word out to the corps," Riley said, returning to the subject of the infiltration unit. "But it won't be hard to find three soldiers who are willing to undertake this mission. My guess is that our best and brightest will be the first to raise their hands."

"But we need four more, not three," Finn said, frowning at the general. "You suggested a team of five, which means me and four others.

"You only need three more because you already have one volunteer," Riley grunted. "Me. I'm coming with you."

Pen threw her head back and let out an exasperated growl of discontent, as if what remained of her will to resist had departed her body as one long wheeze.

"I don't suppose I have any say in the matter, being Principal and all?" Pen said, raising an eyebrow at General Riley.

"If you order me to remain here then of course I will, ma'am," Riley said.

Pen blew a raspberry at the general, which made him flinch and jerk back, as if he'd been shot with a bullet.

"You only said that because you know damned well I won't issue any such order," Pen snapped, still glowering at the general, who was squirming again. "I suppose I can make

Lieutenant Thornfield a temporary replacement, with a bump in rank to Colonel." She paused then leaned in closer to Riley. "And I mean temporary, Will. I don't care for this 'one-way-mission' nonsense. You're coming back and that *is* an order."

Riley bowed his head. "Yes, ma'am."

"As luck would have it, we have recently made a new contact in Makehaven who may be able to provide a way into the city," Pen continued. She had given up protesting and was now turning her attention to the mission. "The contact's codename is 'Trip'."

Finn scowled and thought for a moment. "I knew a guy called Trip. He was the only other person to survive my test trial. But he was from Metalhaven, not Makehaven."

"It's the same man," Riley revealed, his rich bass tone rumbling Finn's chest. "Trip managed to escape the test crucible and was picked up by Metals on the edge of Makehaven. He was adamant about joining the cause and we believe he will make an effective operative. He now acts as a gatekeeper."

"A what?" Finn asked. He'd never heard that term before.

"We have people inside Zavetgrad who act as custodians, guarding the various ways in and out of the city," Pen explained. "Trip, or Erik Fuller to give him his actual name, was deemed missing presumed dead by the Authority, making him a perfect gatekeeper."

"So, how do we get in?" Finn asked.

"It won't be easy," Riley replied, though the general didn't appear dissuaded by this fact. "There is an underground lake and tunnel system that originates outside of the city fence and runs beneath Makehaven. It's a major source of clean drinking water for the city, which is used in part for producing the vast quantities of Zavetgrad's nuclear strong ale."

Finn laughed. "Well, Trip did like his beer," he said, recalling how the man's nickname referred to the fact he would drink three pints for each one his worker pals consumed.

"We have another Metal in Makehaven, who works in a Recovery Center," Riley continued. If we can get into the city through the Makehaven brewery, then this second operative can get us to the location of Elara's trial."

"How?" Finn wondered. "Makehaven and Metalhaven aren't especially close and there's no way to cross sector boundaries without going through a prefect checkpoint."

"We will travel concealed inside a beer truck," Riley answered, and Pen laughed.

"Well, it seems that you already have everything thought out," Pen said, eyeing Riley suspiciously. "How long have you been planning this little scheme of yours, General?"

"A while..." The general replied, looking sheepish. "But it wasn't until Rostova told us about Elara's trial that everything fell into place. Finn is right, ma'am. This could be our chance to bring the Authority to its knees."

Pen sighed again but the decision was made, and she was finally behind it.

"Very well, General, you have my approval to proceed," Pen said. "The people of Zavetgrad will finally see us. It's time we came out of the shadows."

13

AN OLD FRIEND

Finn left the principal's office so that Pen and General Riley could discuss the finer details of the operation to return him to Metalhaven. He imagined that the principal of the Pit was more than happy to see the back of him, at least for a time, but he had no regrets. He felt confident that his decision to return was the right one and that rescuing Elara from the trial would be the catalyst for a wider rebellion. It was merely a convenient side-effect that his choice also helped to alleviate the guilt he felt over abandoning his former mentor and the only human being left on the planet he truly cared about.

Or am I doing this for purely selfish reasons? he asked himself, as he strode toward the inner circle walkway on level one, drawing inquisitive glances from everyone he passed. *Is this the right choice for the workers of Zavetgrad or a selfish choice for me?*

In the end, it didn't matter because he wasn't going to change his mind. He wouldn't be a puppet on a string, play-acting the role of liberator when he could stir shit up and free the workers of the city for real.

"Finn okay?" Scraps queried. The robot remained clamped to his shoulder pauldron.

"I'm fine, pal," Finn said, patting the robot's foot. "I've just got a lot on my mind."

Scraps nodded and Finn watched out of the corner of his eye as the robot wrung his little metal hands in worry.

"I'll be okay, Scraps," Finn said, in an effort to reassure his friend. "I know you want to come with me, but I really do believe you can do more good here."

"Scraps want stay with Finn," the robot said, forlornly. "But Scraps do what is best."

"Thanks, pal," Finn said, patting the machine's foot again. "Now, since we appear to have some time to kill, what do you say we do a little exploring?"

Scraps beamed a smile at him. "Yes-yes! We go level five-five!"

"What's on fifty-five?" Finn asked, frowning.

"Cora!" Scraps replied, throwing his hands up in the air.

"Good plan," Finn said. Scraps always had a good plan. "It's technically the evening in the Pit, so she might be off shift."

"Cora off-shift," Scraps confirmed. "Scraps check with pit 'puter."

"Of course you did," Finn laughed. "Don't go poking around in there too much, though, or Pen might get cross."

"Pen already cross-cross," Scraps said, forlornly again.

"She'll get over it, she's just angry I'm not following her original plan," Finn said, changing course and heading for the closest bridge to the central pillar. "I think in her heart, she knows me going back is the right choice."

"That not it," Scraps said. "Pen sad Finn leaving. Pen likes Finn."

Finn's eyes widened. "You think so?"

"Scraps knows so," the robot replied.

"Well, that makes two people who like me then," Finn said, nodding and smiling to other citizens, who quickly got out of his way as soon as they saw him coming. "You plus Pen makes double the number of people who don't think I'm a worthless asshole."

"And Cora!" Scraps corrected him.

Finn stopped at the elevator and hit the call button. The car was on floor seven and already on its way up.

"Okay, I guess Cora too," Finn admitted. "I must be more popular than I thought."

"And Elara-good..." Scraps added, softly. "Elara likes Finn mostly."

Finn turned to the robot, his face suddenly hot, but Scraps was looking away, scuffing one of his feet against his shoulder pauldron as if the robot were more embarrassed than Finn was.

"I don't think so, pal," Finn said, remembering how harshly Elara had spoken to him before they parted. "I got her in trouble, and I left her to die. Even if I do save her, and even if she does forgive me, I don't deserve it."

"Finn too hard on himself," Scraps said. The elevator door pinged and slid open. "Finn good man. Scraps knows. Scraps clever!"

"Yes, you are," Finn laughed, and this time he gently squeezed the robot's metal foot, which made Scraps swell with pride and happiness, as if his oil can body had expanded like a balloon.

Finn stepped into the elevator and moved to the back of the car to allow others inside, though half of the people waiting were too intimidated by his presence to enter. Eventually, the doors closed, and they began their stop-start journey to Cora's residential level. It took several minutes longer to reach fifty-five than was expected because at each floor they stopped at, citizens would see Finn then dither and hesitate, adding ten or twenty more seconds to what would normally be a quick process. Across fifteen stops, those extra delays added up and Finn was more than glad to squeeze his armored body out of the claustrophobic elevator when Cora's floor finally arrived.

At first, level fifty-five didn't seem much different to level one, but as soon as Finn headed off the inner walkway, the differences between the business and residential areas became abundantly clear. Fifty-five was a bustling, thriving community unlike anything Finn had seen before. In Metalhaven, no-one congregated outside of the recovery centers because the law prevented gatherings of more than two people, and even then, it had to be for justifiable reasons. Fifty-five was a different world in comparison. Most people had left the doors to their apartments open and many had tables and chairs set up outside in the corridors, where the residents sat and drank tea and chatted. Children, still an alien sight to Finn, charged around the place freely, laughing and playing like they didn't have a care in the world.

"This nice!" said Scraps, as a ball rolled along the corridor in Finn's direction.

"Yes, it is," Finn agreed.

He trapped the ball with his foot then bent down to pick it up. The material felt cool to the touch, but it was also malleable, like the doughy algae bread he used to eat in Metalhaven.

"Throw it!" a boy of perhaps six or seven cried out.

The boy was standing with a group of six other children, who all seemed to be playing together. It took Finn a moment to realize the boy had been shouting to him, and he lobbed the squashy ball back in their direction to loud cheers of approval. Finn smiled and laughed too. The joyful sound of their play was infectious, and Scraps was caught up in the emotion too. Then Finn's mood darkened as he realized how close the special prefects of Zavetgrad had come to destroying this virtual paradise. *Surely, even a prefect wouldn't sink to the depths of murdering a child?* Finn asked himself, but the answer he came up with gave him no solace, and the bitterness in his heart remained.

"Finn!"

He looked through the crowd and saw Cora waving at him from outside an apartment toward the far end of the corridor. He wondered how she had managed to see him given the hubbub, before remembering he was still wearing his chrome prosecutor armor, which made him stand out like a naked flame in a dark room.

He worked his way through the mass of bodies, dodging playing children, tiptoeing over toys, and side-stepping tables filled with people who were sharing a meal. He expected his passing to disrupt the occasion and was pleased to find that everyone was too caught up in their own merriment to give him a second glance. Finally, he reached what he assumed was Cora's apartment and the woman threw herself at him, pulling Finn into a tight embrace that made his armor creak.

"I heard that you were instrumental in saving the Pit,"

Cora said, finally drawing back and allowing Finn to breathe. "Though, I'd expect nothing less from the Hero of Metalhaven..." she added, with a sly smile.

"I was just in the right place at the right time," Finn said, his face flushing hot again.

"That seems to be your superpower," Cora said, smiling.

Finn then noticed that Cora wasn't alone; another young woman sat at the small bistro table outside the apartment. He smiled and nodded to her, but the woman seemed rapt with terror, as if she'd just seen a ghost.

"That's Gisele, she got out from Seedhaven about four years ago," Cora said, hooking a thumb toward her guest. "She works on the science floors with me, helping to devise new agricultural techniques and optimizing our food supply programs."

"Hey, Gisele," Finn said.

The woman waved and a croak escaped her lips that Finn thought sounded something like "hey," or "hi," or maybe it was just an incoherent babble, he couldn't be sure.

"Haven't they managed to find you any normal clothes yet?" Cora asked.

She was pouring Finn a cup of what smelled like herbal tea. He recognized some of the floral notes and it reminded him of the teas in the prosecutor barracks, and by extension, Juniper Jones. It was a memory he quickly pushed to the back of his mind.

"They gave me some military fatigues but I'm sort of used to this now," Finn said, only realizing that fact just then. "Besides, I've barely gone longer than twenty-four hours between fights, so it makes sense to keep it on."

"You don't sleep in it, do you?" Cora asked, scowling at him, and Finn laughed.

"No, I'm not that far gone," he replied, before flashing his eyes and adding, "yet..."

"So, to what do I owe the honor of a visit from the fabled Finn Brasa?" Cora said, handing him the cup of tea, which he accepted gladly. She then smiled at Scraps. "And the even more famous Scraps, of course."

"Hi-hi!" Scraps said, waving at Cora.

Finn shrugged and blew out a sigh. He didn't have a particular reason for visiting, other than it being a use for his free time, while Pen and General Riley plotted the mission. Then it struck him that he might be gone from Haven sooner than he'd expected and that this might be the only chance he'd have to say goodbye to one of the few people in his world he actually knew.

"I'm going back to Zavetgrad," Finn said, blurting the words out with less nuance than he'd planned. "I think I have a real chance of rallying the people behind me, but only if I go soon."

Cora's face fell and she set down her teacup on the table. Gisele sensed the shift in mood and quickly excused herself, though it seemed to Finn that she was more than glad to escape his orbit.

"You're going back for her, aren't you?" Cora said. There was no judgment, only sadness. "The prosecutor who mentored you and kept you alive?"

Finn nodded. "It's not the only reason, or even the most important one, but I owe it to Elara to try."

Cora reached out and held Finn's wrist, squeezing it gently.

"It's the most important reason to you," Cora said, "and that's okay. You're allowed to be a little selfish."

"Being selfish is what got me into this mess," Finn said, "and it's what got Owen killed."

"Corbin Radcliffe killed Owen, not you," Cora said, her tone firmer. "Sooner or later, you're going to have to forgive yourself for that."

Finn smiled and nodded, though he was just pretending to agree with Cora so that they could change the subject. She narrowed her eyes at him, seeing his apparent capitulation for the ploy it was, but mercifully didn't push him.

"How was it down here, during the attack?" Finn asked, taking the opportunity to talk about any topic so long as the subject wasn't Finn Brasa.

"We're fairly deep here but we felt the missiles and we knew what was happening, so people were naturally scared," Cora said. "But they trust the Haven soldiers to protect them, and they trust you too, Finn."

Finn suddenly noticed that people were watching them, some covertly and others without attempting to hide it. "I'm surprised they even knew I was involved," he said.

"They didn't." Cora shrugged. "But they knew you were here in the Pit and that was enough."

Finn understood how his name had become near mythical and that his actions inspired people, but it was still difficult to accept the adulation that came along with it.

"I'm still that same dumb asshole from Metalhaven who pushed his luck too far," Finn said, hiding behind his teacup. "Maybe I'm a little wiser and I've certainly got a few more scars, but I'm just a chrome."

"You could stay," Cora said, and her suggestion stunned

him into silence. "You don't owe anything to anyone, Finn. You've already done enough. Why not let the soldiers fight the wars, and you have a normal life?"

Finn laughed under his breath. "I think I'm already way beyond the chance for a normal life, whatever that even means."

"It's pretty simple," Cora said, gesturing to the dozens of people nearby, who continued to watch them talk. "You go to work, doing a job you like, instead of one that was assigned to you, and you spend your free time with the people you choose, rather than those you get lumbered with. It means that you get freedom, Finn, and freedom is more intoxicating than any drug."

"That's why I need to go back," Finn said. Rather than convince him to stay, Cora had simply reinforced why he had to fight. "There are hundreds of thousands of workers in Zavetgrad who deserve what these people have."

"But freeing them doesn't have to be your responsibility," Cora said, almost pleading with Finn. "You've lost so much already. It's okay to take something back."

"Maybe you're right," Finn said, smiling at Cora. "But I'm not ready yet."

He finished his tea, which continued to evoke unhappy memories of Juniper Jones, then set the cup down. Cora watched him place the crockery onto the table and her eyes fell to the floor, knowing that it meant he was leaving.

"Promise me something, Finn," Cora said, still looking down. "Promise me that you're not going back out of some misguided need to punish yourself." She looked into his eyes though it was a struggle. "Promise me that you're not planning to be a martyr, because killing yourself won't bring

Owen back. I didn't know him well, or barely at all, but I'm certain he wouldn't have wanted that for you."

"I know," Finn said. He smiled and held Cora's shoulders. "And I'll come back. I don't know when or how, but I promise that I'll try."

Cora grabbed him again and this time she hugged him so tightly that he could barely breathe. It was the sort of embrace a person gave when in their heart, they believed they may not get another chance to hold that person close. Reluctantly, she broke away then held Finn's eyes for a few seconds before shaking her head and turning to Scraps.

"Take care of him, okay?" Cora said.

"Scraps will!" the robot replied, cheerfully. "Scraps always does."

They hugged again, and Cora kissed him softly on the cheek, then Finn said his goodbyes and worked his way back through the crowds of people lining the corridor. Everyone was watching him now, even the boy, who was standing in front of his friends with the squishy ball tucked beneath his arm. The boy saluted and Finn saluted back. The smiles he received in return filled his soul.

Before long, he was back on the inner walkway, heading toward the central pillar with the intention of returning to his little bunk room on level three and perhaps getting some rest. Then as he approached the elevator, someone called out his name. The voice was vaguely familiar, like something from a dream, and he looked across the sea of faces on the bridge until his attention was drawn to one person in particular. The woman had large, hazel eyes and her hair, as dark as the soil beneath Metalhaven's yards, fell almost to her waist, curly at the ends but laser straight as it ran past her face.

"Sienna?" Finn asked, though he already knew it was.

"Hello Finn," Sienna replied.

"You... got out..." Finn said, struggling to form the words because he was smiling so broadly. "I mean, I was told you did but I wasn't sure, until now."

Sienna had been the wellness center worker Finn used to visit in Metalhaven. She had risked her own neck to discreetly conceal the fact he never actually did the legally-mandated 'deed'. And now there she was, looking exactly the same as he remembered her, in all but one important detail – she was no longer sad.

"Khloe told me you got out," Finn said. "You look good. Strong."

"Thank you," Sienna replied. She held up her left hand and there was a simple gold band around her left ring finger. "I got married!"

Finn laughed and he almost ran to Sienna and hugged her, but the pair had practiced abstemiousness for so long that the habit made him hold back.

"Good for you, Sienna," Finn said, meaning every word. "You deserve some happiness."

"So do you," Sienna replied. "Whatever else you do, remember that."

For a second, Finn worried that he was going to get another lecture on forgiving himself and not choosing to become a martyr, but Sienna was not Cora, and an existence in the wellness centers of Zavetgrad was a far cry from the offices of Spacehaven.

"I heard you're going back," she continued. Finn frowned wondering how she knew, and the woman looked repentant. "I live on fifty-five too and saw you get off the elevator."

"You were spying on me?" Finn said, smiling.

Sienna shrugged. "Maybe a little. I wasn't sure whether to speak to you or not. I didn't know how you'd feel about..." She shrugged and held up the wedding band again.

"I'm glad you did, and I meant it when I said I'm happy for you," Finn replied. Then he frowned at Sienna again. "But if you're not here to talk me out of doing something stupid, then why stop me?"

Sienna stepped closer and it was suddenly like the years of humiliation and degradation she'd experienced during her hard years in Zavetgrad were radiating out of her like an unstable nuclear reactor.

"I want you to bring it down, Finn," Sienna said, forcing the words out through gritted teeth. "I want you to bring the Authority to its knees. Not just for me, but for all of us."

"I will," Finn said. There was a lump in his throat and his voice trembled. "I'll free Zavetgrad or die trying. Then, if I can, I'll crush Nimbus too."

"I know you will." Sienna smiled and it was like he was back in their little room in the wellness center, talking their hour away, just the two of them plotting to change the world. "I know because you're the Hero of Metalhaven."

14

THE VOLUNTEERS

Finn spent three hours in his cramped cabin trying to get some rest, but sleep had evaded him like an irritating fly that refused to be swatted. Time was his enemy. He had too much time on his hands while every minute he lay, tossing and turning on his rock-hard cot bed, Elara's was running out.

Thanks to Metals inside Zavetgrad feeding information to the Pit through secure channels, General Riley had learned that Elara's trial had been set for ten o'clock the next evening in what would be the largest gladiatorial spectacle the city had seen for decades. That gave Finn and the other volunteers only twenty-hours to get inside Zavetgrad and reach Metalhaven in time to save Elara from his former classmates, Herald and Inferno. That the Regents had chosen Ivan Volkov and Tonya Duke to hunt and kill Elara was another sure sign that they wanted to lure Finn back, but he didn't care if he was walking into a trap because traps only work if you don't know about them.

Suddenly, Scraps jumped off the desk beside Finn's bed and landed on his stomach. He'd removed some of his armor in an effort to get more comfortable, which meant the surprisingly dense robot winded him.

"New message!" Scraps said, jumping up and down and pressing more air from his lungs. "Riley ready-ready!"

"How do you know that?" Finn said, lifting the bot off his stomach so he could sit up. "The computer is sat right there on the desk, and it hasn't made a sound since we got here."

The computer bleeped on cue and the screen flickered on to show that a message had been received. Scraps smiled and waggled his metal eyebrows.

"Nobody likes a smartass," Finn said, carrying Scraps to the desk. "Especially a robot smartass."

Scraps reproduced the sound of someone blowing a raspberry then tapped away at the computer's keyboard to bring the message up on the screen. It was from General Riley and was characteristically brief.

All volunteers prepped and ready. Meet me in hangar seven, garage level. Wheels up in thirty.

"Wheels up where?" Finn asked the little robot. "And thirty what?"

"General means skycar," Scraps explained. He knew the lingo because he knew everything. "Mission go in thirty min-mins!"

"Thirty minutes!" Finn said, springing out of the chair. "I've been bumbling around in this room for hours waiting for Riley to give me the word, and now we go in thirty?"

Scraps shrugged. "Plenty of time."

"Maybe for a robot that thinks a billion thoughts per second, but for us humans, it's not much time," Finn said, searching for the armor panels he'd removed. Considering the compact dimensions of the room, he was impressed – and annoyed – that he'd managed to lose them.

"Here-here!" Scraps said, hovering beside the bed and pointing beneath it. The items Finn was looking for were tucked in under the shallow bed frame, exactly where he'd put them. "Laser charged too!"

"Thanks, pal, you always have my back," Finn said, scrambling under the bed to reclaim his missing items.

"Then Scraps should come too," the robot replied. Scraps was still sulky about Finn demanding he stay in the Pit and help from operations.

"We talked about this," Finn said, setting to work completing his armor. "You're many things, Scraps, but a soldier isn't one of them."

Scraps folded his arms in a huff. "Scraps shot Casteel…"

"And look how much of an effort that was," Finn said. He figured that the robot would bring up the subject of blasting the infiltrator, whose actual name was Special Prefect Evelina Rostova, in the chest with his laser cannon. "You did great back there but in Zavetgrad we'll be fighting dozens of prefects like her. I can't be worrying about you and focus on saving Elara at the same time, and you want me to save Elara, don't you?"

Scraps scuffed his foot on the desk and looked down. "Yes-yes."

"Then we're agreed." Finn collected his baseball bat and attached it to the magnetic scabbard on his back then affixed the laser cannon to its holster. It snapped into place with a reassuring *thunk*.

"You can still come and send me off, though," Finn said. He couldn't stand to see his robot buddy looking sad.

"Okay-kay," Scraps replied, shrugging.

Finn sighed and felt even worse, but he wasn't going to give in. He needed Scraps safe and somewhere he could help Pen to monitor the insurgent team's progress and, hopefully, find a way to get them out of the city again.

"Then let's go," Finn said, picking up Scraps and placing the robot on his shoulder. "We only have another twenty-five or so minutes before 'wheels up' and I don't want to be late and make General Riley even more gruff and surly than he already is."

Scraps laughed meekly, which made Finn feel a little better, but if the price of keeping Scraps alive was to make him feel a little sad, at least in the short term, it was a price worth paying. He couldn't lose his robot companion on top of everything else.

Finn chose to take the stairs from the barracks on level three to the garage on level zero, where General Riley and the other volunteers were waiting for him. It would have technically been quicker to take the elevator but the sight of Finn in his prosecutor armor still garnered too much attention and he didn't want to be waylaid. It felt better to be constantly on the move, instead of stuck between floors as people dithered about whether to enter the elevator car or wait for the next one.

Pushing though the submarine-style blast door, Finn entered the garage area and saw General Riley in the distance, standing under one of the few active overhead lights in the cavernous, dark space. He set off toward him but felt something hard underfoot that gave a little as his heavy boots pressed down. Shifting position, he saw that it was a shell casing left over from the battle between Haven's soldiers and the special prefects that had invaded the Pit. He picked it up but couldn't be sure whether it was the remains of a friendly bullet or an enemy one. Then he noticed many more signs of the fight and the longer he looked the more obvious they became. From the holes in the pillars, to scorch marks on the deck, and even blood stains that had stubbornly refused to clean off, the garage area told the story of a battle hard fought and won.

Finn continued toward Riley with Scraps still clamped to his shoulder, his keen electronic eyes scanning every inch of the space. At first, Finn didn't notice the skycar because it had been painted an inky black like the special prefect vehicles that had descended upon the Pit like vultures. In contrast, Riley and the other three soldiers were wearing an urban-pattern camo that made them stand out against the dark background like bright window slits on a castle wall.

"Good, you're on time," Riley grunted, dispensing with any pleasantries, which was how Finn preferred it. "Let me introduce you to the rest of the squad," the general added, stepping aside to reveal three soldiers with mean and serious-looking expressions.

"This is Sergeant Ren Kellan from my unit," Riley began, gesturing to a middle-aged soldier with a thick, black mustache covering his top lip. "He was born here in Haven and is one of the longest-serving and most decorated warriors we have."

"Good to meet you, sir," the sergeant said, standing to attention and saluting.

The sergeant's voice was almost as gruff as Riley's and he matched the general in surliness too. Finn chose not to return the salute and instead offered the man his hand.

"Thank you for volunteering, Sergeant, I appreciate it," Finn said.

Kellan scowled at his hand for a moment but eventually shook it, figuring the break in protocol was warranted, given the unique circumstances.

"Next is Ensign Mara Thorne, who also happens to be our pilot," Riley continued. "But she's much more than just a stick jockey. Mara is one of the toughest bastards in the Pit, isn't that right, Ensign?"

"You know it," Mara said, giving Finn a stiff salute then being first to offer her hand. "It's an honor to be part of this fight, sir."

"Thank you, Ensign," Finn said. It was while he was shaking the woman's hand that he recognized her face. "You were with the general when we fought to secure the garage against the special prefects, weren't you?"

"I was," Mara said, appearing to appreciate the fact Finn had noticed. "I saw you fight too, which is why I know this mission will work."

"That's the first time Thorne has ever seen a proper fight," the third soldier cut in, with a smirk. "She's usually so far up in the air that she needs binoculars to see us grunts on the ground."

"I don't need binoculars to know you didn't fight up here," Thorne said, nudging the third man in the ribs. "I heard you were fighting a battle of a different kind sat on the can with your pants around your ankles when the alarm came through."

"Hey, it ain't my fault I was stuck down on sixty without comms," the third soldier said, feigning offense. "Besides, I won my battle the same as you won yours, though it took three flushes to finally make it go away..."

"That's enough," Riley grunted, while Thorne and Reyes shivered with laughter and Sergeant Kellan shook his head in dismay. "This here is Private Kai Reyes, who despite sounding like a jackass is one of our of best soldiers."

"I *am* your best soldier, sir," Reyes said with pride and confidence. "That's why I volunteered. I missed my chance when those special bastards invaded, and I intended to make up for it in Zavetgrad."

"Don't worry, Private, there will be plenty of opportunities to fight," General Riley said, sounding an ominous and cautionary tone.

"Well, thank you all, again," Finn said, nodding respectfully to the three volunteers. "I know this is asking a lot, but I promise it's not for nothing. I truly believe that if we can stop this trial, we can spark something that will set all of Metalhaven alight."

"I don't know anything about that, sir, I just signed up so I can kick some prefect ass," Private Reyes said. The man held up a closed fist, perhaps expecting Ensign Mara to bump it, but the woman just raised her eyebrows and left Reyes hanging.

"On that note, I think we should get going," Riley said, though Finn thought he could detect the faintest hint of a smile cracking his age-weathered features.

"Just before that, we need to sort out this officer business," Finn said, stopping everyone before they broke up to embark. "It's not the first time I've been addressed as 'sir' but I'm just a guy from Metalhaven who can swing a bat."

"Not anymore," Riley said. The man reached into his

pocket and removed a golden oak leaf, which he proceeded to attach to Finn's chest plate. It was magnetic and stuck in place firmly. "This is a military operation so until we return, you will be Major Finn Brasa," Riley added, stepping back.

Finn felt like protesting but he knew it was pointless to argue with the general, who was more stubborn even than Elara, and they also didn't have time to waste.

"Fine, if it makes you happy," Finn said. "I'd still rather you just call me Finn, though."

"No can do, Major," Reyes said, still smiling, despite his earlier humiliation. "Hey, can I get a field promotion to LT, just so I can outrank the bird dog, here?" the private added, hooking a thumb to Thorne, who rolled her eyes.

"No," Riley said, definitively. "Now, if we're done, I suggest we get on board."

Finn almost climbed on-board the skycar before remembering that Scraps was still attached to his shoulder. He figured that the little robot had stayed quiet for precisely that reason, and he looked disappointed when Finn detached him and allowed the robot to settle into a hover in front of him.

"I'll be back before you know it, pal," Finn said, offering the robot what he hoped was a reassuring smile.

"Scraps scared..." the robot said.

"Don't be, I'll be fine," Finn answered. "Besides, once we free Elara, she'll be so furious that she'll bring down the entire Authority all by herself."

"But what Scraps to do?" the robot said. He wasn't going to be placated, not this time.

Riley then marched over and Finn expected the man to hurry him up but instead the general did something unexpected. He reached into his pocket and removed a pair of captain's bars.

"I took these off the body of Captain Lyra Harken," Riley said, juggling the rank bars in the palm of his hand. "She was part of my unit and a friend." Riley then picked up one of the sets of bars and attached it to Scraps' oil-can body. It clipped on with the same powerful magnetic force that was keeping the oak leaf stuck to his chest. "Finn is right that we need you here, *Captain* Scraps," the general continued. "I'm making you special advisor to Principal Everhart. You're our secret weapon, and I expect you to figure out a way to get us out of Zavetgrad again. Can you do that, Captain?"

Scraps beamed a smile at the general and saluted. "Scraps can! Scraps honor Lyra name."

"I know you will," Riley said, nodding. "Now, report to the Principal of the Pit. She's expecting you."

"Okay-kay!" Scraps said, saluting again.

Riley returned the salute and Finn did too. Then Scraps raced toward Finn and hugged his chest as best he could, considering the armor plating that was between them, before zooming away into the darkness so rapidly he was gone within a couple of seconds.

"Thank you for that," Finn said.

"I've never been much of a fan of robots, and I'm the sure the same is true of you, but that little machine is a difference-maker," Riley said, returning to his trademark gruffness. "The rank may have been a bit of theatre but making your robot an advisor was not for show. Scraps can help here. He knows more about the Pit than any of us and it wasn't for him, we might have already lost Haven."

"Then we see eye-to-eye," Finn said. "On this and the need to rescue Elara."

General Riley narrowed his eyes. "I know this woman means a lot to you, *Major Brasa*, but I need your word that the mission comes first."

"Elara is the mission," Finn hit back. He was done with being lectured, from Riley, Pen, Cora or anyone else. "We save Elara and Metalhaven falls. It's that simple."

Riley continued to scowl at Finn for several more seconds but, tellingly, the general didn't refute what he'd said, because he knew Finn was right.

"Then we'd better hope The Shadow is as resourceful and defiant as you make her out to be," Riley said. "Because if she dies then all hope of freeing Zavetgrad dies too, and our bones will litter the yards of Metalhaven right alongside hers."

15

THE RETURN

THE SKYCAR'S rotors spun up and Finn had to shield his face against the downdraught as he struggled toward the craft with General Riley at his side. The Haven skycars were older and more utilitarian than the sleek vessels the special prefects flew, but it was sturdy and with its jet-black livery, Finn felt confident they could slip by in the night without being noticed. He was about to climb inside the rear compartment when a troubling thought entered his mind. Black was ideal for hiding in the darkness but the barren terrain surrounding Zavetgrad was covered in a thick blanket of blinding white snow.

"Won't this thing stand out like a prefect in a recovery center bar once we reach the other side of the Davis Strait?" Finn asked the general, who was working through a checklist on a clipboard.

"You'd think so, but this old skycar has a few new tricks up its sleeve." Riley held the clipboard against the hull of the craft and a patch of metal immediately surrounding it changed to blend in with the bleached white paper Riley had been working on. "It's a new type of reactive armor. Well, it's new to us, anyway. I understand that your old mentor already had something similar."

"She did!" Finn said, then he laughed remembering how Elara was always able to sneak up on him even without her chameleonic armor. "It freaked me out how she always followed me wherever I went, like a literal shadow, but now that she's not there, it's like a part of me is missing."

"We'll get her back, Major," Riley grunted, returning to ticking items off his checklist. The skycar's armor turned black again. "Then we just have to hope the people of Metalhaven are willing to fight for her, and for you."

"They will," Finn said.

Riley paused his pen-stroke mid-tick then narrowed his eyes at Finn. "How can you be so certain?"

Finn laughed again. "Because there's nothing that the people of Metalhaven love more than a good fight. We just need to give them a reason."

"Pre-flight is done, General, we're ready to lift off when you are," Ensign Thorne shouted from the cockpit.

"Then clear us for immediate take-off," Riley called back. He made one final tick on his piece of paper then stowed the clipboard inside the skycar's cabin and grabbed the handrail. "Last chance to back out of this," the general said.

Finn shook his head. "I never thought I'd be going back to Zavetgrad so soon, but I know this is the right thing to do."

Riley nodded then pulled himself into the rear cabin alongside Sergeant Kellen and Private Reyes. Finn was about to climb in alongside him when Ensign Thorne leaned over and pushed open the passenger side door.

"You want to ride shotgun, hero?" Thorne said. She was

wearing classic aviator sunglasses, despite the garage being pitch black. He recognized the design from his studies of popular culture on his now long-gone data device. "I could use the company."

Finn saw no reason to refuse, so climbed into the cockpit alongside the pilot and pulled the door shut. It needed slamming twice before it closed and locked.

"Don't worry, she might not be as shiny as the skycars the Authority rotorheads fly but she's got it where it counts," Thorne said, smiling at him. "She'll get us there in one piece. It's getting back again that will be the tricky part."

The radio crackled and Thorne pressed a hand to one of her headset earcups to listen to the message.

"Copy that, Haven control, we are cleared to depart," Thorne replied into her microphone. "Buckle up, hero, it's blowing a gale outside so there might be a little chop."

"Something tells me that 'a little chop' might be an understatement," Finn said, struggling to attach his harness.

Thorne smiled at him again then her hands began moving faster than a barman pulling pints for a thirsty worker crew, as she flipped switches and set dials. Then they were moving but Thorne's hands were not on the controls, and it took Finn a second to realize that a hydraulic platform beneath the skycar was lifting them toward the surface. Slabs of metal slid back to facilitate their ascent, all layers of Haven's dense armor, until finally the surface door opened, and snow tumbled onto the craft, covering the canopy and being chewed into tiny ice crystals by the fast-spinning rotors. Compared to the gloom of the garage, the daylight was dazzling, despite the thick cloud cover and swirling blizzard that was already battering the skycar, and Thorne's aviators suddenly made sense.

"Are you sure we can take off in this storm?" Finn queried.

"Piece of cake," Thorne replied, and Finn could just about make out a wink through the tinted lens. The ensign then twisted her neck and peered into the rear compartment. "Clench up, folks, we're about to get airborne."

"Huh, I thought we already were?" Private Reyes mumbled through a mouthful of algae chips.

"How the hell can he eat at a time like this?" Finn wondered.

"He's always eating; the guy is an animal," Thorne said, eyes front again. Then she hesitated and pulled open a drawer in front of Finn's seat. There was a brown paper bag inside. "But if you think you might lose your lunch, use that," the pilot said. "I just had this baby cleaned."

Finn bristled at the notion he couldn't handle a little skycar flight when Thorne threw open the throttle and pulled the skycar into a steep climb. Finn grabbed the arms of his chair and clenched up, just as Thorne had suggested, though it was an involuntary action. Pressed into the back of his seat, he could do little other than stare forward, but all he could see was a chaotic mess of sleet and snow that completely obscured the view ahead. He wanted to call out to Thorne, to seek reassurance that everything was okay, but all that escaped his lips was a muted squeak, like a timid mouse.

Then the skycar punched through the cloud layer and the weather cleared in an instant, like God had just turned off a faucet, but the new view ahead was no more comforting than the blizzard they'd left behind. Nimbus, the Authority's orbital citadel and home to the genetically pure produce of the regime's inhumane DNA-harvesting program, was dead center, as bright and as clear as a full moon. It was always looming, always watching, and Finn wished he could just reach out and pull the abomination out of the sky with his bare hands. Then the skycar leveled off and banked sharply to the right and his view of the citadel was gone, though its image remained burned into his retinas.

One step at a time, Finn, he told himself. *First Metalhaven, then Zavetgrad, then, if I'm still breathing, I'll find a way to destroy Nimbus too.*

"See, nothing to it," Thorne said, winking at Finn again from behind her shades. The Ensign then flicked open the internal comm system. "We've got about another half-hour at this altitude to clear the storm then I'll descend and hug the Davis Strait so close you could drop a net and do some fishing."

"Hell, yeah, I could eat some tuna," Reyes called out. "I'm still hungry."

"You're always hungry," Thorne called back, laughing.

"No-one is eating raw fish in this cabin," Riley said, using his gruffness to dispel any notion that the private might take Thorne up on her offer. "I suggest we all get some shut-eye, duties permitting, of course."

"I can only do three things well, sir... sleep, eat and kick prefect ass," Reyes replied. "And since I can't do the last two right now, some shut eye sounds good."

"Great, then he'll finally shut the hell up," Sergeant Kellen grunted to muted laughter from Thorne and, to Finn's surprise, Riley too.

"No can do, sarge, I talk in my sleep," Reyes said, shuffling down in his seat and closing his eyes.

"Talk in your sleep and you'll wake up in the ocean," Kellen replied to more laughter.

The sergeant then also got comfortable and pulled his cap down over his eyes. Finn glanced into the rear cabin and saw that General Riley had also adjusted his position and was resting his head against the side wall of the skycar with his eyes closed.

"I assume you won't be following suit?" Finn asked Thorne, hooking a thumb aft.

"Not yet, I'll wait till we've cleared the storm and leveled off over the strait," Thorne said. This time there was no wink or smile and the pilot noticed Finn's obvious concern. "Don't worry, the autopilot can handle flying straight and level but if it makes you feel better, you can watch over me."

"If you're asleep at the wheel then I promise you I'll be wide awake," Finn said, firmly.

Thorne laughed then dug a neck pillow out of a compartment to her side and tossed it onto Finn's lap.

"Then you'd better get some sleep now," Thorne said, beginning a gradual descent, since the storm was abating. "You might not get another chance once we reach land."

Finn picked up the pillow, which smelled faintly of carbolic soap, and maneuvered it into place behind his neck. He didn't think much of his chances of falling asleep but once Thorne had settled the skycar into a smooth glide over the choppy, black water of the Davis Strait, he found himself starting to relax. Only thoughts of Elara kept him awake. He interrogated his motives for the mission, wanting to be certain that his choice was the right one for the rebellion and not just the convenient choice to ease his guilt, but the answer was always the same – now was the time to strike. Bringing down the Authority was more important than anything, even Elara. Even so, he would have been lying to himself if he believed he could let her go.

Despite his busy mind the soft glow from the instrument panel and dim, silver light from the moon quickly soothed his frayed edges and Finn found his eyelids growing heavy. His first night in Haven aside, he hadn't slept much, and the drone of the engines and gentle rocking of the skycar as it travelled through the bumpy air knocked him out like an uppercut.

In his dreams Finn was back in Zavetgrad, in the trial crucible. He was watching himself and Elara running toward the skycar that had belonged to Juniper Jones, while a fleet of other prefect skycars raced toward them. He saw the look on Elara's face and remembered the elation he felt as if he were reliving that moment. They were less than a minute away from escaping, together, then a bullet split the air and punched through Elara's armor, sending her crashing to the ground. He flinched as she fell and pressed his hand to his side, as if the bullet had struck him too. Then, to his horror, he felt wetness against his skin and saw that he'd been shot instead of Elara. His eyes darkened and he fell, then the next thing he knew he was looking up at the face of his old mentor.

"What's wrong?" Elara said, desperate. Finn realized he was lying on concrete, slumped over to one side, arm wrapped around his body. "Come on, I'll help you," Elara added.

She tried to get him up, but Finn was a dead weight, and he waved her away.

"It's over, Elara," Finn said, the words forming automatically.

Elara shook her head, then finally saw Finn's blood leaking into the snow and she realized he'd been shot.

"Sniper..." Finn said, nodding toward the skycars. "A lucky shot." He snorted a laugh. "Not so lucky for me." Already his face felt numb, and his words were becoming slurred. "Go, Elara," he added, trying to push his mentor away. "Go, before they get you too."

Elara's green eyes became hard and her expression cruel. "No, I'd never leave you," she said, bitterly. "I'd rather both of us die here, together, than run away..." there was a pause then she added, "... run away like you did from me..."

Finn felt a stab in his gut and at first, he thought it was guilt, until he realized that it was Elara's roundel dagger piercing his flesh.

"You ran out on me, Finn," Elara said, pulling the knife out of his gut. "I thought you cared about me. I thought I mattered... but you left me to die."

"Elara, I'm sorry!" Finn said. He tried to reach out a hand, but it was a dead weight. "Please forgive me..." Then he watched as Elara raised the dagger to her neck and cut deeply into her own flesh. "Elara, no!" Finn cried, but her throat was already cut, and she collapsed onto his chest, blooding pouring from the wound and mixing with his own.

"Hey, hero?"

Finn's eyes shot open, and he jolted upright in the co-pilot's seat. Ensign Thorne was looking at him, this time without her aviators, so he could see her concerned frown clearly.

"You okay there, hero?"

"Yeah, just a bad dream," Finn said, rubbing his face and flexing his muscles. It felt like he'd been in a fight. "They're the only kind I get."

Thorne nodded but she didn't push him. It might have been because she wasn't interested but the look in her eyes suggested she understood his trauma all too well.

"We're over land," Thorne added, pointing out of the window. "We'll be setting down in a few minutes, so I thought I'd better wake you."

"I slept the whole way?" Finn asked and Thorne nodded. "But what about you? Don't you need to get some sleep too?"

"Oh, I slept plenty," Thorne replied, casually. "Don't worry, we were never in any danger," she added, reacting to Finn's aghast expression. "All the risky shit comes next."

Finn blew out a sigh and scanned the horizon but there was no obvious sign of Zavetgrad. Then he spotted the smoke from the factory chimneys and the light pollution from the city in the far distance.

"I think you're going in the wrong direction…" Finn said, unable to judge the distance since the city was simply too far away.

"We have to land a good ways out to avoid their radar and scout drones," Thorne said, adjusting her controls and slowing to a hover. "The Authority sends out little roving robots to search their perimeter for people just like us."

Finn nodded and stayed quiet so as not to distract Thorne from landing the craft, which she did rapidly and without incident, their rotors kicking up snow over the windows and causing a white-out. Then the engines powered down and the pilot flicked an array of switches to shut down their systems, one by one.

"Last one inside Zavetgrad buys the beers!" Private Reyes said. The soldier threw open the door and jumped down, rifle in hand. Sergeant Kellan followed, armed with a shotgun, and the two soldiers quickly scouted and secured their landing zone.

"We're clear, General," Kellan called out. "I'm reading some scout drone activity, but they haven't seen us yet. Even so, I don't recommend hanging around."

Riley nodded then jumped down and slung a compact rifle over his shoulder before checking a computer device attached to his wrist. "The entrance to the cave system is three miles southwest of here," he said, pointing the way. "Let's hustle."

Finn disembarked and waited for Ensign Thorne, who slapped him on the back then moved out ahead, weapon held ready. Her aviators had been left on the cushion of her pilot's seat.

"Stay close, hero," Thorne called back to him. "This place isn't as dead as it seems."

Finn frowned but didn't have a chance to question the pilot, who was already ten meters ahead of him. A low hum then emanated from the skycar, and it morphed from black to snowy white in an instant. Finn had to rub his eyes and squint to even know it was there at all.

"Finn, let's move!" Riley called out.

Finn jogged to catch up, though progress was slow thanks to the thick snow. Riley led from the front, setting a furious pace that Finn struggled to match, despite the high level of fitness he'd attained during prosecutor training. Twenty minutes elapsed without a word spoken between any of them, but the rocky, snow-covered terrain had barely changed, making it seem like they'd made no progress at all.

Suddenly, an alarm sounded, and Sergeant Riley called for the squad to stop, using a hand signal. Riley and the others gathered round, and Finn joined them, feeling his heart thump harder in his chest.

"What it is?" Finn asked, feeling like everyone else knew except him.

"We have a scout drone incoming..." Kellan said, not taking his eyes off his tracker for a second. "Shit, it's right on top of us!"

"Everyone down, now!" Riley yelled, dropping into the snow and dragging Finn down with him.

Private Reyes pulled a satchel-sized bag from his pack, which burst open like a self-inflating dinghy to form a wide canvas that seemed to cling to their bodies and pin them to the snow. It set like quick-drying glue then shimmered like Elara's chameleonic armor.

"Stay perfectly still," Riley whispered. "This tarpaulin will camouflage us and confuse the drone's heat sensors."

"Then what?" Finn whispered back.

"Then we wait..."

Finn barely took a breath for the next full minute, then he heard something buzzing overhead, like a swarm of insects. He tensed his muscles and waited as the sound waxed and waned and eventually disappeared into the distance. Kellen's device bleeped again then all five of them sucked in desperate gulps of ice-cold air.

"It's gone," Kellan confirmed. "Though for how long, who knows."

Private Riley recovered the camouflage tarp, which returned to the satchel like a balloon deflating, and everyone took a moment to dust the snow from their uniforms.

"That was a close call," Finn said.

Unlike the others, who'd shrugged off the encounter, he felt the urge to comment on what had happened, but Riley just grunted a laugh in reply.

"That was nothing," the general said, readying his rifle. "Believe me, there are far worse things in these wilds than surveillance drones."

Finn scowled at the man. "And you're only telling me this now?"

"If I'd have told you before, would it have stopped you from coming?" Riley asked.

Finn huffed a laugh and shrugged. "No..."

Riley smiled and took the lead again. "Well then, follow me..."

16
MUTAGENIC LUPUS

Finn was no stranger to Arctic conditions, having spent most of his life working outside, but the rocky, undulating terrain and thick blanket of snow underfoot was a challenge even for him. Even so, his progress toward the cavern system that would lead them beneath Zavetgrad was swifter than that of the others, who trudged forward, wrapped in thermal cloaks in an effort to stave off the bitterness.

"How are you not freezing your balls off?" Private Reyes wondered, looking at Finn like he was a freak of nature. "I can't feel my feet or my hands, and daren't even look at what's between my legs in case it's snapped off."

"There was nothing much there, anyway," Ensign Thorne said, waggling her little finger like it was a worm. "I've seen you in the shower, remember?

"Yeah, well the water was cold!" Reyes snapped back. "It was nothing compared to this though."

"I worked fourteen to sixteen-hour shifts in Metalhaven for longer than I care to remember," Finn said, smiling at the two soldiers, who clearly liked each other, despite the snippy banter. "You get used to the cold because you don't have a choice."

"The Pit is warm, too warm for my liking," Riley grunted. Ice crystals had formed on his silvery hair and beard, making the general look like a prehistoric man who'd been thawed out. "It's nice to get some fresh air."

"If you say so, sir," Reyes said, continuing to lumber forward with his arms wrapped around his body. "Personally, I like things hot and steamy." He winked at Ensign Thorne. "I know you know what I'm talking about..."

Thorne snorted and shook her head. "How about you do us all a favor and close your mouth for a couple of minutes. With any luck, it'll freeze shut."

The group laughed, though this quickly descended into chalky coughs as the ice-cold air tightened their airways and made them gasp for breath. After that, they walked in silence for a time with only the howling wind for company.

After two hours of trekking, Finn had developed a long lead over the others, despite efforts to moderate his pace so he didn't lose them completely. Reaching the top of a hillock, he stopped to rest and wait for the squad to catch up when he saw what looked like the remains of a settlement a few hundred meters down the other side.

"Are you seeing that too?" Finn asked Riley once the general had caught up.

"Yes, there are still the scattered remains of some settlements out here," the general said, struggling to get the words out while regaining his breath. "Sometimes, we use them as camps or shelters when a storm hits."

"Are they from before the Last War?" Finn asked but Riley shook his head.

"Zavetgrad wasn't the only attempt at civilization, it was just the most successful," the general explained. "It wasn't only the ancestors of the regents that made it out here; many other survivors did too. Those who refused to abide by the laws of the fledgling Authority chose to settle elsewhere. As you can see, they didn't survive for long. Many only lasted weeks or months but even the strongest succumbed after only a few years. For all Zavetgrad's many faults, what it did right was to protect its resources and quickly harvest new ones."

"But it did that by exploiting people," Finn said, angered that the general was giving the Authority any form of praise. Riley picked up on Finn's hostility, but the man didn't backtrack on his statement. If anything, he doubled down.

"It's a hard truth to swallow, but if it wasn't for the Authority then humanity may not have survived at all," Riley said, shocking Finn again. "If everyone who arrived in this frozen wasteland centuries ago chose to go their own way, like the people of that settlement out there did, then all of them would have died and there would be no Haven. No hope for the future."

"You can't know that for sure," Finn said, unwilling to give the brutal regime that had tortured and subjugated him all his life any credit. "And even if you're right, it doesn't excuse the Authority for their actions."

"I didn't say it did," Riley grunted. "I'm just pointing out facts, as difficult as they may be to accept."

"Hey, a village," Private Reyes said, lumbering up the hill just ahead of Sergeant Kellan and Ensign Thorne. "Maybe, we can drop in and say, 'hi'?"

"The dead don't speak, and if they could, you wouldn't like what they had to say," Riley grunted. Their conversation had soured his mood and Finn's. "But the caves we need are beyond that settlement, so we have to pass through it anyway."

Riley moved out ahead and Finn walked slower to make sure the squad all arrived at the settlement together. Despite it being abandoned for what looked like an age, everyone approached with weapons ready, and Finn was reminded of Riley's comment that they weren't the only living creatures in the wilderness.

"Split up and search the huts," Riley ordered. "I doubt we'll find anything useful, but it doesn't hurt to look, and it will give us all a rest break too."

Finn nodded and was about to work his way toward the far side of the settlement when he saw something poking out of the snow. He bent down to smooth the powder away, like an archeologist uncovering a relic from a dig site, revealing an old, gnawed-looking bone.

"What the hell did this?" Finn said, holding up the bone, which was either from a leg or arm, and scowling at the deep teeth marks. Then he had an unsettling thought. "These settlers didn't eat each other, did they?"

Reyes and Thorne exchanged anxious sideways glances, but Sergeant Kellan and General Riley remained stoical, as if they knew something the others didn't.

"That may have happened in some camps, but I don't think so here," Riley said, looking more on edge than usual. "Radiation-induced mutations are normally detrimental, so few animals survived the fallout, but those that did became effective predators. We shouldn't linger here long."

"Surely, any animals that survived the Last War would have died out long ago, even mutants?" Finn said.

"Many did," Riley grunted, "but not all."

The general's statement did nothing to ease Finn's mind and he was suddenly far less keen to explore the ancient habitat, despite his natural curiosity.

"We move out in five," Riley added. "Whatever you need to do before then, do it now."

Riley moved away to speak with Sergeant Kellan, while Thorne and Reyes approached Finn.

"Safety in numbers, right?" Thorne said, revealing her motivation for joining him.

"I feel like I need to pee, but there ain't no way I'm whippin' out my john-thomas now, not with some freaky monsters lurking around," Reyes said, hopping on the spot.

"There isn't enough meat on that thing, anyway, so you'll be just fine," Thorne said, nudging Reyes and almost knocking him over.

"Shit, I can't hold it, and I ain't pissing myself or my pants will freeze to my legs," Reyes said, dancing even faster. "If I'm not back in two minutes, send out a search party."

"Later!" Thorne said, waving at Reyes as he scooted off to relieve himself behind one of the buildings. "Come on, hero, let's see what treasures this old place holds," the pilot added, slapping Finn on the back then heading toward the far side of the settlement.

Finn was reluctant at first to leave Reyes alone, but the euphoric groans and plume of steam that were emanating from the spot where the private was relieving himself convinced him to give the man some privacy. He found Ensign Thorne inside the largest of the huts, sifting through age-decayed shelves and storage boxes, which all looked to have been crudely hand-made by the former occupants.

"This whole place is no bigger than my apartment in the prosecutor barracks, but it looks like maybe a dozen or more people slept here," Finn said, standing in front of what remained of a row of cot beds.

He spotted a faded photograph on one of the beds and picked it up. It was damaged by the cold and brittle around the edges, but he could still make out the faces of a man and a woman, and two children, perhaps in their early teens. Despite their ragged clothing and gaunt, starved expressions, they were smiling.

"What was it like?" Thorne said, tossing an old canteen aside. "Living with the golds, I mean. It must have been tough?"

"It was at first, but you get used to the lying and pretending," Finn replied, working his way along another shelving rack, but age and cold had degraded most of its contents so badly they were unrecognizable. "After a while, I actually started to feel like I belonged there but the weekly interrogations by the special prefecture kept me grounded."

"Were the golds as bad as the stories make them out to be?" Thorne asked, more interested in Finn's experiences than the possibility of finding buried treasure.

"Not all of them," Finn said. "There were one or two that I even grew to like."

Thorne pouted her lips and nodded. "Well, Riley used to be a gold, a bad one too, and look how he turned out. Maybe more of them than we think are capable of change."

Finn thought about the prosecutor mentors, and Chief

Prosecutor Voss in particular, and how in nine weeks he'd seen nothing good in any of them. Then he thought of Ivan Volkov and Juniper Jones, and he felt bile rising into his throat.

"I think most of them are exactly as rotten as your stories suggest," Finn said.

He recalled how Riley had made excuses for the Authority and it occurred to him that there was an appetite for forgiveness in Haven. Pen seemed to be the forgiving, tolerant type, and her governance would have permeated every tier of the Pit's leadership, but to Finn, forgiveness was a luxury they could not afford.

"The general speaks about mutant beasts as if those creatures are the worst thing this fucked up world has produced, but I promise you they're not," Finn said. His tone was laced with anger, and Thorne was both captivated and unsettled. "Those who wear gold are worse than animals, Mara. Animals act on instinct. Golds use and exploit and kill out of choice, and they don't give a shit how much we suffer, so don't for one second think they're worth saving. If I had the chance, I'd drop a bomb on that place and blow the entire fucking city to dust, and not shed a solitary tear."

Thorne stood as still as a statue, as if the cold had seeped into the soles of her boots and frozen her to the ground. He'd never seen the cocksure, quick-witted pilot without a smirk on her face, until then.

"If you ever you get the notion that the Authority can be redeemed, just look at this," Finn said, pressing the photo into Thorne's hand. "Pain and abuse are the Authority's legacy, and as soon as they get the chance, they'll blast themselves to

Nimbus, and leave the rest of us here to die, just like the family in that photo."

Thorne frowned at Finn then held up the photo and studied each of the four faces in turn, her expression a twisted mix of sorrow and anger that intensified the longer she looked.

"Stand-to! Stand-to!"

General Riley's warning command cut through them like a knife and Finn pulled his laser cannon free from its magnetic holster. Thorne shoved the photo into her pocket then stood ready with her rifle.

"Follow me!" Thorne called out, color flushing her skin from the sudden surge of blood and adrenaline. "We're being attacked!"

"By who?"

Finn's call went unanswered, and he ran outside after the ensign to find her and the rest of the squad in cover, aiming their rifles into the frozen wilderness. Finn couldn't see their targets until he realized that it wasn't special prefects who were closing in, but four-legged animals with snarling rows of jagged teeth. Finn had seen images of creatures like them on his data device and the beasts most closely resembled wolves, except larger and more powerful, and with dense fur that helped to insulate them against the harsh environment. Like the squad, the beasts were hunkered behind cover, using the rocks and natural terrain features to mask their advance.

"I take it these are the animals you mentioned?" Finn said, taking up position close to General Riley.

"I'm afraid so," the general replied. "The scientists in Haven call them 'mutagenic lupus' and I'd hoped to avoid them. I've lost good men to these monsters."

"Their metabolism can switch between fats and carbohydrates as energy sources, allowing them to survive long periods without food," Sergeant Kellan added. More than any of the others, Kellan appeared most afraid of the wolves, and Finn wondered if this wasn't his first experience of them. "And their cells repair at a highly accelerated rate, so they live for maybe forty or fifty years, or even longer, we really don't know for sure."

Finn watched the mutated wolves, but the wolves were watching them just as closely. They'd managed to get within fifty meters of the old settlement before General Riley's sharp eyes had spotted them, but now that their assault had been discovered, they seemed unwilling to commit to it.

"They don't seem like much of a threat right now," Finn said, wondering why Riley had sounded the alarm so urgently given how timid the wolves seemed.

"Don't be so certain, they're smarter than you think," Riley answered, tracking the largest of the five wolves, which appeared to be the pack leader. "Their mutations also changed their social behavior, and we believe they've developed a system of communication that allows them to learn and adapt in real time." The general laughed coarsely. "They're effective soldiers. I wish we could train them."

"I'll settle for not being eaten by them," Finn replied.

Suddenly, one of the wolves broke cover and darted closer. Sergeant Kellan aimed and fired his shotgun, but the blast smashed into a rock as the animal found cover again before it was hit. At the same time, the other wolves retreated and spread out, encircling the village while continuing to use the terrain for cover. Finn suddenly got the sense they were being herded like sheep.

"Fall back, slowly," Riley ordered. "There's another entrance into the cave system a hundred meters south of here, so we head for that. It will make reaching Zavetgrad harder, but now that the wolves have our scent, they'll follow us until they taste blood."

"I agree," Finn said, his own senses climbing.

"I wasn't asking, Major, it's called an order," Riley said. "Now move out!"

A few months ago, the old Finn Brasa would have told General Riley to shove his order up his ass, but he was now able to control his temper. It had been a lesson learned the hard way.

The squad formed a circle and retreated, back-to-back, so that they could cover all angles. The biggest of the five wolves remained the furthest away, while the others managed to inch closer with each burst of speed, the closest wolf always leading the charge. Finn fired his laser at the animals, hoping to tag one or at least scare it off, but if was as if the wolves could sense his attacks, and his blasts always landed wide.

"Save your ammo, Major," Riley said. "Shooting these things will only piss them off."

The squad continued to fall back, and the wolves matched them every step of the way, creeping ever closer while remaining out of the line of fire. Soon, they were descending into a steep ravine at the bottom of which was the system of caves Riley had mentioned. The uneven footing meant that they slipped and stumbled every other step, causing their aim to falter too, and allowing the wolves to close in.

"Sir, we have a problem," Ensign Thorne called out as the group finally reached the edge of the cave system and could no longer back away from the predators hunting them. "It looks like a recent rockslide blocked the entrance."

"Sergeant, cover me," Riley said, before moving to the rear of their formation.

Finn kept half his focus on the general, who was scrambling toward the collapsed entrance, and the other on a wolf that was eyeing him hungrily.

"Major, I need you," Riley called out.

Finn pressed his back to a rocky outcropping and trained his laser on the wolf, but this time held his fire. The beast's unblinking eyes were staring at him with hypnotic intensity as if it were pulling his thoughts and intentions out of his mind through some sort of telepathy.

"Major, get your ass down here!"

"You're up, hero," Thorne said, nudging him.

"Shit, I'm not used this rank crap yet," Finn said, hustling toward the cave entrance while Thorne took up his spot. Then he heisted, realizing that if he left, only three remained to fend off five wolves.

"We've got this, Major, now go," Thorne said, sensing Finn's unease. "You and the general are the strongest and have the best chance of clearing those rocks."

Finn nodded then aimed his cannon at the wolf that had been stalking him. "Keep a close eye on that one. It seems to know what I'm thinking."

"I'm thinking you should start hauling rocks," Thorne said, a touch impatiently. She then smiled and added, "...sir."

Finn worked his way down to where Riley was already busy trying to clear the blockage. He snapped his laser cannon to its holster and got to work, lifting and displacing hulks of stone that were at least fifty-percent larger than those the general could manage.

"It looks like those beasts aren't the only genetic marvels around here," Riley said, impressed by Finn's feats of strength.

"Thanks for not saying 'freak'," Finn replied, tossing another boulder the size of a beer barrel. "More often than not, my genetic purity has felt like a curse."

"It's not," Riley replied, as gunfire began to crackle around them, punctuated by the snarl of the wolves. "It proves that life can still exist, even in this. It's why the Authority prized your DNA, and it's why they're afraid of you too."

"Afraid of me?" Finn said, frowning at the general while continuing to dig.

"None of the golds are like you, Finn, not even the Regents," Riley said, sweat managing to overcome the freezing temperatures to bead on the man's brow. "They hate you for being something they're not and can never be. Trust me, I know these people because I used to be one."

A cry of, "On your left, look out!" snapped their focus to the fight that was going on above them, and Riley threw down the rock in his hands, and grabbed his rifle.

"Keep digging!" the general shouted, before clambering back toward the others.

Finn's instinct was to follow Riley and help fight the beasts, but he knew they were all dead if they couldn't escape into the cave system, so he bore down and clawed rock after rock free until his fingers started to bleed. The harried shouts and gunfire increased then there was a cry of pain, as chilling as any Finn had heard during a trial. Hauling the final rock clear of the opening he threw it down then climbed, heart thumping in his chest. Reaching the top of the cave entrance he saw Sergeant Kellan being dragged away by the wolfpack leader, the beast's jaw clamped around the man's calf. Reyes and Riley were both aiming shots at the beast, even with the risk of hitting Kellan instead, but the wolf's thick hide shrugged off the bullets like his prosecutor armor.

Finn climbed higher to get a clear shot with his cannon then saw Thorne get swiped by another wolf and knocked to the ground. He turned and fired, lasering the animal in the back of the neck and forcing it to run, howling and screeching like a banshee. The second wolf pounced, and Thorne raised her weapon, holding it crossways like a staff, and the beast bit down on the metal and tried to tear it from her grasp. Finn threw himself off the rocks and landed on the wolf, his armored mass acting like a battering ram, but in the fall his laser slipped from his grasp.

The animal yelped and clawed itself away but didn't run. Finn recognized the same hungry eyes that had stalked him since the beasts had first appeared and he knew the wolf would not back down. Drawing his baseball bat, Finn swung at the animal as it charged, striking it hard across the jaw and stunning it. He swung again and again, smashing the heavy metal club into its head and flanks but the beast wouldn't go down. Then it pounced again, and Finn was knocked to the ground, the wolf pinning him with its muscular front legs. Its mouth opened wide, and saliva dripped onto his face, then a blast of laser light hit the wolf in the eye socket, and it fell off him, like it had been struck by lightning.

"Get up, hero!" Thorne yelled. She offered Finn her hand, and she hauled him up.

"The entrance is clear," Finn called out, accepting the laser cannon back off Thorne with a grateful nod. "Fall back!"

"What about the sarge?!" Reyes yelled, dancing toward them while firing from the hip and holding back the other wolves.

"Kellan is gone!" Riley answered.

Finn chanced a looked toward where the sergeant had been hauled away and wished he hadn't. Kellan was already being ripped to pieces by the pack leader and two of the other wolves, their dark grey fur painted red with the man's blood. Riley grabbed Finn's arm as he ran past and together, they struggled toward the entrance, sliding and stumbling over the snow-covered rocks before tumbling awkwardly into the cave.

"Private, seal the entrance!" Riley ordered from the flat of his back.

Reyes sprang into action and grabbed an explosive charge from his webbing, while continuing to suppress the remaining two wolves with bursts of fire from his weapon. The man had switched from joker to steely-eyed warrior in the blink of an eye and without him, Finn doubted that the squad would have made it past the wolves alive.

"Fire in the hole!' Reyes called out, while running back into the cavern.

The explosion, intensified by the confines of the cave walls, knocked Finn off his feet and he landed hard in a pool of ice-cold water. Dust covered his face and stuck to his teeth, and he clawed it away, using the pool water to help wash the grit from his eyes, but even then, he couldn't see a thing before the cave turned pitch black, like the space around Nimbus. Riley, Thorne and Reyes activated torches, and the stark white light revealed their haggard, battle-weary expressions in ghoulish clarity.

"That'll keep them out," Riley said, picking himself up and dusting down his fatigues. "But in case there was ever any doubt, there's no turning back now."

17

DEEP TROUBLE

Finn stopped to fill his canteen from the underground stream that disappeared beneath the rocks ahead of them and eventually filtered its way into Zavetgrad. The water was crystal clear and ice cold, and after more than two hours of hard trekking deep inside the caves, he was more than ready for it.

"I didn't expect it to be so warm down here," Private Reyes said, removing his thermal cloak and packing it away.

"It's not warm, it's just not below freezing like it is outside," Riley commented, while also refilling his canteen. "But we shouldn't rest for too long or our bodies will start to cool off."

"That's a shame, 'cos I could stay here for hours," Reyes said.

The soldier was sitting on a rock and looking around the cave with wide-eyed astonishment, and Finn could fully appreciate why. Despite the fact they were deep underground, light filled the cavern, generated by hundreds of luminescent crystals that bathed the smooth rock in an ethereal glow. Bioluminescent creatures were also scurrying around, perhaps unsettled by the intruders who had disturbed their magical underground domain.

"I didn't have you down as a man of nature," Ensign Thorne said, side-eyeing the private with her familiar smirk. "For all your bravado and big talk, it looks like you have a sensitive side."

"Hey, I can appreciate beauty," Reyes hit back. The man had taken offense for real rather than just feigning it. "It's not like we get to see shit like this every day."

"I agree," Riley said, and everyone looked at the boorish general with surprise. If it had been a shock to learn that Private Reyes had a sensitive side, it was a seismic blast wave of biblical proportions to discover that Riley did too. "It's heartening to know that there is still beauty in this broken world," Riley continued. "I like to think its proof that the planet can heal itself, given a chance and enough time."

A luminescent critter that resembled a crab scuttled past Reyes and the soldier scooped it up into his hands. Curiously, the creature didn't try to escape and instead stood there, peering back at Reyes, while gently swaying its glowing pincers at him in a hypnotic display.

"Don't get too close, these creatures are radioactive," Riley said.

"Shit!" Reyes immediately dropped the critter, which thudded onto the rock then waved it pincers indignantly before scuttling away. "Am I gonna die?"

Riley grunted a laugh. "No, not unless you try to eat the damned thing, anyway. The glow is a side-effect of the fallout, another improbably advantageous mutation, but our bodies have adapted to become resilient too. Our pre-war ancestors wouldn't last more than a week down in these caves before they succumbed to crippling radiation sickness, but we'll be fine."

The critter that Reyes had been holding was still nearby, watching the soldier with interest. Finn noticed that other similar creatures were gathering and though none of them appeared particularly threatening, he didn't like thought of being swarmed by glowing, crab-like organisms and being pincered to death.

"We should probably head off," Finn said, stowing his canteen while continuing to keep a close eye on the growing cluster of crabs. "Based on our progress, I'd say that we have maybe another hour before we pass underneath Zavetgrad's border fence, and the same again to reach Makehaven."

"I concur," Riley said, also standing up. "Though the last stretch will be the most difficult, so make sure to eat and drink something now. You'll need your strength."

Finn looked toward the route ahead and it appeared no more unwieldy than the passage behind them. The cave was undulating and sometimes tight, requiring them to squeeze between rock faces and drag their bodies through tunnels barely large enough to accommodate them, but it was a struggle he'd gotten used to.

"It doesn't look any harder than what we've already done," Finn said, suddenly anxious that he was missing something important.

"The tunnels aren't any more challenging than what we've overcome but the final stretch is," Riley replied. "In order for us to reach the underground lake beneath the ale factory in Makehaven, we'll have to swim."

Finn suddenly felt as cold as the water in the stream. "I can't swim, and the last time I tried to make an escape across water, things didn't exactly work out as planned."

"Don't worry, Major, we've accounted for everything," Riley said. The general nodded to Thorne. "The ensign will take care of you, when the time comes."

The fact the general wasn't fazed by his concerns gave Finn some comfort, but he still wanted specifics. Thorne, however, wasn't about to volunteer them.

"Don't worry, hero, I've got your back," the pilot said, gathering her gear.

"I don't enjoy surprises, Ensign," Finn said, feeling sick to the stomach. "But I trust that you know what you're doing."

"It's okay, Mara's only drowned, what... one or two people before today?" Reyes said, grinning.

Thorne gave Reyes the middle finger and Finn shot the private a suitably menacing look and the soldier held up his hands in submission.

"Knock it off, private," Riley said, in an admonishing tone. "We're getting close to Zavetgrad, so I need you all to focus."

"Yes, sir," Reyes said, shaping up just as the general had ordered.

The squad pushed on for another hour, abrasion from the rocks scraping the chrome paint off Finn's armor and making it look weathered and worn, until they reached a pool of perfectly still water that butted up against a sheer rock face. Finn checked the new cavern, but he couldn't see any way through. Then it hit him, and his gut knotted again.

"When you said we had to swim, you didn't say it would be underwater," Finn said.

"Hey, I said I've got you and I meant it," Thorne answered, setting down her pack. "I'll guide you through. You can do this."

The ensign removed a tightly coiled bundle of rope from her pack along with a box containing two sets of cylinders, the size of small water flasks. Finn watched as Thorne attached the cylinders to mouthpieces and he suddenly remembered that he'd seen a similar object before.

"That's a rebreather, right?" Finn said, and Thorne nodded. "Elara had one when we tried to escape through the Seahaven sub-sector in the test trial, but I didn't use one myself."

"It's simple, really, you just breathe normally through the mouthpiece, and not through your nose," Thorne said, giving a quick demo. "I'll show you once we're in the water, and I'll be with you the whole time."

Finn sucked in a lungful of the cold air then nodded. "It looks like I don't really have a choice."

For the next thirty minutes, Thorne took Finn through how to use the rebreather then fitted the compact scuba gear to his armor. The ensign had strongly suggested he ditch his protective outer layer, but Finn had grown so used to wearing his prosecutor armor that he felt naked without it. He also knew that when the fighting started, it could mean the difference between life and death. As a final step, Thorne physically tethered herself to Finn using the rope she'd removed from her pack. This unsettled Finn almost as much as the prospect of diving underwater because it meant that if he sank like stone, he'd drag Thorne down with him.

"Ready?" the ensign said, making final adjustments to his gear then standing back to visually inspect it.

"Not really, but let's go anyway," Finn said, resigned to his fate.

Riley and Private Reyes had been ready for some time, but the two soldiers had patiently waited while Finn received his instruction, neither chipping in with comments or, in the case of Reyes, wise-ass remarks. Finn appreciated the private's sudden seriousness, though his change in temperament also emphasized the risk they were about to take.

"You'll be fine, Major," Riley said, confidently. "We'll see you on the other side."

Riley entered the pool of glacial water first and within seconds the general had disappeared beneath the water's glassy surface. Reyes gave Finn and Thorne a thumbs up sign then jumped into the pool and vanished as if he had been swallowed by a portal to another realm. Seeing both men disappear so suddenly did nothing to allay Finn's fears.

"I'll go in first then you follow," Thorne said, easing herself into the pool. When the water reached her waist, she let out a gasp, like air escaping from a punctured tire, before gently easing herself in to shoulder depth. "Now you…"

Finn let out another uneasy sigh then stepped into the pool. He'd expected the water to be cold, but it was a still a shock, and by the time he was chest deep, he could barely breathe.

"Just try to relax," Thorne said. "Your body will adapt and get used to the cold, but we need to be fast. At this temperature, you're going to feel exhausted after ten to fifteen minutes."

"How long after that until we freeze?" Finn asked, and straight away wished he hadn't.

"About thirty minutes, more if we're lucky," Thorne said, her lips already chattering. "But I suggest we don't take that long. If we work fast, we'll be through to the other side in five or six minutes, tops."

Finn nodded then placed the mask over his eyes and the rebreather into his mouth and gave Thorne the signal to go. Dipping his head under the water felt like someone had placed it into a vice but he knew he had to commit. Thorne signaled to ask if he was okay and he signaled back, then the ensign turned and began swimming. Finn pushed off the rocks and kicked his feet like Thorne had shown him but the further away from the entry point he moved, the faster his heart beat until he thought it might explode in his chest. The cave walls closed in around him as the tunnel narrowed, adding a crushing sense of confinement to his dread fear of drowning.

Finn grabbed the walls and dragged himself forward. The equipment Thorne had fitted provided buoyancy as well as breathable oxygen, and the rope tethered to the ensign occasionally tugged at his waist to remind him that the pilot was still there. Then the tunnel widened, and Finn swam out into a vast underground lake that seemed to stretch below him without end. Light came at him from all angles, and he saw that the plants growing beneath the surface of the lake were luminescing, like the critters in the cave. Then a shoal of fish weaved through the water ahead of him, their shimmering scales glowing like fireflies, and he was mesmerized. For a moment, he forgot his fear and the deathly cold that was seeping into his bones and just floated, awestruck by the alien underwater domain he'd invaded.

A tug on his rope broke his trance and he looked up to see Thorne signaling him. Her hand movements were flustered and insistent and he couldn't understand them. Then a shadow pierced the veil of darkness deep below him and Finn cried out, pushing air from his lungs into the water and sending it bubbling urgently to the surface. The creature bearing down on him was as large as a wolf but its jaws, lined with rows of dagger-like teeth, were three times the size of the mutagenic lupus that had claimed the life of Sergeant Kellan. Finn tried to scramble for his laser, but his hand was frozen, and he couldn't close his fingers around the weapon's grip. The monster accelerated like a torpedo and Finn pushed out his hands to protect his face, but its jaws clamped themselves around his body instead. He felt a crushing force squeeze his chest and back as the bite pressure increased, but his armor resisted the monster's piercing attack.

Survival instincts kicked in and overcame the paralysis that had crippled his body. He pulled his knife from the stow on his armor, forcing his frozen fingers to grip with enough force to deal a deadly blow. The blade sank into the monstrosity's flesh and Finn cut deeply and raggedly until finally the creature released him and spun away, thrashing its tail and vanishing through the plume of blood-clouded water. In the process, the monster's scaly fins thrashed Finn's face and the rebreather was knocked out of his mouth. He pawed at the cloudy water, desperately searching for the mouthpiece, but he couldn't find it, and he began to panic, knowing that he'd soon drown.

Suddenly, another shape approached through the murky

water and Finn readied his knife, though he could barely hold it. The shape darted toward him, and Finn tried to lunge with the weapon, but his strength failed him, and it fell from his grasp and spun away into the abyss. Then his vision blurred and the need to suck in a breath became overwhelming, despite knowing that he would simply inhale water and drown. Then something was pressed into his mouth and a burst of oxygen cleared the water from inside it. The urge to breathe became irresistible and he gulped, but instead of water, he sucked in life-sustaining air with the fervor of a newborn lamb suckling milk from its mother's teat.

His vision cleared and he saw Ensign Thorne in front of him, signaling for him to swim up, and he kicked his legs with all the strength he had left. The ascent seemed never-ending but eventually he saw a light shining above him then his head burst though the surface of the lake like an arrow piercing a target. General Riley and Private Reyes gabbed his rebreather harness and dragged him out onto the rocks, like a prize fish they'd just netted, and the rebreather was yanked from his mouth.

"Thorne!" Finn croaked, trying to sit up, and Riley supported him. He couldn't see the ensign anywhere. "Where's Thorne?!"

Suddenly, the officer's head burst though the surface and she began dragging herself over the rocks toward them but another ripple in the water was chasing her. Then a jagged dorsal fin pierced the surface, followed by another, and another, and the shape of three more monsters began to push through the lake, forming bow waves like a speeding boat. Finn jumped up and drew his laser, and Riley and Reyes had already pulled their weapons into their shoulders. The creatures lifted their bodies out of the water and opened their gaping jaws and Finn fired directly into one beast's mouth, burning a furrow from throat to tail. The monster sank then a burst of gunfire engulfed the other two and the water was turned red. Thorne clawed herself out of the lake and Finn grabbed the ensign and helped to pull her clear, before the two of them collapsed on the rock and lay in a heap, their panicked breathing fogging the air like smoke from a fire.

18

THE PUMPING STATION

Private Reyes wrapped an emergency blanket around Finn's freezing body and activated the power core. Electricity coursed through the heating elements woven into the fabric and he was suddenly enveloped in warmth, like stepping into a sauna in the prosecutor barracks. Reyes then helped Ensign Thorne, carefully wrapping a blanket around her shoulders, and activating the power cell, since the officer was too frozen to do it herself. There were no bullshit comments or sly jokes, only calm professionalism, and concern for his fellow soldier.

"Thanks, Mara," Finn said to the ensign, through chattering teeth. "You weren't kidding when you said you had my back."

Thorne did her best to approximate a smile. "Don't mention it. Though, if I'd known there were giant killer fish down here, I might not have made that promise."

Finn wheezed a laugh and Reyes cracked a smile too, though the private was now busy pouring liquid from a flask into four cups. Steam billowed from the container and each cup, as if he were pouring molten lava.

"Get this down you, Major," Reyes said, handing one of the cups to Finn before giving another to Thorne. "It's loaded with meds that will thaw your insides and give you a solid kick up the ass too."

"I think I could do without the kick, thanks," Finn said, sipping the liquid. It burned as it went down but he didn't care, it was hot and sweet and immediately started to make him feel human again.

"You'll be glad to know the worst is over," General Riley said, huddled inside his blanket while drinking from one of the remaining cups. "It's a short climb from here to the factory in Makehaven and we've made good progress, so we can afford the time to recover."

Reyes picked up his cup and wandered close to the water's edge, though not close enough to be prey. The shot-up carcasses of the three killer fish had washed up on the rocks, which were stained red with their blood. Finn watched as the same bioluminescent critters he'd seen in the earlier cave crab-walked out of the water and began to devour the remains.

"It makes you wonder what other freaks of nature the war created," Reyes said, kicking a chunk of glowing fish flesh toward a critter, who gratefully accepted the offering. "Besides the Authority fuckers, I mean."

"I'm very sure I don't want to find out," Finn said, finishing the sweet, life-giving drink.

Out of the four of them, the private had been least affected by the icy swim and had quickly reverted to his usual cocksure self. This transformation contradicted Reyes' earlier and all-too frequent complaints about the harsh weather conditions outside the cave. The soldier could switch from being an ass one moment to a steely-eyed warrior the next, and Finn struggled to reconcile these contrasting facets of the man's personality. The private remained an enigma, but Finn was certainly glad to have him on the squad.

"I wonder what they taste like..." Reyes mused, still watching the critters have their feast. "I bet they taste good."

"We're not eating bullet-ridden, mutant fish, so get that thought out of your head, Private," Riley said, quick to dispel any notion they might take a snack break.

"Besides, the radiation will probably make your cock drop-off," Thorne added, managing a smile. She then reconsidered her warning. "On second thoughts, go ahead and chow down, private."

Reyes gave Thorne the bird and even General Riley managed a phlegmy chuckle, though the general was sounding like a geriatric with a chest infection.

"Break's over, people," Riley said, finishing his drink and standing up, with the thermal cloak still wrapped around him. "The climb will help us to warm up, then once we're inside the ale brewery, we'll hanker for the cold of this cave."

"I very much doubt that, sir," Thorne said, wincing as she pushed herself up. "If I never see another goddamn snowflake again, I'll die happy."

The squad packed their gear and Riley led from the front, guiding Finn and the others along a steep path that lead up the cavern wall, following the course of a river that branched off from the massive underground lake. The general had been right about the climb, and soon Finn's blood was pumping, and his skin was hot and dry, making the thermal cloak feel stifling and uncomfortable. He removed the blanket and handed the life-saving item back to

Reyes, who folded it like an origami expert and slid it back into his pack.

Thirty minutes into their ascent, Finn started to see evidence of civilization above them. Huge pipes, supported by rusted iron and steel works, plunged through the roof of the cave and into the many deep tributaries that bled off from the main lake. The rhythmic thump of powerful machines pulsed the cave walls and before long Finn saw the first sign of man-made structures ahead of them.

"What's that?" Reyes asked, as they climbed toward the scaffold that held up the structure.

"It's an old pumping station and maintenance accessway to the facility above," Riley said. "It was sealed up decades ago, after it fell into disrepair."

Finn looked at the rusted metal, which was covered in moss or algae that glowed blue like the fish in the cave and wondered how the structure had not already collapsed into the water and been washed away.

"It doesn't exactly look safe," Finn commented.

"It's not," Riley grunted in reply. "So, watch your step."

The general reached the scaffold first then began to pull himself up, but with each step and handhold that Riley took, the metal creaked and groaned like an ancient shipwreck. Finn followed next, taking a slightly different route to the general so as not to add stress to the same sections of the crumbling structure. Then Thorne and finally Reyes climbed onto the scaffold and suddenly Finn felt the entire pumping station began to tip and he pulled his body tight to the metal.

"Stop!" Riley called out, as the platform rocked and teetered like a car on the edge of a cliff. "There's too much weight on this side of the station. We must climb up one at a time to balance it, starting with Major Brasa."

Finn nodded to them resumed his climb, but he didn't know whether to proceed slowly and carefully or just scramble to the top as fast as he could, and the indecision was paralyzing. Below him, Reyes and Thorne had wrapped themselves around the scaffold, suspended above the ravine and fast-flowing river a hundred meters below them. Chunks of rusted metal were raining from the platform like giant hailstones, before being consumed by the rapids and swept away to God knows where.

"Don't hurry on our account, Major," Reyes called up, but despite returning to his wisecracking persona, the private looked terrified.

Finn sucked in a deep breath then climbed, finally choosing haste over care, but half of the handholds he reached for crumbled in his grasp like dried leaves. Just over half-way up, the platform tilted again, and Finn's feet slipped off the moss-covered metal, leaving him hanging over a sheer drop. Despite the rush of water below him, he heard Riley gasp. Legs flailing to find purchase, he finally hooked his ankle around an upright and pulled himself back onto the scaffold. He made the mistake of looking down and was overcome with vertigo, his trembling hands refusing to relinquish their hold on the metal but his will was stronger than his fear, and he forced himself to climb. Close to the top, Riley crept to the edge of the platform on the flat of his stomach and stretched out his hand.

"Take it, I'll pull you up!" Riley called out.

Finn grabbed the general's hand and it was reassuringly firm. The soldier pulled with all his considerable strength and soon Finn was on his back on the platform, gasping for air. It felt like emerging from the icy lake all over again, only this time his body was burning hot instead of freezing cold.

"Thorne, you next!" Riley shouted.

Ensign Thorne started climbing, but with two bodies acting as a counterbalance, the platform remained steady. Finn slid to the edge and stretched out his hand, as Riley had done to him, and Thorne grabbed his wrist, squeezing with the force of a pneumatic press. Gritting his teeth, Finn pulled the soldier and pilot on to the platform.

"Hey, no sneaking off without me!" Reyes shouted. The soldier had already started his climb.

"Wouldn't dream of it..." Thorne called back, sarcastically.

With two bodies on the far side of the platform, Finn stayed on his stomach, peering over the edge with his hand outstretched, as a target for Reyes to aim for. The extra gear that the private was carrying made his climb more challenging, especially considering that most of the good footholds had already crumbled to dust.

"Come on, Private, you're almost there," Finn urged, stretching his arm as far as he could reach.

Reyes climbed three more steps then stopped and reached out, but their fingertips barely managed to touch. The private cursed then searched desperately for another foothold that would get him an extra inch or two higher, then the groan of metal became deafening as bolts snapped and a support beam was torn from the cave wall. The platform dropped sharply, and Finn slid further over the edge before managing to lock his foot through a rusted deck plate. At the same time, Reyes lost his footing and slipped but Finn's reactions had stayed sharp, and he snatched the man's wrist before the scaffold fell away and crashed into the ravine.

"Help!" Finn yelled, as the full weight of Private Reyes threatened to pull his arm out of its socket.

Hands grabbed his ankles and Finn was dragged over the deck, his armor screeching against the rusted metal plates like a derailed train grinding across the track, but he clung onto Reyes, despite his arm burning with pain. The private scrambled onto the platform then more bolts snapped, and the pumping station dropped another two degrees.

"We have to get off this thing!" Reyes yelled, scrambling away from the edge. "It could go at any second!"

Finn climbed to his knees and looked for Riley but instead of trying to get off the platform, the general had run inside the pumping station and was darting up the stairs to the top level.

"Hurry, this is the only way out!" Riley shouted, waving them on.

"But this entire platform is about to fall!" Finn said.

"If we get trapped in the cave, we're dead anyway, now move!" Riley yelled.

Thorne helped Finn and Reyes to stand then all three of them raced after Riley, the thump of their boots on the stairs causing the pumping station to bounce like a rope bridge. When they reached the upper level, Riley was already at the hatch, hands gripping the locking wheel, teeth gritted.

"It won't budge!" Riley growled. "Help me!"

Finn and the others grabbed the wheel and their combined strength slowly managed to overcome the decades of rust that had seized it shut. Metal grated against metal and slowly the gears turned until the hatch was unlocked. Finn was about to push on it when the door swung open, and the barrel of a gun was pressed through the opening.

"Blood!" a voice called out.

"Metal!" Riley called back. "Now take my hand before this whole fucking thing crashes down!"

The gunman hesitated but the shriek of bolts snapping convinced the operative to dispense with any further security challenges. Riley was hauled through the hatch first then Finn helped Thorne and Reyes to escape next, hooking his hands underneath their boots and lifting them into the opening. Finally, it was his turn and he reached up his hands just as the final bolts snapped and the pumping station fell away beneath him. Riley and Reyes caught hold of an arm each, and for an agonizing few seconds Finn was left dangling over a sheer drop, as the pumping station smashed into the ravine and was pulverized, its remains quickly swept away downstream, as if the cave had swallowed them.

Finn was pulled through then the hatch was slammed shut and locked behind him. Suspended over the abyss, he'd worried that the screech of metal would have alerted half of the prefects in the city, but the relentless pounding of machinery from Makehaven's towering factories could have drowned out the sound of nuclear detention.

"You guys sure know how to make an entrance," the Metal who'd opened the hatch said. The man was sitting in shadow with his back to wall, but Finn recognized the voice right away. It was Trip, the worker who'd fought with him against the prosecutors in the test trial, and without whom he'd have never survived. "I don't know about you guys," Trip added, breath labored. "But I could use a pint or three."

19
HARD TRUTHS

Trip, the former Metalhaven worker turned operative for Haven, shuffled out of the shadows, and nodded a greeting to Finn.

"I must admit, I didn't expect to see you again," the former Metalhaven worker said. "But I'm happy to see you're still alive."

"That goes for us both," Finn said, clasping wrists with the man. "I'm glad you managed to escape the test crucible, though you seem to have chosen a dangerous new line of work."

Trip shrugged. "That goes for the both of us."

"Thank you for being on time," Riley said to the Metal, gruffly understating just how critical Trip's timely intervention had been. "Is everything ready?"

"It's all in hand," Trip said, taking a carefree tone with the general. "But we've got a few hours till the truck departs for Metalhaven, so take a breather, it looks like you need one."

"A few hours?" Finn said, suddenly alert. "Elara could be dead by then."

"Don't worry, we'll have you inside the crucible in time for the trial," Trip said, still smoothly reassuring. "Now kick back and let me do my job."

Finn blew out a heavy sigh and let his back thud against the wall and take up his weight. Between dangling over a precipice and almost being eaten by a murderous fish, he admitted to being a tad strung out.

"A pint of Metalhaven ale wouldn't go amiss, right about now," Finn said, flexing his aching shoulder, which was thankfully still attached to its socket.

"Now that is something I can arrange!" Trip said, a broad smile on his face.

Finn had been joking but then he remembered how Trip had gotten his name by outdrinking everyone else in the Recovery Center by three pints to one. It stood to reason the man would have ale close to hand. Finn expected Riley to instantly shoot down the idea but to his surprise, and relief, it seemed that the general was in the mood for a pint too.

Trip led them through the basement levels of the Makehaven brewery, carefully avoiding any areas that were staffed with workers, though most purples were toiling the floors above them. They quickly reached a storeroom that appeared to be disused, containing only dusty old boxes and empty, useless beer kegs. Trip pushed through the detritus and activated a false wall that led them inside another space that was decked out like the operations center in Haven, except on a much smaller scale. Toward the back of the room were a couple of old sofas and chairs and a row of four cots.

"This is my new office," Trip said, proudly introducing them to the room. "Needless to say, I like it a shit load better than the last one."

"Does your new job involve pulling pints?" Finn said, hopefully. He'd spotted a couple of barrels in the corner of the room and the refrigeration system was plugged in.

"It does now!" Trip replied.

Riley, Thorne and Reyes collapsed onto the sofas and sank into the well-worn padding, like they were sitting on a cloud. Trip fetched a round of ales, which were ice-cold, just as Finn remembered. The first sip was always vile but once the alcohol and drugs kicked in by the third and fourth sips, it was like drinking molten ambrosia. True to form, Trip had sunk a couple of pints before the others were done with their first, and Finn was astonished at how casual and relaxed the man was, considering that less than a week ago, he'd been in a desperate fight for his life that he had barely survived.

"Drink up," Trip said, looking at Finn directly as he said this. "Us chromes have to show everyone else how it's done."

Finn laughed then sank his pint and offered the glass back to Trip for a refill. Riley's scowling eyes followed the progress of the glass all the way to the barrel.

"Go easy, Major, we may have a few hours to kill, but you need to stay sharp," the general said.

"Don't worry, it'll take more than a couple of pints to dull my edge," Finn said, accepting the fresh, frothing pint back from Trip.

"I've got some probiotic goop in the fridge that'll counter the effects of this crap long before you need to fight," Trip cut in, dropping heavily onto a wooden chair by his operations station. "Mind you, it won't take away the filthy beer taste."

"I don't know how you drink this stuff," Ensign Thorne said. Unlike the others, she'd barely touched her pint. "It tastes like dish water."

"Dish water would be an improvement," Trip said, grinning. "Trust me, I know. Sometimes, I came back from the center so pissed and thirsty that I drank the contents of my kitchen sink."

Finn laughed, taking the story at face value, and believing it to be true, while Thorne and the others looked suitably suspicious, and repulsed.

"So, what are your stories?" Trip said, well into his third pint. No-one appeared willing to volunteer but Trip was nothing if not persistent. "We all know about Finn, so how about I start, because my story is simple," Trip continued. "I was born in the birthing center twenty-six years ago then raised in the workhouse, not that I remember any of it, then spent fourteen years in the yards, before fate brought me here."

"I'm sure there's got to be more to it than that?" Thorne said.

Trip shook his head. "Nothing worth telling."

Thorne sighed and shrugged. "Okay, I'll go next, the pilot said, sitting more upright. "I'm Ensign Mara Thorne, Haven born, though my mom was from right here, in Makehaven. She was sentenced to die for skimming protein bars off the production line and giving them to workers who'd lost foot chits betting on the trials. My dad was a Haven native too, descended from the first Metals who founded the colony." Thorne's head drooped and she took a sip of beer to wet her lips, despite hating the taste. "He died a year back from rad sickness, but I know he'd be proud of what we're doing."

Reyes sat up and straightened to attention. "The name's Kai Reyes, and both my folks were Haven natives. My mom was the daughter of a worker from Seedhaven. Her crime was refusing to fuck a prefect." The anger suddenly radiating from the private could have boiled the beer in his glass. "My old man was an ancestor of a first Metal, just like Mara's. He died on an operation in Zavetgrad when I was nine."

"Didn't that put you off signing up to the military?" Finn asked but Reyes shook his head.

"He believed that this fight was worth the risk, and I do too," Reyes said. The soldier raised his glass. "Metal and Blood."

There was a reprise of "Metal and Blood," then everyone drank, including Thorne, though it made her pucker up and pout like she'd drunk salt water. Trip then looked to General Riley, but it was obvious the man was trying not to meet the Metal's eyes, and it didn't take a genius to work out why. Thorne and Reyes were Haven-born and bred, but Riley was a former gold, and the man had more skeletons in his closet than were buried beneath the irradiated soil of every continent on the planet.

"What about you, General?" Trip said, pushing Riley to respond. "A man doesn't reach your age without a few stories under his belt."

There was another awkward silence and Riley looked like he wanted the sofa to open up and swallow him whole. Reyes and Thorne knew some aspects of the general's background and were glancing at each other awkwardly until the tension became unbearable and Finn tried to intervene.

"The advantage of being a general is that you don't have answer to anyone, isn't that right?" Finn said, smiling at Riley and trying to lighten the mood. "Apart from maybe Pen, but she's hundreds of miles away."

"It's okay, Major," Riley said, holding up a hand. "I'm

ashamed of what I was, but I'd also be a coward if I didn't admit to it."

Trip shifted uncomfortably in his seat, suddenly comprehending the possibility he'd just opened a Pandora's box. Reyes and Thorne also looked like they'd rather be anywhere else, but Finn wanted to know. He'd already busted the general's balls about his background as a former head prefect, but Riley had stopped short of explaining why he switched sides.

"Up until twenty-five years ago, I was Head Prefect of Stonehaven," Riley began, and Trip almost dropped his pint. "I wasn't a good man. I hurt people. I killed people. I sent people to die."

Riley's voice was even gravellier than usual, and it was clearly a struggle for the general to talk about his past, but Finn needed to hear it.

"So, what changed?" Finn asked, not letting Riley off the hook. "What was so bad that it made a bastard gold like you realize their mistakes?"

Riley glowered at Finn, but the insult was calculated. He wanted to get under the general's skin. In a few hours, they would be fighting, side-by-side, and he needed to know that the man was all-in, and that no trace of gold remained.

"I saw something..." Riley grunted. "Something I'll never forget until the day I die."

"You mean like I saw my best friend being murdered in front of me?" Finn said. He shrugged. "We'll all seen things, General. So what?"

"This was different," Riley said. He had shrunk even deeper into the fabric and no longer looked like the powerful, commanding general Finn knew. "One day, the Regent of

Stonehaven ordered me to a new post. The head prefect of the birthing center was taken ill, and I was to replace him, at least until he was well enough to return. They thought I could handle it. They saw me as a hard man from Stonehaven, and I was."

"What's the matter, General, you don't like kids?" Finn goaded. He knew he was being cruel, but he couldn't help it. In that moment, all he could see was a head prefect of the Authority, the worst of the worst, and it made his gut churn. "Or was sorting babies into workers or golds, based on DNA results and labor shortages too taxing for you?"

"You don't understand," Riley snapped. The conversation was opening a wound but still Finn pushed.

"Then help me to understand," Finn said. "I need to know you won't bail on us if this all goes south. I need to know that you'll fight and, if it comes to it, die alongside us."

"Fine, you want to know, then here it is," Riley said, pushing himself up. "You're right that the birthing center buckets babies according to their DNA and market demand, which is how a double-five like you ended up in Metalhaven instead of Nimbus, but not all of the stock was viable."

"The stock?" Finn spat. "What the fuck does that mean?"

"Many babies were born with defects too serious to correct," Riley said. He'd committed now, come what may. "Those babies were... rejected." The general let that word hang in the air like a witch's curse before continuing. "They were euthanized then incinerated. Dozens of them, every week."

"And you oversaw this?" Trip said. Like Finn, he was revolted by what he was hearing.

"Yes," Riley answered, looking Finn dead in the eyes. "At

first, I signed the orders without even knowing what I was signing. I was just 'filling in' for another guy, going through the motions until I went back to my proper job. Then I witnessed the euthanizations for myself, and everything changed. I used to have unshakable faith in the Authority and its mission. I thought that the hurt I inflicted was in service of the greater good, for Nimbus and the survival of the species." He shook his head and Finn could see he was fighting back tears. "But nothing justifies what I saw, and what I allowed to happen. Nothing. I knew then I had to bring it down, so I defected."

"And Haven just welcomed you with open arms?" Finn said.

"No..." Riley answered, ominously. "I spent the first ten years in a cell, only brought out so that I could offer intelligence and insight into operational matters. I would have been content with that but then Pen became principal." He huffed a laugh. "That woman has a capacity for forgiveness that I will never comprehend. I didn't deserve a second chance, and I know that I'm irredeemable, but if I can destroy this regime, perhaps I can atone, at least in some small measure, for the bastard gold that I was."

"Fuck the Authority," Trip barked, making everyone jump. He went to the barrel and refilled his pint glass. "Fuck those bastards. All of them!"

Suddenly, there was a knock on the door, and everyone reached for their weapons. Trip pressed his finger to his lips then grabbed a pistol that had been lying on his operations station and went to the door. Anxious seconds past then Trip threw his head back and sighed a breath of relief.

"It's okay, it's another Metal," Trip said. A thin-faced man wearing Autohaven overalls poked his head through and nodded to them.

"The trial has been moved up," the Autohaven worker said. "Grab your gear, we have to move out now."

20

STOP AND SEARCH

FINN JUMPED TO HIS FEET, sloshing ale onto his armor, then set down his pint glass and stormed toward the door.

"How long do we have?" Finn directed the question to the thin-faced Metal who had brought the news that the start time of Elara's trial had been moved up.

"Less than three hours, but we can still make it, if we leave right now," the Metal said.

"Is it safe to travel?" Riley cut in. He was back to his old self, at least on the surface.

"It's never safe but it's no more dangerous to leave now than it would be in a few more hours," the Metal replied. "So long as you lie low and stay calm, we'll make it through the checkpoints and reach Metalhaven before they close the yards."

"Squad, gear up," Riley said but Reyes and Thorne were already on their feet, gear in hand. "And drink some of that probiotic to clear your heads. We need to be sharp."

Trip hurried to the flask and handed it to Finn. He drank directly from the container then offered it to Riley. Though he didn't say it outright, he figured that sharing a drink with the general was as close to a peace offering as they could get. Finn was still smarting from what Riley had revealed about his past but as difficult as the story had been to hear, it made Finn more certain than ever that the soldier was with them.

"I like this crap even less than the beer, but thanks," Riley said.

The general raised the flask as if toasting Finn then took two large gulps of the cloying liquid before passing it to Reyes. The private drank deeply then offered the flask to Thorne, but she turned it down.

"Don't worry, I'm stone cold sober," the ensign said, pointing to her almost undrunk pint on the table. "Though I kinda wish I wasn't."

"Sully will take you to the loading bay and get you safely stowed away on the truck," Trip said, gesturing to the thin-faced Metal. "I actually wish I was coming with you. I'd love another chance to fight those prosecutor bastards."

"Be careful what you wish for," Finn said. He offered Trip his hand and they shook. "But if this works, you'll get your chance. Everyone in Zavetgrad will. I just hope they're as willing to fight as you are."

"Ever since your broadcast, the recovery centers have been buzzing with talk of revolution," Trip said. "The people just a need a sign and someone to rally behind. If you pull this off then the workers will take up arms, I just know it."

"We really have to go," Sully said. The man was growing increasingly anxious. "The golds in charge of operations watch everything. I've gotten you onto an earlier truck bound for Metalhaven but if it doesn't leave exactly on time, they'll be suspicious."

Sully led the squad out of the safehouse, and Trip ran ahead to check that the coast was clear. While the lower levels of the brewery were too dark and musty for the administrator golds to grace with their presence, the rest of the factory was teeming with foreman robots who managed operations in the factories with the same tyrannical meticulousness as they did in the yards of Metalhaven.

Sully led them through the storehouses and past the mash tuns into the brewing rooms before signaling for Finn to stop. He and the others got into cover behind one of the enormous vats and saw Sully creep ahead toward the packing area where the strong ale was fed into kegs, ready to ship out to the hundreds of Recovery Centers across Zavetgrad. The allocation of stock and the process of loading the barrels onto trucks was being overseen by a chief foreman, an annoyingly astute and observant gen four model.

"What's the hold up?" Riley whispered.

"Foreman..." Finn replied, and this word on its own was enough to explain the delay. "I see a chief and six other robots between the packing and loading areas. I don't see how we can get past them all, without being seen."

Finn then spotted Trip, who was further toward the loading dock than Sully, skulking across the observation gantry. The Metal let out a sharp shrill whistle then hid before the chief foreman turned its mechanical eyes in the direction of the sound. Finn wondered what the hell the man was trying to achieve when he noticed that the workers in the packing area had also heard the signal and were whispering to one another.

"Hey, watch what you're doing!" one of the factory workers suddenly shouted.

"You watch it!" the man who had been the target of the complaint snapped back. "You're in my area, asshole!"

"What did you just call me?"

"You heard!"

The chief foreman stomped over to the two quarreling men. "What is the meaning of this?" the robot said, twisting its metal features to approximate a stern scowl.

"This fucking moron is in my workspace!" the first worker said.

"Moron?" the second man snorted, before shoving his adversary hard in the chest. "Who are you calling a moron, dickwad!"

Then, all hell broke loose. The first worker threw a punch and the second was sent reeling into a stack of kegs, which teetered and wobbled, threatening to bring the whole lot crashing down. The worker who'd been punched bounced back and threw himself at the first, then they were rolling around on the floor, fighting tooth and nail. If it was all an act, as Finn suspected it to be, then it was a good one.

"Fight!"

The shout rang out from elsewhere in the packing area, then a crowd of workers swelled toward the source of the affray to watch and cheer on the combatants, as if they were spectating a trial. The chief foreman signaled to the other robots and the machines pushed through the crowds to break up the unauthorized gathering. Then Finn saw Sully waving them on.

"Now's our chance, go!" Finn said.

He stayed as low as he could and ran toward the loading area, watching Trip and Sully out of the corner of his eye for any warning signals, but the fight was still in full flow and the foreman robots were too preoccupied to notice them. Sully ran to the open loading dock window and quickly checked outside before standing in front of a truck and waving Finn and the others inside. With the foremen finally starting to get control of the situation, Finn picked up the pace and sprinted the rest of the way, crashing into a stack of cargo so hard that his armored shoulder dented one of the beer kegs. Riley and the others were only a heartbeat behind and as soon as they were safely inside the trailer, Sully closed the shutter to hide them from prying robotic eyes.

"Quickly, down here," Sully said, pulling back a tarpaulin to reveal a narrow corridor running between the stacks of beer kegs. The Autohaven worker went in first but stopped midway down the trailer to open a panel in the floor. "In here. It's a smuggling compartment, though usually it's for equipment and other supplies, rather than people."

"Will we all fit?" Finn wondered, lowering himself into the hole, which was barely wider than his body.

"It won't exactly be comfortable, but it'll keep you hidden from the checkpoint patrol prefects," Sully replied. "Now please, hurry. I'm scheduled to depart in two minutes, and I guarantee one of those asshole robots will stop whatever it's doing to make sure I leave on time."

"Go, we'll manage," Riley said, ushering the driver toward the rear of the trailer. "But don't drive slowly. I've spent enough time in confined spaces."

Sully ran to the shutter door and eased it open just enough to squeeze underneath before the door was slammed shut and locked. Finn struggled into the compartment, which was every bit as cramped as Sully had suggested, but there was room enough to wiggle around and get comfortable. Then he heard voices, one Sully's and the other the unmistakable authoritarian drone of a foreman, and the truck's engine roared into life. Before long, the vehicle had pulled away from the loading dock and entered the main autoroute toward Metalhaven, rattling and bumping along the poorly-maintained road at a rate of knots.

"How far is it to Metalhaven?" Reyes asked. As the last to enter, the private had the least amount of space.

"Maybe thirty minutes, assuming no hold ups," Finn said. "But the road networks are littered with checkpoints and prefect patrol cars who love nothing more than to interfere and fuck up a worker's schedule."

"Great..." Reyes said, sarcastically. "I hope it's not too long. After that beer and probiotic crap, I really need to pee."

Thorne rolled her eyes at the private, which was about all she could move, but while Finn hoped that Reyes had been joking, he wasn't convinced the soldier was. Then the sound of skycar rotors drowned out even the rumble of road noise and Finn looked up, even though all he could see was metal decking. He waited and listened, but the sound didn't diminish.

"I think we're being followed," Finn said.

"Followed by what?" Riley grunted.

"If we're lucky, it's a just a regular prefect patrol being an asshole," Finn replied.

"And if we're unlucky?" Thorne added.

Finn sighed and shrugged. "If we're unlucky then that skycar above us will be black, instead of gold, which means the special prefecture have taken an interest in us."

Another minute elapsed with the sound of the skycar still

close, then Sully's voice cut through over a speaker in the trailer compartment.

"I'm being pulled over," the Metal from Autohaven said, and Finn cursed under his breath. "They're special prefects. You might want to get ready."

The speaker cut off and Riley scowled at Finn. "Get ready for what?"

"To fight," Finn said. "Special prefects don't conduct traffic stops, so if we're being pulled over it's because they know something, or at least suspect."

"Fuck," Reyes said, hammering on the panel above his head to open it. "But if we get into a firefight out on the road, how are we supposed to sneak into Metalhaven?"

"If we're discovered here then the plan is sunk, and we need a plan B," Finn said, speaking plainly.

"But I didn't see a plan B in the briefing," Thorne said, frowning.

"There is no plan B," Riley grunted, matter-of-factly. "If we're discovered here then we have to improvise to survive." Finn glowered at Riley, but the general was adamant. "We can't rescue Elara Cage if we're dead. If the prefects find us, our plan B is to stay alive and run. Everything else, we figure out from there."

Reyes clambered out of the compartment then helped the others to scramble free, before each of them took up positions in the rear of the trailer, but it was so full of beer kegs there was nowhere to hide. The truck pulled off the road and came to an abrupt halt, then the sound of skycar rotors became briefly deafening before the pitch and whine of the blades fell sharply and there was nothing but a yawning silence. A door opened and slammed shut again and Finn heard boots clomping against the asphalt surface.

"They're coming, two of them," Sully said in a hushed voice. Finn figured that the man was standing roughly level with their compartment. "Sit tight, I'll try to bluff our way out of this."

"Give me your identification and haulage permit." The officer's voice was taut and hostile. *A typical special prefect...* Finn thought.

"Sure, officer, it's all here," Sully said, doing a good job of sounding composed, like it was just another day on the job.

"Where have you come from and what is your destination?" the special prefect asked.

"Brewery seven, and my destination is right there on the permit!" Sully said, in a jovial tone.

Finn heard the snap of artificial leather striking flesh and Sully yelped with pain, then through gaps in the trailer's sidewall, he saw the Metal fall to his knees, clutching his ribs.

"That is for your insolence," the special prefect snarled. "Disrespect me again, and I will break your fingers, one by one."

"Yes, sir... sorry, sir," Sully replied, his words unsteady.

"Now, I ask again. What is your destination?" the prefect hissed.

"I have four stops in Metalhaven, sir," Sully replied, now speaking plainly, his voice laced with fear. "Recovery centers, one-eight, four-five, seven-six and ten-six, sir."

A voice crackled across the prefect's radio, but it was too muffled for Finn to hear.

"Remain there, I shall return shortly," the prefect ordered, then Finn heard regulation issue boot-heels snapping against the asphalt, coming closer. The prefect had walked away from Sully and was by chance now standing only meters away from where Finn was hiding.

"This is SP192K, go ahead, control," the special prefect said.

"SP192K, be advised that surveillance drone analysis has confirmed the body found outside the perimeter fence was a rebel from Haven." The voice on the other end of the comm-channel said. *"It's too badly mauled to make a definitive ID, but the corpse is fresh, maybe hours old, a day or two at most."*

"Received and understood, control, what are you orders?" the special prefect said.

"In light of this evidence, we believe operatives may have already infiltrated the city, perhaps with the objective of disrupting tonight's trial," the controller said. *"You are ordered to stop and search all ground and air traffic attempting to enter Metalhaven. Your C.O.N.F.I.R.M.E computer has been programmed with your new patrol sector. This comes direct from the Head Prefect."*

"Orders received and understood," the special prefect replied, promptly. "SP192K out."

Finn looked at Riley then at the others, but there was no need for words. They all knew that they would have to fight their way out, but even if they took down the special prefects and managed to escape, they were in the middle of an Autohaven road that ran between sectors, where there was almost nowhere to hide.

"Open the trailer," the special prefect ordered.

"But, sir, I'm on the clock, and this cargo needs to be delivered before..."

Sully's sentence was cut short by a gasp, as if he'd been

punched in the gut. The crackle of an electrified nightstick buzzed, and Finn heard more yelps of pain.

"Open the trailer," the prefect snarled. Finn heard the sharp, metallic sound of a pistol's slide being pulled back then snapping into its original position to chamber a round. "If you make me ask again, you get a bullet in the brain."

"Yes, sir, of course," Sully said.

The man had done his best but there was no point arguing with a special prefect, who was more than willing to make good on his threats. And a dead driver did them no good at all.

"Weapons ready," Riley whispered. "Fire only on my mark..."

The locking bolts on the shutter door snapped open and Finn aimed his laser, trying to predict where the two special prefects were standing. The shutter inched open then another message crackled through the officer's radio.

"Go ahead control," the special prefect said.

"SP192K, we have a priority one alert, rebel infiltrators have been sighted in Seedhaven," the controller said, rushing through the words. *"You are ordered to proceed to the destination with maximum haste. This supersedes all other orders."*

"Message received, control, SP192K en-route," the prefect replied, excited at the prospect of the chase ahead. "Proceed to your destinations," the officer added, now speaking to Sully. "Do not deviate off course or you will be flagged as a traitor and fired upon."

"Yes, sir, I understand," Sully said.

Finn heard bootsteps rushing away, then moments later the skycar's rotors began to power up, drowning out all other sounds. The canvas walls of the trailer were then buffeted by the skycar's downdraught, as the vehicle took off and accelerated toward Seedhaven.

"Well, ain't we just the luckiest sons-of-bitches on the planet," Reyes said, almost collapsing against a stack of kegs. "I thought we were screwed for sure."

"So did I," Finn said, fixing his laser back into its magnetic holster. "But why did they get ordered to Seedhaven? We don't have any Metals trying to break in there, do we?"

Riley shook his head. "No, we do not."

"Hey, guys, the coast is clear," Sully said, speaking through the tiny gap in the shutter door. "And you have a visitor."

"A visitor?"

All four members of the squad spoke the word at the same time, before shooting one another befuddled looks. Then the shutter door was inched open, and Sully ducked inside, followed by Scraps.

"Hi-hi!" Scraps said, waving at Finn as if it they were just casually hanging out in Haven. "Scraps make bad men go away!"

"Damn it, pal, I told you to stay in the Pit!" Finn said, and Scraps' eyes fell to the floor, making him feel like dirt. "I mean, I'm happy to see you, but it isn't safe here."

"Scraps didn't listen, learn that from Finn..." Scraps replied, in what Finn admitted was an impressive burn. "Scraps help Finn now. Finn needs Scraps."

"Wait, so did that little robot just spoof the priority one call that got those special prefects off our asses?" Reyes said, and Scraps nodded, proudly. "Well, shit. If you ask me, the robot is right, we do need him!"

Finn shot Reyes a dirty look but before he could admonish the private for encouraging more insubordination from Scraps, Riley also spoke up in the robot's favor.

"You might not like it, but Reyes is right," the general said. "Without Scraps, this mission would already be over."

"Captain Scraps!" the robot said, then giggled and saluted.

Finn had forgotten about the robot's impromptu promotion and saw that the captain's bars were still firmly attached to Scraps' oil-can body.

"How did you even get here?" Finn asked.

"Snuck onto skycar, but cold-cold make Scraps freeze!" Scraps said, setting down on one of the beer kegs and folding away his rotors. "When thawed, Finn gone!"

"But how did you get into the city?" Reyes asked. "We barely made it here alive and there were five of us, God rest the sarge."

"Scraps flew over fence," the robot said, casually. "Very high. Scraps scared!"

Finn couldn't help but laugh. He didn't want to put the robot in danger, but he realized that decision had been selfish. Scraps had the right to choose and if he chose to be a Metal, he had no right to deny him.

"Well, since you're here, I guess we could use a fifth member of the squad," Finn said. Scraps jumped up and waved his hands in the air. "But..." Finn added, wagging a finger at the robot, "you follow orders, okay? I'm a major and you're a captain, which means you do what I say." Finn then doubted himself and frowned at Riley. "Major outranks captain, right?"

Riley nodded. "Yes, but general outranks you all." The soldier than walked up to Scraps and rested a hand on the robot's head. "And I think it would do us all good to listen to Captain Scraps."

Scraps giggled and saluted again, and Finn couldn't help but notice how everyone was smiling, as if they'd woken up on their birthday to find a stack of gifts at the foot of their beds. As usual, the robot's effervescent charm had won everyone over.

"We should get going," Sully said, breaking up the reunion. "The asshole prefect that sucker punched me also stamped my travel permit, so we won't get any more trouble from checkpoints or roadblocks. It'll be smooth running from here on in, maybe ten minutes at most."

"Thank you, Sully, then let's not delay any further," Riley said.

Sully nodded then closed and locked the shutter door. A few seconds later the truck's engine sparked into life, and they were moving again.

"Thanks to Scraps, plan A, our only plan, is still a go, but let's not kid ourselves that the next part won't be the most difficult," Riley said. "Even so, we've come this far, and I truly believe we can go the rest of the way." Riley then looked Finn dead in the eyes. "We'll find Elara Cage, then, in full view of the Regents and every worker in the city, we'll stop the prosecutors and show everyone that the Authority can not only be beaten, but that they can be humiliated too."

21

SEVEN SIX

FINN WAS BUMPED and jolted as the truck lurched down the dilapidated roads that crisscrossed Metalhaven like a chaotic spider's web. The narrow streets made maneuvering a vehicle the size of Sully's ale truck even more of a challenge but eventually the brakes were applied, and the engine was switched off. Finn and Riley glanced anxiously at one another and readied their weapons just in case the stop had been ordered by another overzealous prefect but when the shutter door was opened, it was only Sully's face he saw outside.

"It's okay, you can come out now," Sully said. "I've parked the truck down an alley so no-one will be able to see you."

Finn moved ahead then ducked underneath the shutter and squinted his eyes as he emerged from the gloom of the trailer into Metalhaven. There was never much daylight from the perpetually low, cloud-obscured sun, but a thick blanket of snow on the ground reflected what little light there was into his eyes. Riley and the others climbed out next, but Finn was already mesmerized by the sight of his old home. Even with the truck wedged down an alley, Finn could still see enough of his old sector for it to feel all too familiar. From the drab buildings with their leaking roofs and chipped brickwork, to the smell of burned metal lingering in the smoggy air, it was like he'd never left. Then he looked at the recovery center that Sully had parked outside and laughed.

"What's so funny?" Riley asked.

"This is Recovery Center seven-six, I used to drink here sometimes," Finn said, pointing to the building. The stench of stale beer and sweat was oozing out of the door like pus from a sore. "It wasn't my regular bar, but I know it well enough."

"Why do they have weird names, like seven-six?" Private Reyes asked. "Wouldn't it be easier to just call it the Worker's Rest or something more memorable like that?"

"The name corresponds to the reclamation yard and residential zone that the recovery center was built to serve," Finn explained. "So, seven-six is intended for workers from yard seven, who live in residential block six. You can technically drink anywhere in Metalhaven, but most people just go to their closest bar, since it's quicker and it's usually where your worker buddies drink too. My regular recovery center was seven-nine, a couple of blocks away."

"So how come you came here sometimes?" Reyes asked.

The faces of Soren Driscoll, Corbin Radcliffe, and their obnoxious associates invaded Finn's mind. It felt like an age since he had sat in a recovery center like the one opposite, taking shit from Soren and giving it back, before inevitably getting into a fist fight. It was not a happy memory.

"Let's just say there were some people in seven-nine that I

preferred to avoid," Finn explained. "And those particular assholes were too lazy to venture further afield."

"It doesn't actually seem that bad," Thorne said. The ensign had been quietly listening in while taking in as much of their surroundings as the blockading wall and beer truck would allow. The soldier then noticed that Finn was looking at her, eyebrow raised. "I mean, it's obviously not great," she added, backtracking. "But in my mind, I was half-expecting to see buildings on fire, dead bodies in the street, and mutant rats running all over the place."

Finn laughed. "You'd need to be here on a trial day for that." Then he stopped and realized that it *was* a trial day. "Actually, if we manage to stick around long enough, you'll probably get your wish."

"On second thoughts, it's just fine as it is," Thorne said, smiling.

"You know, I actually miss this place," Finn said, shaking his head. He hadn't realized it until just then. "How weird is that?"

The months he'd spent in the luxury of the Authority sector and his short time in Haven had both felt like layovers, like he never really belonged, but despite how much suffering he'd endured within the confines of its sector boundaries, Metalhaven still felt like his home.

"You spent most of your life here, and the habits you established and friendships you made aren't easily forgotten," Riley cut in. "So, it's not weird at all. No matter where you end up, Metalhaven will always be a part of you."

"Is that how you feel about Stonehaven?" Finn said. He was risking opening the old wound again, but he'd spent his life being frank and honest with people and wasn't about to change now.

"No," Riley grunted, solemnly. "Golds are brought up to believe these sectors are beneath us, and designed for a lesser class of human, so I spent a good part of my life detesting Stonehaven, and its workers. For me, Zavetgrad is just a reminder of the monster I was, and I would gladly see it all burn." The general sighed then glanced at Finn. "But what I want is inconsequential. What I can do for the people I once hated is now all that matters."

Finn nodded then caught movement in his peripheral vision. He looked up and scanned his eyes across the dark, cloudy sky before spotting a surveillance drone flying in a circuit a few hundred meters south.

"We need to get inside," Finn said, moving against the wall of the alley and urging Riley and the others to do the same. "The sector is on high alert and those drones will be searching for anything out of the ordinary."

"We certainly qualify," Riley grunted.

"No worries, we okay!" Scraps said, zooming out of the back of the trailer. "Scraps jam bad flybot. Won't see unless get closer."

"Are you sure it can't see us?" Finn asked, as Scraps landed on his shoulder and folded away his rotors.

"Sure-sure!" Scraps replied, cheerfully, while narrowing his mechanical eyes in the direction of the surveillance drone. "But Scraps keep eyes on it."

"This way," Sully said, waving them over. The driver had been talking to a worker from the recovery center, and both Metals looked eager to get the squad of Haven soldiers off the street.

Finn approached the Autohaven driver and the stranger, who looked like a typical chrome, especially next to the slender-framed Sully. The man was rugged and heavy-set, and while the worker was likely in his late twenties, the scars and lines on his face suggested an age that was at least twenty years beyond that. Finn could also see evidence of injuries caused by laser cutter accidents, most notably a mangled right hand, which had been crudely repaired.

"I had a cutter blow up on me five years ago," the man said, perhaps noticing that Finn and the others were staring. "Luckily, I have a genetic rating of three, otherwise I'd have been sent to a wellness center, or to trial, though I don't know which is worse."

"This is Briggs," Sully said, hooking a thumb at the man. "He does have a first name, but apparently no-one remembers it."

"Not even me!" Briggs joked, before patting his over-large gut. "That's what you get for working in a recovery center and drinking half the contents of the cellar all by your lonesome." The man shrugged. "At least it helps me to forget."

Finn caught another glimpse of the surveillance drone and he got the sense it was inching closer. "We should get inside," he said, feeling suddenly exposed. "Assuming we're to lay low here until the trial begins?"

"That's the plan," Briggs nodded.

Finn started toward the rear door of the building, but the worker held up his good hand to stop him, then pointed to a trailer in the courtyard. It was the same style of trailer used in the reclamation yards to collect salvaged metal and ferry it to the processors.

"But first, you need to put all your weapons in there," Briggs added.

"Are you mad? We can't give up our weapons," Riley said, suddenly angry.

"Look, there's no chance of you getting those firearms past the gate scanners without being detected, but I have a Metal who can get them in."

A figure moved out of the shadows toward them, and Finn was shocked and embarrassed to admit that he hadn't spotted the third person before. The silhouette resolved into a woman wearing Metalhaven coveralls.

"That's close enough," Riley grunted, as Reyes and Thorne aimed their weapons at the new arrival. "Identify yourself."

"Xia…" the woman mumbled, ignoring the guns pointed at her and looking right back at Riley. She then approached the trailer and opened a compartment in its base. "Weapons…"

Finn struggled to make out the words the Metal had spoken before noticing deep scars on the woman's face, running from the base of her ears to the corners of her mouth. When she'd spoken, her jaw had barely opened.

"Xia had a run-in with a prefect's nightstick a while back, so she can't talk much," Briggs explained, answering the question on Finn's mind. "Though that does also mean the foremen and prefects don't bother asking her questions, which has its advantages too."

"I'm sorry about that," Riley replied, not sounding especially sorry, "but what does this have to do with our weapons?"

"Xia works in yard seven, emptying reclaimed metal from

trailers like this one into the processing hoppers then returning empties back into the yard. This one was taken out for maintenance, so if you stash your weapons inside, Xia will get them through the gate scanner."

"That sounds like an awful risk," Riley said, still unconvinced. "If our weapons are discovered, the plan fails. What's to say this trailer won't be searched, or that it won't just trundle off in the wrong direction, taking our weapons with it?"

"Re-program..." Xia mumbled; arms now folded across her chest. She'd taken Riley questioning the plan as a personal insult.

Scraps was still diligently observing the surveillance drone and Finn tapped him on the shoulder, interrupting the robot's vigil.

"Hey, pal, can you check out that trailer's programming, and make sure everything's okay?" Finn asked. "Then we can all be satisfied that our weapons will be safe."

Riley narrowed his eyes at Finn then nodded his agreement, and Scraps leapt off Finn's shoulder and flew to the trailer. Xia scrutinized the robot's work over his little shoulder, but it didn't take Scraps long to interrogate the trailer's basic programming and get the answers Riley needed.

"All good. Few tweaks. Xia did good job!" Scraps said, giving the Metal a thumbs-up sign. Despite her wired jaw, Xia still managed to smile.

"Very well," Riley said, pulling the sling on his rifle over his head and placing the weapon into the trailer. "But these had better find their way back to us, or this won't be much of a fight."

Finn placed his laser cannon and baseball bat into the

trailer then went to collect his knife, before remembering it was at the bottom of the cave pool, deep beneath Zavetgrad.

"Take…" Xia said, removing a knife from her coveralls and dropping it next to his laser cannon.

"Thanks," Finn said, noting that the knife looked well-used, but sharp.

Reyes and Thorne relinquished their weapons too, albeit with the same reluctance Riley had shown. Xia then activated the trolley and steered it along Metalhaven's narrow backstreets toward the yard.

"Flybot close!" Scraps said, and everyone looked skyward. The flight path of the drone was bringing it closer to the recovery center. "Inside-inside!" the robot added.

Briggs ushered them toward the back door of the building and Finn waited for the others to enter first, before picking up Scraps and following. Sully was going in the opposite direction and the man stopped and grabbed Finn's shoulders.

"Good luck, Finn," the Metal from Autohaven said. "I'd like say I wish I was coming with you, but I'm not even a very good truck driver, never mind a fighter."

"You've done more than enough, thank you," Finn said. The man may not have held a gun or thrown a punch, but he'd still risked his life to get the squad to Metalhaven, which made him as brave as any soldier. "Now go, before you miss your next delivery."

The men shook hands then Sully rushed back to his truck and got it ready to move out. Briggs stood by the door waiting for him and the Metal quickly ushered Finn inside before closing and locking the heavy door behind them. Finn was then led to a cellar room, where the others were waiting, gathered around a table built from empty beer kegs. Briggs hurried to a trunk in the corner of the room and threw open the lid before grabbing five sets of Metalhaven work coveralls and dumping them onto the makeshift table.

"Xia will take care of your weapons, but we still need to get the five of you inside yard seven," Briggs said, adding five fake worker IDs to the pile. The man then scowled and counted the people in the room, his lips twitching as he did so. "Wait, there's someone missing."

"Sergeant Kellan," Riley said, taking a suitably grave tone. "He didn't make it."

"I'm sorry," Briggs said.

"We'll mourn the dead later," Riley said, unmoved. "Now, explain how we get inside the reclamation yard."

From the way Riley had shrugged off Sergeant Kellan's death, Briggs would have been forgiven for thinking the general heartless, but Finn understood the man's reaction. They had to remain focused and unemotional, though the latter was a skill Finn was still working on.

"Put these on, they should be large enough to fit over your uniforms," Briggs continued, sorting the coveralls and identification badges according to their intended recipients. "You all have fake identities, and if stopped and questioned by a foreman or prefect, you must remember to give the name on your ident."

Finn picked up his badge and the name read, Clark Tyrell. General Riley was Kian Addams, Thorne was Erin Wheeler, and Private Reyes was Lane Howley.

"Sorry about the smell, but at least it's authentic," Briggs added, perhaps noticing that Reyes and Thorne were holding up the coveralls like they were disease-ridden rags. "Once you're dressed, you'll head out and join shift rotation three, which begins in twenty-eight minutes. That shift will be cut short so that all thirteen reclamation yards can be closed and made ready for The Shadow's trial."

"If they're clearing the yards then what happens to us?" Thorne asked, tentatively pushing her foot into the leg of her coveralls, while pulling a face. "We need to still be inside when the trial begins."

"Your work loggers have the location of a burned-out APC," Briggs explained, tossing four of the wrist-mounted computers onto the table. "When the klaxon sounds to end the shift, get inside that APC as fast as you can and hunker down. Your weapons will already be there, waiting for you."

The squad exchanged nervous looks. The plan was full of risk, not least of which was the part where they hid inside a destroyed armored personnel carrier from the Last War, which was rusted and on the verge of collapse.

"Your little robot can maybe help hide you from scanners," Briggs added, nodding at Scraps, who saluted in return. "I didn't see a robot mentioned in the mission briefing I got from Haven, but it was a good idea to bring him along."

"See..." Scraps said, smugly. "Scraps told Finn so..."

"Yes, you did, now shut up," Finn said, playfully, and Scraps giggled.

"Wait, how will Scraps get inside?" Reyes asked. He patted the spare set of coveralls on the table. "I'm pretty sure these aren't his size."

"Reyes-Reyes no worry!" Scraps said, nonchalantly. "Scraps sneaky."

"Too damned sneaky for your own good," Finn added, narrowing his eyes at the robot, but Scraps just giggled again.

"I can't walk you to the gate because I have to get ready

for the influx of workers who are about to flood this place, ready for the trial," Briggs said before nodding to Finn. "But you already have your own expert guide. Finn will get you inside. After that, it's up to you. I'd say, 'good luck' but you're going to need a miracle."

"We don't need a miracle or luck," Reyes said, adapting a confident swagger. "A few magazines of nine-millimeter hollow point and a grenade or ten should do the trick."

"Hooah to that!" Thorne said, bumping fists with Reyes in solidarity.

Finn was glad they were geared up for the fight, but no-one knew better than he did that cockiness and Metalhaven prefects were an explosive mix.

"I suggest you keep that enthusiasm bottled up till we're safely tucked away inside the APC," Finn said. "First, we have to get into yard seven and survive a few hours of work, and I promise you that's not as easy as it sounds."

"Come on, Major, we're almost there," Private Reyes replied, undeterred by Finn's cautionary tone. "How hard can it be to slice up a few old tanks?"

Finn laughed and so did Briggs, who was quick to remind Reyes of the dangers by waving his mangled hand in the soldier's face.

"I suggest you don't get cocky," Briggs said, backing Finn up. "Besides, laser cutters aren't the most dangerous things in this sector. If you see a prefect, I suggest you keep your head down, and your lips sealed, unless you want to have your face smashed in, like Xia did."

22
A DAY AT WORK

Finn led the squad out of the recovery center and onto the streets of Metalhaven. Even as a native chrome, he felt unsafe out in the open, so he could only imagine how the others were feeling, as Haven operatives at large in enemy territory. Even General Riley, normally so unflappable in the face of danger, appeared jittery and worried, while Reyes and Thorne looked practically petrified.

"You guys are going to have to relax," Finn said, guiding them toward the gated entrance to yard seven. It was a walk he'd done a thousand times before and he could navigate blindfold. "Prefects can smell fear from a mile away, and right now you look like people with something to hide."

"No shit we have something to hide," Reyes said, adjusting his coveralls, which hung heavily off his athletic frame. "Now I wish I'd downed a pint of that disgusting ale to take the edge off."

"We need to start chatting, like normal worker buddies on the way to a shift," Finn said, trying to think of a way to ease the tension and make them act more naturally. "What do you all like to do in your spare time?"

"Reyes likes trying to add notches to his bunk post, isn't that right, stud?" Thorne said, and Finn saw her familiar smirk return. "He's not especially good at it, but he gets an A for effort."

"Fuck you, Mara, I'm a prolific swordsman, and everyone knows it," Reyes hit back. Suddenly, it was like he'd forgotten where he was.

"It doesn't count if you jerk yourself off, you do realize that, right?" Thorne hit back, and Reyes gave her the bird, though he was smiling too.

"What about you, Ensign?" Finn asking, trying to keep the momentum going. "I guess when your day job is flying skycars, it's hard to find anything else that measures up."

"I actually like to read," Thorne said, surprising Finn with her chosen hobby.

"Color-by-numbers books don't count as reading, Mara..." Reyes cut in, leaping on the chance to get his own back.

"What would you know? The only thing you've read in the last year was your shitty performance evaluation," Thorne said.

Finn huffed a laugh, scoring it two-zero to Thorne so far. He then glanced at Riley, but the general had barely blinked since leaving the recovery center and he still looked like a man harboring a guilty secret.

"What about you, General?" Finn asked, trying to engage Riley and make him loosen up. "What do you do in your off time?"

"I don't have any off time," Riley grunted, clearly

unwilling to play Finn's game. "I work when I'm on duty, and when I'm not on duty, I work."

"Come on, sir, you must do something for fun?" Reyes asked.

"I do not," Riley replied, stiffly. "Now stop asking."

Private Reyes may have been cocky, but he wasn't stupid, and he knew when to shut his mouth. Finn considered pushing the general for an answer, since he wasn't afraid of the man's bark or his bite, then he remembered Riley's confession and the dark past that still weighed heavily on his broad shoulders. Considering the atrocities that the former head prefect had witnessed and been party to, engaging any of his time for personal enjoyment would seem tactless and improper. It would be like dancing on the graves of those who had died either directly or indirectly because of his actions.

Finn then saw the gate to yard seven up ahead and he breathed a sigh of relief, knowing that once inside they would only have the asshole foremen to contend with, instead of prefects. Then he spotted a patrol loitering nearby and cursed under his breath. There were only two officers, but they were taking an unusual amount of interest in the workers who were approaching the gate.

"What's wrong?" Riley said, perhaps noticing that Finn had become tense.

"Prefects don't normally patrol by the gates," Finn said, slowing his pace to give himself more time to think. "It's usually just the foremen who scan people in and out."

"What does that mean?" Riley asked. "Should we turn back?"

"No, if we try to walk away now, they'll tag us for sure,"

Finn said. "Just keep your heads down, walk straight for the gate, and present your work logger to the chief foreman. And whatever you do, don't look the prefects in the eyes."

"But what if we're stopped?" Thorne said, speaking urgently but in hushed tones.

"It's like Briggs said, answer their questions but don't antagonize them. Just be deferential and keep your responses short and to the point. I'll try to step in where I can."

Finn continued walking, adjusting his route so that he'd pass through the gate as far away from the prefect patrol as possible. With any luck, the officers would be too preoccupied harassing another group of workers to notice them. They weren't lucky.

"You four, stop!" one of the prefects called out.

The squad did as they were ordered, and Finn tried to maneuver himself to the front of the group, in the hope that he would get quizzed instead of the others. It was a risk, since he had perhaps the most recognizable face in the entire sector, but he also knew that the streets of his old home were the very last place the Authority would expect to find him and was banking on the officers not looking too closely. Even so, he kept his chin down and eyes fixed on the ground in front of his boots.

"Names," the prefect demanded.

"Clark Tyrell, sir," Finn answered.

He spoke calmly despite the disdainful tone of the prefect's voice triggering deep-rooted feelings of rage and hatred.

"Lane Howley, sir," Reyes said, answering with a level of humility that Finn thought the soldier incapable of. "Erin Wheeler, sir," Thorne added, straight faced and with the same deference. Then General Riley grunted the words, "Kian Addams." The honorific, "sir..." did not follow, nor had Riley's answer conveyed the respect Finn had urged, and sure enough, the prefect squared up to the general, fingers wrapped around his nightstick.

"You're old for a worker," the prefect said. "Just how old are you, anyway?"

"Thirty-five, sir," Riley grunted, this time with the proper respect, though Finn feared it was already too late.

"Thirty-five!" the prefect bellowed, before nudging his partner. "You look more like sixty-five!" he added, and both officers laughed, cruelly. The prefect then grabbed Riley's work logger and scanned it. "Kian Addams, rating three-three, age thirty-five," the officer said, still laughing. "You must have had a hard life, worker." The prefect leant in closer. "Do you frighten yourself when you look in the mirror? I'm surprised it doesn't shatter!"

The two prefects laughed but Finn could see that Riley was struggling to keep his cool. He was a man used to being obeyed not ridiculed.

"It must be nice to be young," Riley said, and the prefect squared up to him again. "Such lovely smooth skin..."

Don't do it... Finn thought, trying to urge the man to stop with the power of his mind. *Don't give him a reason...*

"Tell me, son, when do you expect to reach puberty?" Riley added, his lips curling into a smile.

The crackle of electrified nightsticks split the air then in the blink of an eye, Riley had been set upon by both prefects, one jabbing the electric probes into his gut, while the other hammered his baton across the general's exposed back. Riley went down and for a second, it looked like Reyes and Thorne were going to intervene, but Finn held up his hand to stop them, and by some miracle they obeyed.

"Let's see how you manage your work shift with broken hands, chrome scum!" the first prefect roared.

The officer grabbed Riley's limp wrist and prepared to smash his baton into the bone. Then the officer's radio squawked an alert and both prefects immediately dropped what they were doing to answer the call.

"P434A responding, what's wrong?" the prefect said.

"There's a disturbance outside Recovery Center seven-six, proceed at once, priority one!" a voice on the other end of the communicator said.

"P434A, received and understood. We're en-route," the prefect replied. "It's your lucky day, asshole," the man added, dropping Riley's arm then spitting on his coveralls. "Now, keep your nose clean, or I'll cut it off."

With that, the two prefects sprinted away from the gate before quickly disappearing around a corner in the direction of the recovery center where Finn and the others had been hiding only minutes earlier.

"Fuck, that was lucky," Reyes said, helping Riley to stand.

Finn was about to agree, when he spotted Scraps, perched on a third-floor windowsill of a nearby building. The robot waved at him then held his hand up to his ocular holes, simulating an old-fashioned telephone.

"You're right about that," Finn said, grabbing Riley's other arm to steady the general. "I think we have a guardian angel watching over us."

Reyes frowned then Finn covertly gestured toward Scraps and the private smiled.

"Shit, that little robot did it again!" the soldier said.

"Scraps shouldn't have needed to intervene," Riley said, angrily dusting himself down. "I should have just done what you said, and kept my mouth shut."

"Are you okay?" Finn asked.

"It's mostly my pride that's wounded," Riley said, sheepishly. "But I don't know how you lived with this for so long without snapping."

Finn laughed. "I didn't, I just got a hell of a lot of beatdowns."

"We should head inside, while it's quiet," Thorne said.

As diligent soldiers, Thorne and Reyes had been watching their surroundings, but there were no other jackbooted thugs in sight. The general's thrashing had also garnered little attention from other workers, though Finn wasn't surprised, since such beatdowns were commonplace.

"You are late," the foreman on the gate said, as Finn approached, work logger presented for inspection.

"We got held up by prefects," Finn said, scowling at the machine. "You were literally standing right there when it happened."

"That is no excuse, worker Tyrell," the robot replied, scanning his work logger. "One hour has been added to today's shift."

"But that makes no sense; today's shift will be cut short because of the trial," Finn pointed out. He couldn't help arguing with the tyrannical robots. It was habit.

The foreman thought for a moment and Finn could practically hear the transistors fizzing inside its electronic brain.

"In that case, one shift hour has been added to tomorrow's shift," the foreman said. "Now get to work."

Finn shook his head at the robot and sighed heavily to punctuate his disappointment, then marched through the gate. It felt like he'd never left. Riley and the others followed, and none of them spoke, even when the foreman berated them for being tardy and added an extra shift hour for the following day, just as Finn had received. He got the general's attention then led the squad to a rack of laser cutters that were stacked up close to the entrance and showed them how to use their work loggers to release a tool. Dozens of other workers were piling in alongside them, grunting their displeasure at how long it was taking Finn's newbie worker buddies to get sorted.

Laser cutters in hand, Finn then led the squad into the reclamation yard, which was already in full swing, with hundreds of workers toiling in the low afternoon sun. The scale of the operation was bewildering to Riley, Reyes and Thorne, and the soldiers ambled through the yard, mouths agape. Finn made sure to keep a close eye on his fellow Metals to make sure they didn't wander off or fall into a pit while they were mesmerized by the sizzle and flash and hundreds of laser beams. The smell of burned metal was so intense that even Finn struggled to stomach it, and he wondered how he'd ever coped working sometimes as many as sixteen hours a day in such horrific conditions.

"I had no idea it would be like this," Reyes said, his face already blackened by smoke. "It's like something out of a nightmare."

"Except it's not a nightmare, it's the reality for tens of thousands of people," Finn said. "You can see now why this has to end."

"Fucking A..." Reyes said, shaking his head. "I want to tear it down, all of it."

"First, let's stop this trial," Riley cut in. Even as a former head prefect of Stonehaven, the general looked shocked by what he was seeing. "Then, maybe we can do just that."

Finn found their allocated work zone then quickly located the burned-out APC that was to be their hideout once the klaxon sounded. It was still several hours until their shift would end and the yard cleared and made ready for Elara's trial, which meant they had work to do.

"Stay busy, but stay safe," Finn said, igniting his cutter and starting to slice off a section of a destroyed French tank. "Watch me and watch carefully. These cutters can be as deadly as any gun. One slip, and you could lose a leg, just like that..." He snapped his fingers and Thorne jumped in fright.

"How long do we have to do this for?" Reyes asked, already holding his cutter further away from his body, like it was a live grenade.

"Four hours, give or take," Finn said, and Reyes looked like he was about to pass out. "It'll be hard, but we'll get through it. I'll show you how."

Finn got to work, and he was pleased to discover that the others were all quick studies. Even so, the work was backbreaking, even for him. After months away from the yard, and despite his trained physique, his tolerance for the work had fallen sharply, though it was still far easier for him than it was for the rest of the squad. Then, just under four hours into the shift, the klaxon sounded, and foremen began ushering workers out.

"They're a little ahead of schedule but nothing seems out

of the ordinary," Finn said. He'd expected to be working for another hour at least.

"I ain't complaining," Reyes said, resting on the side of an armored car. "I'm dead on my feet."

"We need to reach the APC before the foremen see us," Riley said, shouldering his cutter and shuffling into cover.

Finn nodded but the robots were already swarming the yard and it didn't seem possible. Then four foremen began to approach, from each corner of the yard, boxing them in and making it impossible to hide.

"All workers must exit the yard at once," one of the foremen called out, still stomping closer. "This shift is over. Repeat, exit the yard at once..."

"Fuck, what do we do?" Reyes said, holding the cutter like it was his rifle.

Finn looked for Scraps, searching the highest points of the yard in the hope his robot pal was lurking close by. *Come on, buddy, if ever we needed you, now is the time...*

The foremen continued to close, shouting their orders with increasing volume, then suddenly all four of them stopped dead, as if their power cells had given out at the same time.

"What's going on?" Riley grunted. "Why aren't they moving?"

"Quick-quick!" Scraps yelled, zooming out from whatever hiding place the robot had squirreled himself into. "Foremen offline but only for sixty-seconds!"

Finn didn't need telling twice, and he ran for the APC, laser-cutter slung over his shoulder, the heat from the barrel scorching his face like it was a naked flame. He reached the burned-out vehicle first and pulled open the side hatch, before waving Riley and the others inside. The bulk of the cutters made entering difficult, and with each second of struggle, Scraps grew more anxious.

"Hurry-hurry!" Scraps said, waving his hands in the air.

Thorne finally squeezed through the hatch then Finn tossed his cutter through the opening and began to climb inside.

"Pal, come on!" Finn said, calling out to Scraps, who was still standing guard, using his electronic countermeasures to disrupt the quartet of robots. "We're all in, now hustle."

Scraps zoomed through the opening at the same time the foremen reactivated and resumed their march, then Finn slammed the hatch shut.

"All workers must exit the yard at once," the robot called out, its speech starting slow then getting faster, like an old-fashioned tape machine that had suddenly been turned on in the middle of a track. "This shift is over..." the machine added before its voice trailed off.

"Where are workers Tyrell, Addams, Wheeler and Howley?" one of the robots queried.

"Unknown. They were just here," another robot with a near identical voice replied.

"I will interrogate the gate computer," a third foreman said. "Processing."

The wait was agonizing, especially in the cramped confines of the wrecked APC. Then the foreman delivered its verdict.

"Workers Tyrell, Addams, Wheeler and Howley have exited the yard," one of the foremen said. "This zone is clear. Moving on to the next zone."

Finn let out the breath he hadn't even realized he was

holding then flopped onto his back and closed his eyes. It wasn't long before he felt the weight of Scraps pressing down on his chest.

"We safe-safe!" Scraps said, cheerfully. "Plan went well!"

Finn laughed and so did the others, even Riley.

"Captain Scraps, I do believe I may have to promote you," the general said.

23

LET THE TRIAL BEGIN

Finn kicked off his overalls then collected his laser cannon and baseball bat, which were waiting for him inside the APC, just as the Metals from the recovery center, Briggs and Xia, had promised. Riley and the others were also gearing up, and Finn realized that his prosecutor armor was far more conspicuous than their digital-camo-pattern fatigues, despite its chrome color scheme.

"We're going to need a way to stay hidden for as long as possible," Finn said, attaching his cannon to its magnetic holster. "The camera drones recording the trial will be focused on Elara and the prosecutors hunting her, but we can expect there to be foremen and prefects standing watch at the entrances and exits to every reclamation yard. If they see us and raise the alarm, we'll be surrounded in seconds."

"What about Scraps?" Thorne nodded to the robot, who sat twiddling his little thumbs. "He's managed to hack the authority's communications and jam their scanners before; maybe he can help to keep us off their radar until we reach Elara?"

"What do you think, pal?" Finn asked. "Can you do it?"

Everyone looked to Scraps but despite the sudden attention and pressure that was being heaped on him, the robot did not appear concerned.

"Scraps can," the robot said, with a shrug. "But need foreman. Chief-chief!"

Riley scowled. "You need us to get you a chief foreman?"

"Yes-yes!" Scraps said, before tapping the side of his head. "Need FLP."

Finn understood his robot's plan. "So, if we can get you the head of a chief foreman, you can hack its FLP, tap into the security systems in the yards and scrub our images from their cameras?"

"Yes-yes!" Scraps said. "But trial TV drones harder. Special prefect system."

"We can worry about that later, but by the time we risk being spotted by camera drones, we should already be in range of our target," Riley said, sounding convinced. "By that point, it might actually help us to be seen. We need the people of Metalhaven and beyond to know we're fighting for Elara, and for them."

Riley removed a puck-shaped device from his pack that looked heavy and only just fit inside the palm of the burly general's hand.

"This is an extraction beacon," Riley explained. "Once we secure Elara, I'll activate this, which will trigger the skycar's auto-recovery program. Assuming the surveillance drones that found Sergeant Kellan's body didn't also find our skycar, it should then auto-pilot into the city and fly right to us."

"What are the chances it will make it past the border fence?" Reyes asked.

Everyone looked to their resident pilot to answer, but Ensign Thorne did not look hopeful.

"Honestly, the odds of the skycar making it inside the city are slim," Thorne said. "Most likely, it'll get tagged by the border scanners and blown to pieces by sentry guns before it even gets close." She shrugged. "But we knew that already. We took on this mission knowing it might be a one-way trip."

"We might not escape but that doesn't mean we get captured either," Finn said, keen to put a more positive spin on their chances of survival. "Briggs said the whole sector is ready to go up like a powder keg, so all we need to do is provide a spark, and maybe we can take Metalhaven from the golds and make this our new base."

"First, let's find one of those worker robots," Riley said, turning his attention to their immediate problem. "Then Captain Scraps can work his magic."

"Major Scraps!" the robot said, saluting. "I promoted!"

"Hey, don't get ahead of yourself, pal," Finn said, scowling at his robot buddy, who appeared all too eager to climb the ranks for his liking. "The general said *may have to* promote you. Don't get delusions of grandeur."

"Major Brasa is correct," Riley said, and Scraps looked crestfallen. "But hack a foreman's FLP and keep us hidden, and I'll make it official," the general added, and Scraps grinned.

Finn eased open the APC's side hatch and peeked outside, but the reclamation yard was eerily quiet. He took a chance and pushed it open fully, wincing as the battle-damaged and rust-worn hinges creaked and groaned like an old iron gate.

"It looks clear," Finn said, poking his head outside and taking a breath of cold air. "What do you think, Scraps?"

"Scraps check!"

The robot sprouted his rotors and zoomed through the opening before Finn could caution his buddy to be careful, but if anyone knew how to sneak around, it was Scraps.

"Clear-clear!" Scraps said, suddenly dropping in front of the hatch and slowing to a hover. "But bad-robots close... Stay sneaky!"

Finn climbed outside, happy to be finally free of the acrid-smelling confines of the burned-out APC. He stayed low and edged along the side of the vehicle while Scraps snuck ahead and pointed into the distance. Finn took a quick peek and saw a foreman standing guard on a lookout tower. It was one of many platforms that were set up across all the yards to allow the robotic middle-managers to spy on workers and spot those who were taking unauthorized breaks or generally slacking off. On this occasion, the robot was looking out toward yard one in the distance, and Finn could see giant TV screens being hoisted into the air, ready to show the trial.

"They're getting ready to start the ceremony," Finn said, whispering despite them being too far away even for the foreman's electronic ears to detect. "We have to snag that robot quickly. It looks like a gen-four, though I can't tell if it's a chief."

"Bad robot is chief," Scraps said, before growling at the foreman like a dog. "Scraps distract!"

"Pal, wait, we need a plan..." Finn said, but Scraps was already moving.

"Shit, that little robot is not one for following orders!"

Reyes said, though the comment implied admiration rather than criticism.

"I wonder where he gets that from?" Riley added, side-eyeing Finn, who made a point of showing offense.

Suddenly, a rock flew at the foreman and hit it on the back of the head. The machine jerked in surprise then spun around. "Who is there?" it demanded.

Another rock thudded into the foreman, then Finn saw something speed away from the lookout tower, heading in their direction. The object was moving so fast it was little more than a blur, but he felt sure it was Scraps.

"Get ready, I think Scraps is luring the foreman to us," Finn said, drawing his baseball bat.

"What should we do?" Riley asked.

"Grab it when it gets close, then leave the rest to me," Finn said.

He'd left his answer intentionally vague, but he doubted that Riley would like what he had in mind, and there wasn't enough time for the general to quiz him further. The foreman had already climbed down from the tower and was stomping in their direction.

"If there is still a worker in this yard, you must exit immediately," the foreman said, its heavy footsteps shaking the ground. "Four hours will be added to tomorrow's shift for disobeying a direct command."

Finn waited for the foreman to get close then sprang out from behind the APC, baseball bat drawn back. The foreman's glowing, mechanical eyes widened in surprise then Finn clobbered the machine so hard it pancaked the robot's face flat.

"Now!" Finn yelled.

Riley and the others ran out, each grabbing an arm or a leg to restrain the foreman, who had been teetering, on the verge of falling over. Finn dropped the bat then drew his cannon and flipped the setting to 'continuous beam'. Hot laser light spilled from the barrel of the weapon and smoke clouded his eyes as he sliced through the foreman's thin neck and removed its head. Straight away, the machine shut down and the body fell limp in the hands of Finn's squadmates, while the head thudded into the snow, melting a patch around it due to the residual heat.

"How are we supposed to hack a headless robot?" Reyes said, tossing down the metal leg he'd been holding.

"The head contains the Foreman Logic Processor, which is all we need," Finn explained, holstering his cannon, and returning his bat to his back scabbard. "Scraps can power up this thing's brain and take it from there, right Scraps?"

"No problem!" Scraps said, leaping onto the foreman's head then sprouting the tools he needed to prise open its cranial flap. "Foreman stupid. This quick!"

Music suddenly began to blare out from the speakers attached to the massive TV screens that were hovering above yard one, and Finn instinctively hustled into cover. The screens flickered on, and instead of the commentary team that would usually provide some inane analysis in the run up to the trial, the Regent of Spacehaven was displayed in all his abundance. The aristocrat was wearing ceremonial clothes and gold chains to signify his status as Regent and Mayor of the Authority.

"That's Maxim Volkov, the most senior gold on the planet," Finn said, spitting the words. "I trained with his son, Ivan. He's an even bigger prick than his father."

"You mean Herald, one of the two prosecutors in this trial?" Thorne asked, and Finn nodded.

The TV feed cut away from Volkov as the regent waved to the stony-faced crowd, and instead focused on a small army of prefects and foremen, who were gathered around the perimeter of yard one, tossing prize bundles into the assembled crowds. Usually, this would create a frenzy of activity, as weary and often starving workers fought amongst themselves to claim the bundles, hoping to find one containing the most coveted prize of all – reductions to their shift hours. However, on this occasion, there was no fighting and no scramble to claim the prize bundles, even as they landed at the feet of some workers. The crowd remained deathly silent.

"I think the Authority has fucked up," Finn said. "I've never seen the people of Metalhaven like this. Chromes lap up the trials and would normally punch-out their own worker buddies to claim a prize bundle, but it's like they're frozen in ice."

"I can feel it," Riley grunted, scowling up at one of the screens. "As Head Prefect, I could always tell when a crowd was about to turn violent. You learn to recognize the signals, like tuning in to radio waves."

Maxim Volkov continued his preamble, and his officious tones droned out across Zavetgrad, but besides the regent's voice, the city was still. Finn had tuned out the speech almost from the beginning, since it was a script he'd heard hundreds of times before at every other trial he'd been forced to attend. It talked of how the Last War began because the people of Earth's once great nations were given too much power. Freedom was a drug, the regents would say, a drug that once consumed would taint a person's very soul and make them willful and greedy. And once power resided in the hands of the people, rather than the ruling class, civilization was doomed. The Last War was proof that freedom was the world's only true evil and that to survive, a civilization required strict order and control. Zavetgrad had endured where all other nations failed because the Authority believed unflinchingly in the rule of law and the righteousness of justice. The trials were a frequent and bloody reminder that the workers of the city had no choice but to obey, and by surrounding the executions in glitz and spectacle, this message was reinforced time and again, without anyone even realizing it. Not anymore, Finn thought. Now, the Authority's parlor tricks were no longer working.

Maxim Volkov finished his speech then the image pulled back, and Finn saw Captain Viktor Roth, Head Prefect of Metalhaven, on the stage with him, flanked by four prefects. There was someone else there too, but the camera angle wasn't wide enough to capture them. Volkov then gestured to something or someone just out of shot on the other side of the stage. Finn's gut knotted into a lump like rock. He knew what was coming.

"And here she is, your offender!" Volkov announced, as Elara Cage was marched onto the stage, hands bound in front of her, and wearing a chrome-colored jumpsuit, the same as Finn had worn during his trial. The crowd broke into a low murmur, like the sounds of bees buzzing around a hive. "You know her as The Shadow, or perhaps the Iron Bitch of Metalhaven..." Volkov paused then laughed. "You may even believe she's one of you, and in that you are right, but everything else you think you know about this woman is a lie."

"You're the liar!" someone in the crowd shouted. "We know who she is, and we know what she did!"

Captain Roth signaled to his officers on the ground, and they pushed into the crowd, protected by two columns of foremen.

"Elara Cage is a chrome!" the man shouted, as prefects grabbed the protestor's arms and dragged him away. "Haven is real! Redeemer told us!"

Finn flinched at the mention of his prosecutor name, but a bag was quickly pulled over the man's head to muffle any further protests, before nightsticks were thumped into his gut to press any remaining air from his lungs.

"There is an example of how cruelly misled you have all been," Volkov said, pointing to the worker who was being beaten unconscious in front of the crowd. "There is no Haven. It is a lie you have told yourselves so often you have come to believe it. The truth is there is no escape from Zavetgrad. All that awaits you beyond our protective fence is death."

"Liar!" a worker called out, and the crowd murmured their agreement. "We saw the broadcast! We know Haven exists!"

A gunshot cracked the air and Finn gripped his laser cannon, head on a swivel, alert to threats nearby, but the sound of the bullet had originated far away, amplified by the speakers surrounding yard one. The TV screens then showed the worker who had called out fall to his knees, blood draining from a hole in his chest.

"You will all be silent!" Captain Roth roared into the

microphone. "The Regent demands your respect and attention, and I *will* have it!"

The shooting of the man in front of everyone was shocking, even for Finn, who was no stranger to seeing workers beaten and abused, and the crowd was silent again.

"Finn Brasa fed you lies," Volkov continued, unmoved by the death of the man who'd interrupted him. "Brasa survived his trial and in return the Authority, in our benevolence, spared his life, but he was not worthy of the color gold. Finn Brasa believed in the myth of Haven, and he convinced Elara Cage it was real too. This cost him his life."

"Redeemer lives!" a woman shouted, pushing to the front of the crowd. "We all saw his broadcast!"

A crack of gunfire reverberated around the yard and the woman fell, shot to the head. Captain Roth then stormed off the stage and barked orders to his officers, who quickly marshaled five more workers out of the crowd and pushed them to their knees beside the dead woman.

"For every one of you that speaks lies, five workers will die!" Roth pressed his pistol to the head of the closest worker and fired. Finn flinched and Riley cursed, but they could do nothing but watch. "Order will not be compromised!" Another gunshot, and another dead. "Justice will not be sacrificed!" *Crack...* Another dead. "The Authority will be obeyed!" *Crack...* A fourth worker fell, her blood painting the front line of the crowd red. "The myth of Haven will die!" *Crack...* The fifth worker was shot. Then Roth marched back to the stage, leaving the bodies to go cold in the snow, where everyone could see them.

"You want proof that Brasa is dead, I understand," Volkov said, continuing as if nothing had happened. The

Regent then turned to one of the giant screens hovering above the yard. "See for yourselves..." Volkov boomed, and the image switched.

"What the fuck?" Private Reyes said, turning from the image of Finn Brasa, hanging by the neck from a scaffold in the Authority sector central plaza, to the real Finn Brasa beside him. "How are they doing that?"

"I've seen this trick before," Finn said, cursing under his breath. "They manipulate the feed from the trials all the time, to hide when people escape and to tell the story they want people to see."

The crowd had begun to murmur again, and the camera drones panned wide across a sea of distraught faces, eyes moist with tears, frozen in shock, hands pressed over their mouths.

"Don't believe them!" Elara called out. Roth's hand flew and struck her cleanly, but The Shadow would not be so easily silenced. "They're liars, all of them!" Elara yelled, as she was dragged off the podium and away from the microphone. "Finn is alive! You must believe!"

Volkov shook his head and laughed, and the sound of the man's ridicule sent shivers down Finn's spine.

"See how delusional your precious Iron Bitch is?" Volkov said, pointing to Elara as she was manhandled to the starting position. "Even as Finn Brasa swings, she still believes his lies. I urge you not to be taken for a fool, as The Shadow was. Finn Brasa was executed for his crimes, but Elara Cage will face trial. And in this trial, the sentence of death has already been passed."

Volkov stepped aside and the cameras pointed at the Regent then panned back to reveal the figures who Finn had only managed to glimpse in earlier shots. Two stood front and center, proudly wearing their prosecutor armor. With her flaming red hair and striking beauty, Tonya 'Inferno' Duke was unmistakable but Finn only had eyes for Ivan Volkov. In his musketeer-inspired regalia, Herald looked even more pompous than this father did, but the look in his fellow trainee's eyes spoke only of a desire for vengeance.

"Here are your prosecutors," Volkov said, as Herald and Inferno stepped forward. "Show them your appreciation." No one in the whole of Metalhaven made a sound. "I said show them your appreciation!" Volkov bellowed, but still there was nothing.

Finn looked for Captain Roth, expecting the tyrant to rush toward the crowd and kill more innocent people, but the Head Prefect of Metalhaven was still with Elara, who kicked and clawed and struggled against the army of officers trying to hold her back. Instead, another figure approached the microphone, dressed in black carapace armor with gleaming gold shoulder pauldrons.

"Juniper…" Finn hissed, but none of the others heard him, as they were too caught up in the broadcast.

"Cheer for your prosecutors!" Juniper Jones said.

Whereas Roth had growled his orders with force, Juniper's demand was spoken with quiet malice. Despite the different styles, the response was the same. Silence. The special prefect drew her pistol and fired, shooting dead a man in the front row. Another worker stepped forward and took the dead man's place, staring back at Juniper, as if willing her to shoot.

"I said, cheer!" Juniper snarled, this time so loud the speakers crackled with distortion.

Still, no-one spoke and Juniper fired twice more, but the

dead workers were replaced by others who had been standing behind, and the defiance continued. Her nostrils flared and she jumped off the stage and marched toward the crowd.

"Cheer!" she demanded, shooting a woman dead. "Cheer!" she repeated, shooting another, then another, until six more lay dead in the snow.

"They can't kill everyone," Finn said, wondering when the senseless murder would stop. "We must do something. We can't wait."

"What can we do?" Riley said, and Finn could hear the despair in the man's voice. "We're six yards away, and even cutting across the middle yards, it would take us twenty minutes to reach then. And then what? There's an entire division of prefects down there, against the five of us."

"Six!" Scraps said, but this time even the robot's charm was not enough to dispel the gloom that had descended on them.

"We have to do something," Finn said again. "We can't just stay here."

"Cheer for them!"

Elara's voice was barely audible over the speakers, but Finn knew it was her speaking. He turned back to the TV screens, and the camera drones had focused on her face. Roth had his hand clamped around the back of her neck, but the sadistic prefect was allowing her to speak.

"Clap for their prosecutors, if that's what they want," Elara called. "Then wait until the trial begins, and I will give you something to really cheer for!"

Roth lashed out again then the camera switched, leaving the image of the prefect's hand striking Elara's face etched into Finn's mind. He clenched his teeth and fought the rage bubbling inside him, knowing the time was soon approaching when he could finally unleash it. Then a slow hand clap began somewhere in the crowd and others joined in, disjointed at first, until a natural rhythm was established, and the sound grew louder and louder, like the beat of an executioner's drum. Juniper lowered her pistol and turned to the regent, her eyes asking for orders, but Volkov had had his fun. The regent raised his hands and smiled into the camera.

"Your appreciation is noted, and we will reward your loyalty in kind over the coming days," the regent said, his sarcastic promise foretelling of more death and torment. "But for today, only one more person need die." Volkov, ever the showman, paused for effect, then added, "Let the trial begin!"

24

THE LAST TRIAL

Elara was released with a five-minute head start over prosecutors, Herald and Inferno, who were backed by squads of special prefects in black carapace armor. Finn watched the TV feed as Scraps continued re-programming the foreman's processor to keep them hidden from the camera drones. The shot was currently focused on Elara and though she was unarmed and without her chameleonic armor, Finn could see the determination on her face. She had been released into the crucible as prey, but The Shadow was a predator, and she wasn't going to play by the Authority's rules.

"How are you getting on, Scraps? Because we need to move out, now," Finn said, conscious that even with all the short-cuts he knew, they were still at least fifteen minutes away from reaching Elara.

"Done-done!" Scraps said, jumping back from the robot's head. "Foreman generates fake image. Hide us from cameras!"

"Great work, pal!" Finn said, picking up the robot's head and strapping it to General Riley's backpack. "Now we can move without being seen, at least by anyone watching the camera feed."

"Once we start dropping prefects and foremen, it won't take the Authority trial controllers long to figure out something is wrong," Riley said, as Finn took the lead. "We need to strike hard and fast, and as soon as we have Elara, be ready to drop our cloak so that everyone can see us. This plan only succeeds if the people rally behind us."

"They will," Finn said, laser cannon in hand and set to maximum output. "If we fight for them, they'll fight for us, I know it."

Finn set the pace and began weaving through yard seven, using his home-grown knowledge of Metalhaven to chart the quickest course toward yard one. Despite the linear numbering system, the reclamation yards were not in a single long row from one to thirteen but were instead arranged in a grid configuration. Yard seven was in the middle row on the eastern edge, while yard one was located on the opposite side in the north-west corner. Elara was heading south toward yard four, which put yards five and six directly between the squad and their objective.

"Prefects and foremen in yards two, five, eight and nine," Scraps said, delivering his intel while flying above and behind the squad.

"What about in the other yards?" Finn asked.

"Not many," Scraps replied. "Prefects enclosing yard four."

Finn had to wrack his brain to remember the yard layout, but Scraps was right. If prefects and foremen were guarding the boundaries of two, five, eight and nine, it would mean they were trying to box Elara into yard four.

"I don't get it, why are they trying to trap her in four, if they have all thirteen yards to drag this out over?" Private Reyes said.

Finn had a thought. "Scraps, do you know which yard Elara worked in, when she was still a chrome from Metalhaven?"

"Nope-nope," the robot said, shaking his head. "But will find out..."

Scraps landed on Finn's shoulder and the weight of the robot momentarily unbalanced him, but he didn't have long to wait before his buddy had an answer.

"Elara worked yard four," Scraps said. "That why!"

Finn nodded. "That's what they're doing. They want to end this in the yard where Elara used to work, to send a message about what happens when you defy the Authority. It's just the sort of sick, poetical shit the Regents would pull."

"Then we have to get to yard four at the same time she does," Riley said, his voice juddering with each thud of his heavy boots on the ground. "How many prefects and robots are protecting the border between yards four and five?"

Scraps thought a moment, his eyes flicking from left to right as he interrogated the Authority computer via the foreman's head that was bouncing up and down on the back of Riley's pack.

"Fifty!" Scraps said. "Too many!"

"We'll see about that," Riley grunted, a grim determination showing in the man's hollow eyes.

Suddenly, gunfire crackled across the sky from the direction of yard one and Finn skidded to a stop and peered up at the TVs. One set of screens was showing Inferno and Herald, slowly making their way toward their target, while the other showed Elara, pinned down by special prefects, who had hemmed her in behind a wrecked amphibious assault craft from the Last War.

"She's moved fast," Thorne said, moving beside Finn, hands on hips and breath heavy from the sprint. "She has to be close to the border of yards one and four already."

"Which means we're running out of time," Riley said, eyes twitching as bullets ricocheted off the assault craft, forcing Elara deeper into cover. "They could kill her before we even get close."

"No," Finn said, shaking his head. "Those prefects haven't got her yet, and if they think they have, they're in for a shock."

Finn set off again, though he kept half an eye on the screens. One of the prefects was trying to work their way behind the wrecked assault craft and flank Elara, but she'd heard the officer's approach and was waiting. Grabbing the barrel of the rifle, Elara wrenched the man toward her then crushed her elbow into the officer's face, smashing the opaque visor that was hiding the prefect's eyes. The rifle slipped from the man's grasp and Elara spun it in her own hands before aiming the weapon at the officer's head and pulling the trigger twice. A cheer erupted from the crowd, so loud it was frightening, and Finn felt an energy ripple through the sector, as if every man and woman in Metalhaven was willing Elara to not only survive but to win.

The remaining four prefects tried to rush Elara, but she had already moved, anticipating their attack, and climbing onto the hull of the boat. She fired two tight bursts, killing another prefect, before return fire again forced her to move, but despite being outnumbered, it was clear that she was the aggressor. The prefects tried to regroup but Elara didn't give them a second to think, and soon another was dead, his black carapace armor riddled with holes. The prefects returned fire again, but hit only snow and metal, then their weapons were empty, and the officers hurried to reload. It was a delay of only seconds, but seconds was all Elara needed to make the final kills.

Jumping from the hull of the boat, Elara drove a flying knee in the face of the closest prefect, before rolling through her landing and taking the second down with a gut-wrenching low-blow. A knife was stolen from the downed prefect and the man's throat was cut an instant later. The surviving officer was back on his feet and to the man's credit, he didn't run, but choosing to fight Elara Cage – The Shadow – wasn't brave, it was stupid. The two clashed, Elara blocking the prefect's blows and chipping away at the man's armor with the stolen knife until the prefect was cut in so many places he could no longer stand. The officer dropped to his knees in front of Elara, eyes imploring her for mercy, but none was given, and the knife was sunk into the man's neck, spilling his blood into the snow. The roar from the crowd shook the ground like an earthquake.

"Come on!" Finn cried, punching the air, but his shout was lost in the uproar that had engulfed the entire sector like a hurricane.

The TV screens panned away to show Herald and Inferno, while the trial commentators talked down what everyone had seen. Finn half-expected them to fake images of the prefects recovering and regrouping, as if their brutal deaths at the hands of The Shadow had never happened, but the Authority's digital trickery only worked when people watched the TV feed, and the whole of Metalhaven had come out in force to support one of their own in person. Crowds of workers had surrounded yard four, where Elara was heading, now armed with enough ammunition to take down an entire prefect division. They were held back behind barriers that had been erected after the yards were cleared but it wasn't enough to stop people from seeing what was happening with their own eyes.

Then Finn saw people atop the tenement buildings and recovery centers that littered Metalhaven. Foremen and prefects were rushing to bring them down, but the spirit of revolution was spreading, and Finn could feel the tension in the air, like a pressure wave pushing against him. Decades of violent oppression and abhorrent abuses of basic human rights had left a mark on every man and woman in the sector, building hatred and resentment like electricity being generated inside a thundercloud. And, like a thundercloud, this vital force could only be contained for so long.

"Stand to! Stand to!"

Riley's order snapped Finn's attention away from the TV screens and the tops of the buildings to a cluster of prefects and foremen ahead of them. Without stopping to think, he aimed and fired, hitting one of the robots in the face and causing its head to explode like a grenade. The prefects shouted orders and warnings and ran for cover, Riley and the others already had them zeroed-in and five fell before they even knew what hit them. Finn pressed on, focusing his laser blasts on the prefects instead of the unarmed foremen, until four of the robotic tyrants stood in his path.

"Stop! You are not authorized to be here!" one of the foremen yelled. It was a gen three, and not too bright.

Finn holstered his laser and drew his baseball bat. He told himself that it was to conserve his cannon's battery, but the truth was he'd been itching to smash up foremen ever since arriving back in Metalhaven.

"Stop!" the gen three repeated and Finn clubbed it across the side of the head, bending its metal neck and sending the machine tottering to one side, as if it were drunk.

The other two foremen advanced, arms outstretched, ready to seize and detain him, but he'd been accosted by the robots so many times before, and he knew their tactics better than their own memory banks did. Dropping low, he smashed his bat in the knee joint of the closest robot and sent the machine crashing to the ground like a felled tree, before clobbering another across the shin and sending it flat onto its face. He quick-drew his laser cannon and burned holes into the heads of both machines before they could right themselves, then holstered the weapon again, and turned his attention to the final robot. This was a gen four and a chief, still wearing its high-viz jacket, hardhat and disapproving expression.

"I will detain you," the robot said, tearing a shock-absorber from the chassis of a wrecked delivery truck and wielding it like a club. "You will obey my directive."

"I'm done taking orders from the likes of you," Finn said, holding his baseball bat two-handed. "So come at me, if you dare."

The machine's metal eyebrows frowned. "Why do you resist the Authority?"

Finn smiled. "Because fuck them, that's why..." He flourished the bat then waved the robot on. "And fuck you too."

The foreman stomped forward and swung its improvised club with blistering speed. Finn blocked with his bat, but the blow knocked him off his feet and sent him tumbling backward. The shock absorber weighed the same as a sledgehammer and he hadn't been prepared for the force of the impact. Climbing to his feet, Finn shook his head to clear his vision, but the foreman was relentless, and before he could react the machine had slammed a blow into his chest that sent him reeling over the top of a low wall. His armor held but the shock resonated through his bones and pressed the air from his lungs. Still the foreman came at him, and he swung blindly, managing to deflect the next attack, but it didn't give him enough time to recover and soon the robot was standing over him, weapon held high.

Finn held his bat in both hands in a desperate effort to block the hammer blow that he knew was coming, when bullets pinged off the foreman's armor and it staggered back. He looked toward Riley and the others, but they were still engaged with the prefects, pushing the Authority forces back and carving a path toward the yard border. Then another gunshot rang out above his head, and he looked up to see Scraps, prefect's pistol held in his little metal hands. His buddy had an intense look of concentration on his face as he squeezed the trigger and fired again, sinking a bullet into the foreman's eye socket, and smashing its FLP. The recoil sent Scraps spinning through the air like a fighter jet performing a corkscrew maneuver, then the robot recovered and aimed again, but his target was already defeated.

Finn got to his feet and looked at the chief foreman, disabled where he stood, improvised club still held high above its smoldering head. He walked up to the machine and pushed it in the chest, sending it toppling into the snow like a broken statue.

"Got him!" Scraps said, zooming next to Finn, pistol still in hand. "Bad robot!"

"You got him, alright," Finn said, rapping his knuckles against Scraps' oil-can body. "Thanks, pal. You make a great partner."

"Major!" Riley called out, waving Finn over. "We need you."

It was only then that Finn realized the crackle of rifle fire had fallen silent. He walked over to the squad and witnessed the bloody culmination of their efforts in all its gory detail. More than a dozen special prefects lay dead on the ground, their black carapace armor contrasting sharply against the blood-stained, pure, white snow. With their legs and arms splayed in chaotic arrangements, the men and women of the Authority's most sadistic fighting force looked more like demonic monsters than humans. *Perhaps death has just revealed their true nature...* Finn thought.

One of the giant TVs suddenly caught Finn's eye. It was showing the carnage left over in the wake of their assault, but while the image should have also revealed Riley, Reyes and Thorne, the squad remained invisible. Finn could hear the bumbling voices of the trial commentary team crowing from the speakers, desperate to provide an explanation for the mysterious deaths, but the Authority pundits were unable to make sense of the seemingly impossible.

"We have a problem," Riley said, dispensing with any preamble, as was the general's way. "Elara has stopped advancing and appears to have dug in on the border of yard one," the man continued, pointing to another of the TVs.

"What's she doing?" Finn said. "She could easily break into yard four and keep running; why stop now?"

"She's going to make a stand," Riley said, scowling at the screen. "She won't allow the Authority to chase her around in some sick game of cat and mouse. She's going to face them and go down fighting."

"Then we have to move," Finn said, setting off, but neither Riley nor the others followed.

"We're too far away," Riley said, angry and frustrated. "Herald and Inferno, backed by a detachment of prefects, will be on top of her long before we can get close, and by then this will all be over."

"We have to try," Finn said, furious at the general for giving up. "Elara can hold them off, I know it. We must keep going!"

"Major, the general is right," Private Reyes said. "We're ten minutes out, and with another twenty or thirty prefects between us and Elara. I'd love to be wrong, but we're out of time."

General Riley slipped off his pack and removed the extraction beacon, but Finn refused to accept defeat.

"No, don't give up yet, we'll never get a better opportunity than this," Finn said, turning to the general then pointing to the people lining the rooftops of every building they could see. "Metalhaven is ready, they just need a sign, but if Elara is torn apart in this crucible and we run, our chance is gone, perhaps forever."

Riley hesitated and Finn could see the conflict in his eyes. "It's a suicide mission. What good will adding our deaths to the tally do now?"

"We're not dying here, General, not today." Finn turned

to Scraps, who was close as always. "Pal, can you reach Elara and tell her we're here? You'll need to fly like the wind, faster than you ever have before."

Scraps nodded. "Yes-yes! Scraps can! Scraps will!"

"How soon can you reach her?" Riley asked the robot.

"Two min-mins," Scraps replied, without hesitation. "Scraps fast! But must go now!"

Riley ground his teeth inside his mouth then shoved the extraction beacon back into his pack.

"Then go, and tell Elara to run, and to not stop running until she finds us," Riley said. "We'll make our stand together, in yard four. One way or another, it ends for Elara where it began."

Scraps nodded then threw down the pistol, before jettisoning some of his heavier tools to allow him to fly faster. The robot's rotors accelerated, spinning so fast they were invisible, before the robot angled its body toward Elara Cage and shot away from them like a bullet from a rifle.

25

WHERE IT BEGAN

A BLAST of light from his laser cannon sent another foreman crashing to the ground then Finn leapt over the smoldering frame of the machine and carried on running. Dozens more of the robots stood in the way of him reaching Elara, many acting as shields for prefects who were now closing in on the squad, but Finn charged them down like a raging bull. Bullets pinged off his prosecutor armor, which held fast in the face of an onslaught of bullets, and Finn tore through their ranks, employing every tactic and skill the Authority had taught him to carve a path toward yard four. Men and machines fell at his feet, cut down by furious laser energy, no different to the junk in the yards that Finn had spent his life slicing up for the Authority's gain.

There was a lull in the fighting and Finn paused, boot pressed to the skull of a ruined gen-four foreman, and checked the TV screens. Elara was battling hordes of prefects that were closing in on her, and still there was no sign of Scraps. He cursed under his breath. *Come on, pal, hurry!* Gunfire crackled behind him as General Riley and the others caught up, their weapons barely silent for a second as they picked off targets with pinpoint accuracy and a coolness that put the Authority's supposed elite guard to shame.

"How far?" Riley said. His breath was labored and finally the strains of the arduous journey were beginning to take their toll on the man. *At least it shows he's human, after all...* Finn thought.

"We're about five hundred meters from the center of yard four, but Elara still hasn't moved," Finn said, eyes locked onto the TVs, hoping to see Scraps swoop in, but still there was no sign of the robot.

"Scraps will complete his mission," Riley said, and there was no doubt in the man's eyes. He grunted a gruff laugh. "Then I really will have to promote him to major."

"If he pulls this off then you should make him a general," Finn said, smiling.

Gunfire ricocheted off the junk metal heap they were resting behind, breaking up the moment of levity and forcing them back on the offensive. Private Reyes climbed to higher ground then shouldered his weapon and returned fire, driving the prefects into cover, and allowing Thorne to ambush them from the right flank. Within seconds, five golds were dead in the snow, but there were still dozens between them and Elara.

"Clear," Reyes called out, scrambling down the other side of the junk heap.

Riley acknowledged the soldier and moved into open ground, then a foreman burst out from a junkpile and struck the man hard across the chest. Riley went down and Finn lasered the machine, but another sprang up behind it and shoulder-charged him to the ground. Reyes made a run toward him, but was ambushed by a third foreman, who burst out from the junk heap, throwing off the chunks of twisted metal it had used to hide itself. The robot grabbed the soldier and wrestled Reyes to the ground, but Thorne was there in a heartbeat, hammering shots into the back of the robot's head and putting it down. Two more foremen then exploded out of the wreckage like zombies smashing through crypt walls, and the soldiers were grappled and subdued, but with one of the tyrannical machines also bearing down on him, Finn couldn't do anything to help them.

Finn climbed to his knees and aimed his laser at the foreman, but the robot struck it from his grasp, and it landed in the junk heap beside Riley, who was still dazed. The robot tried to stomp him but Finn rolled to the side and swept at its leg, sending the machine crashing into the snow. His training kicked in, and he was back on his feet before the robot could right itself, baseball bat firmly in his grasp. A two-handed swing rung the machine's head like a dinner gong, then a follow-up bent its cranium so deeply that its FLP was crushed and rendered useless.

The machine crumpled and Finn ran to Thorne and Reyes, who were powerless to resist the crushing strength of the Authority's robot underlings. He clobbered the closest foreman across the back of the neck, breaking electrical connections and causing the machine's circuits to falter enough that Reyes could break free of its grasp.

"Help me with Mara!" the private cried, jumping onto the last robot and trying to prise its metal fingers away from Thorne's throat. The ensign was already turning blue.

Finn threw down his bat and grabbed the machine's other hand. Years of handling laser cutters had made his grip so strong it could crush coal, and Finn was able to free Thorne and wrestle the robot to a stalemate. Its mechanical eyes narrowed, and the gen-three's face approximated a look of confusion, its FLP unable to comprehend how a human could match it in a contest of strength. Then Reyes drew his pistol and rammed the barrel into the robot's metal mouth before squeezing the trigger three times and blowing its electronic brains out.

"Clear!" Reyes said, checking their surroundings and aiming his pistol into every pile of metal that could potentially harbor a foreman. "At least, I think so..."

Finn helped Thorne to stand. Her neck was bruised, and she was looked unsteady, but she gave him the thumbs up. Riley joined them, rifle butt pressed into his shoulder.

"Med kit, right rear pouch," the general said, skipping past pointless questions and comments and focusing on what mattered. "Thorne will know what she needs."

"It's okay, I've had my fair share of experience treating injuries," Finn said. "I know what to do."

Finn removed the med kit from Riley's pouch then set to work on the ensign, while the general and Reyes covered him. He glanced up at the TV screens between administering the meds, but Elara was still dug in, and close to becoming surrounded. He tried to stay strong, but despair was encroaching on him, like the prefects on the TV, and he looked away.

"Wait, is that Scraps?" Reyes said.

Finn scowled and checked the screen again, but from the angle of the camera drone he still couldn't see anything. Then he looked at the TV that Reyes was watching, based on a different camera feed, and the dark cloud enveloping him was burned away. Scraps had landed next to Elara, and she was talking to him.

"Come on, pal, convince her!" Finn said. "They're right on top of you."

Suddenly, Scraps darted away like a missile, and Elara armed and threw two grenades over the wall of her dug-out position. They landed in piles of loose wreckage and exploded too far from the approaching prefects to injure them, but the detonations kicked up vast plumes of dust, turning the air black. Then, shrouded by smoke, Elara turned and ran.

"Let's move!" Finn said, collecting his laser cannon and bat, and ignoring the threat of other foremen that may still have been lurking in the junkpiles, waiting to ambush them.

"Major, wait!" Riley called out, but Finn ignored the command. "Finn!"

The squad was strung out and Ensign Thorne was still recovering and gathering her gear, but Finn was done waiting. He needed to reach Elara, not only for himself, but because the two of them together could end the trail and turn the tables on the Authority without even firing a shot. It all hinged on them, and nothing was going to stop him from getting to her.

Finn had hated the assault courses he'd had to complete at the end of each day's prosecutor training, but those grueling challenges had prepared him for the mission in ways he could never have imagined. He jumped onto vehicles, scrambled over towering junk piles and leapt precipices that would have left any normal human being trembling with fear. Foremen jumped out at him, but he was wise to their ambush tactics and had spotted their hiding places before they could spring their traps. Those closest to him he blasted in the face while others he avoided, jinking and weaving through yard four in the same way he had done to avoid Walter Foster's attempts to drag him down on the assault courses.

Gunfire crackled to his rear and Finn chanced a look over his shoulder to see Riley and the others in pursuit, but without his unique skills, they were far behind. *But at least they're coming...*Finn thought. *This time, I'm not doing this alone.*

Close to the center of yard four, Finn spotted Elara, not on a TV screen, but for real, and the sight of her gave him a boost, like pouring fuel on a fire. Prefects were swarming into the crucible, trying to cut her off, but by focusing their attention on Elara, they hadn't seen him coming. Slowing his advance, he drew his laser cannon and fired, burning deep holes thorough the black carapace armor of the Authority's malignant fighting force. Six were dead before the officers turned their dark visors in his direction, but by then it was too late. Holstering his cannon, he drew his bat and tore through their ranks, crushing muscles and breaking bones with a sickening brutality that would have turned the stomach even of a Regent.

Bodies lay strewn around him like windfalls from the apple trees in the Authority sector's grand arboreta, but still dozens of prefects were hounding Elara, slowing her escape, and forcing her to take cover. Then automatic weapons fire erupted from behind him, and the prefects were mown down like cut grass. Riley, Reyes, and Thorne were with him and unleashing hell, and within seconds the center ground was cleared.

Elara ran, this time unchallenged by gunfire, and Finn raced to meet her. They met in the middle of the yard, their bodies colliding with such force Finn would have been bowled over if it were not for Elara's arms wrapped around him, holding him up. He returned the embrace, pulling her tight, and suddenly all his shame and regret poured out of him like water gushing from a burst dam.

"I'm sorry," Finn said into Elara's ear. "I'm sorry for all of it. I should have listened to you."

"Forget that now," Elara said. She drew back and there was no judgement in her emerald eyes, nor anger, only relief. "Now, we need to get out of here, so what's your plan?" Her eyes narrowed a touch. "You did come here with a plan, right?"

Finn smiled. "We did, and the plan is simple. Revolution."

General Riley approached with Reyes and Thorne to his rear, and Elara released Finn and stepped back, her stolen prefect rifle held ready.

"It's okay, they're with me," Finn said. "They're soldiers from Haven."

"Miss Cage," Riley grunted, offering Elara a curt nod of the head. "It's good to finally meet you. I'm General Riley."

Elara looked the man over with her enquiring eyes then glanced up at one of the TVs. Every screen was focused on her, because according to the camera feed, she was the only person in the middle of yard four.

"It appears that you're a ghost, General," Elara said. "Either that, or I'm hallucinating."

Finn also looked at the TV screens, focusing on those that were showing a wider angle of the crucible, including the hundred or more prefects and foremen that were about to descend on them like an army of ants.

"Maybe now is a good time for this plan of yours," Elara said, hopefully.

"General, you have something I need," Finn said, limbering up his arms in readiness for another swing of his bat.

Riley removed his pack and unhooked the chief foreman's head from the webbing, before tossing the lump of metal into the snow at Finn's feet. While this was happening, Scraps flew into the middle of the fold, but the robot didn't go to Finn, and instead folded his rotors and dropped into Elara's arms like she was catching a ball.

"Elara-good!" the robot said, as she hugged Scraps close and even cracked a smile.

"It's time we lowered the curtain and let everyone see the truth," Finn said, pulling the bat back in a two-handed grip.

"Then what?" Elara said.

Finn blew out a sigh. "Then we hope the workers of Metalhaven are up for a fight."

He brought the bat down on the foreman's head, smashing it open with the first swing before crushing its FLP and power core with the next. The head sparked and fizzed and smoke rose from the destroyed components, then they all looked up and waited. The images on the screens flickered and distorted then Finn, Riley, Reyes and Thorne appeared too. Finn didn't know what to do next, but his former mentor did. She grabbed his hand and raised it together with hers, before looking directly into the lens of the closest camera drone.

"Workers of Metalhaven, I have something to say!" Elara shouted, and her voice was projected across the sector, as if the words had been spoken by the sky itself. "This is not just my trial, it's yours, but they can't kill us all. If you want to be free, then fight! Metal and Blood!"

Suddenly, all the TVs hovering above them switched off at once, and without the light from their giant screens, yard four was cast into darkness. Finn listened but the crowds had gone quiet, and he could no longer make out the rows of people lining the tops of the buildings.

"Did it work?" Riley asked. "Did they hear us?"

"I don't know," Finn said, his hand slipping from Elara's grasp. He could hear something now, it wasn't the chant of the crowd, but the stomping jackboots of an entire division of special prefects. "If they heard, they didn't listen."

The yard four klaxon switched on with a thump then the screech and whine of its shrill speaker cut through the air like a razorblade.

"This trial is over," a voice bellowed, and Finn recognized Maxim Volkov's overbearing tones. "All workers will return to their tenement blocks at once. Failure to comply with this directive will result in summary execution."

The clump of boots stopped, and a ring of black-armored prefects had encircled the center of yard four, like a mini crucible. Then Ivan Volkov and Tonya Duke – Herald and Inferno – stepped through the ranks. They were flanked by Sloane Stewart, Ivan's paramour and bodyguard, and the woman who had seduced, deceived, and made a fool of Finn, Juniper Jones.

"The trial isn't over," Finn said, realizing why they hadn't yet been obliterated in a hailstorm of bullets. "But this isn't about spectacle anymore. It's about settling scores."

"That's fine with me," Elara said, checking her weapon

then reloading it with a fresh magazine. "If the workers of this sector won't fight, I will."

"So will I," Finn said, ejecting the power cell from his laser cannon and slapping in a new one. "I left you once before and I'm never doing it again. Revolution be damned."

"We'll stand with you," Riley said, and though he'd spoken for the other two volunteers, neither Reyes nor Thorne objected.

"There's no need for you to die too," Finn said. He picked up Riley's pack and removed the extraction beacon, before activating the device and tossing it into a clearing behind them. "There's still a chance your skycar can make it past the perimeter fence. It's a chance you should take."

"Even if the skycar makes it inside the city, we'll be dead before it gets here," Riley replied, stoical as ever. "We've come this far. We'll see it through to the end, together."

Finn nodded. "I'm sorry it didn't go the way I'd hoped. I honestly believed that if they saw us, the workers would rise up. I guess the Authority's chokehold is still too strong."

"For now," Riley grunted. "But Haven endures, and so long as it does, hope endures too."

Herald and Inferno began walking toward them and Finn prepared himself for what was to be his final contest against his old classmates, but as much as he loathed Ivan Volkov, his sights were set on Juniper Jones.

"Metal and Blood!"

The cry came from somewhere above them, maybe a rooftop. Finn scoured the horizon, but the buildings were still in silhouette.

"Metal and Blood!"

The second cry was louder, also from a rooftop, and it

was answered with matching calls from all around the sector. Then shouts of "Metal and Blood!" enveloped the yard like a fog, and the encirclement of prefects grew anxious and jittery. Suddenly, the roar of thousands of workers swept through the yard like a storm front and Finn felt the hairs on his body stand on end. It was like a hundred years of pain and suffering had suddenly been given voice. Then soaring fires like beacons exploded on the rooftops of tenement buildings, recovery centers and wellness centers all around them, and in the flicker of their orange light, Finn could see a mass of bodies swell and crash into the wall of prefects like a wave breaking on a shore. The prefects turned and suddenly their guns were no longer pointed at Finn or Elara but at the army of chromes who had rebelled against the Authority and were fighting for their freedom.

26

A SOLDIER'S DUTY

For a time, Finn and Elara were lost in the moment, swept up by the coming together of thousands of workers, united in common purpose against a common enemy. But like all waves once they've crashed to shore, the water receded, dragged back by another inevitable force that was even more powerful. Gunfire erupted all around the sector and electrified nightsticks crackled in numbers that Finn had never even imagined possible, yet the chromes of Metalhaven stood firm and fought, and Finn knew he had to do the same.

"We have to get out there," Finn said, having to shout over the background noise of the battle. "They're fighting for us, and we have to fight for them too."

"There's only one fight I care about," Elara said.

Despite the uprising, Herald and Inferno were still inside the encirclement, along with Ivan Volkov's bodyguard, and Juniper Jones. Finn tried to work out which of the four Elara was focused on, before realizing it was the special prefect who had captured her attention. He wondered what Juniper had done to Elara whilst imprisoned and at her mercy then tried to put that thought out of his mind, for fear it would drive him to rage and carelessness.

"Ivan and I have a score to settle," Finn said. He wanted to take down Juniper, but Elara's need was greater. "So long as you leave that privileged prick to me, the rest are fair game."

"Agreed," Elara said.

Suddenly, Juniper began running up and down the wall of prefects that were holding back the worker horde, like Roman centurions blocking a barbarian attack with their shield wall. Slowly, officers were pulled out of the formation, one by one, until a dozen were standing to attention beside the prosecutors.

"That might complicate things," Finn said, as the squad of special prefects expanded riot shields and moved ahead of the others to protect them. "General, I know I told you to leave, but we could use your help for a little while longer."

"My pleasure, Major," the general said, slapping a fresh magazine into his weapon and chambering a round.

The general bellowed the order, "Stand to!" then without hesitation Private Reyes and Ensign Thorne took up firing positions atop a towering junk heap. Finn wished he had more time to thank them for what they had done, and he kicked himself for all the moments he'd wasted on the long journey to Zavetgrad that he could have used to make them understand how grateful he was.

"Major, something's happening," Riley said.

Finn climbed the junk heap with Elara to where Riley was lying prone, looking down the iron sight of his weapon. The dozen special prefects who were advancing ahead of the others had split apart at the center, and Inferno had slipped between them. Her shotgun was pointed toward their position but aimed high.

"That blunderbuss is no good at this range," Riley grunted, clearly unsettled by the unusual tactic. "I don't suppose you know what the red-head's game is?"

Suddenly, Tonya Duke fired, but instead of shot, her custom-made shotgun launched a burning fireball at them, like a miniature flaming missile from a medieval trebuchet.

"Dragonfire rounds!" Finn said, remembering Inferno's special incendiary ammunition. "Take cover!"

The projectile slammed into the top of the junk heap and exploded with a violence that belied its small size, spreading flames over the summit and raining fire down on their bodies. The shotgun boomed again, and another round soared over their heads and landed behind them, creating a curtain of fire that ignited another of the hundreds of junkpiles that littered yard four. Finn tried to look over the summit of the junk heap, but another round exploded, and a wall of red-hot heat beat him back. Then the persistent crackle of gunfire started up and the dozens of carapace-armored special prefects began laying down suppressing fire in even, controlled bursts that kept them pinned down and trapped.

"Scraps, go high and let me know what you see!" Finn shouted, brushing burning debris off his armor.

The robot nodded then shot upward, acting as their eyes and ears. Finn chanced another look over the junk heap and saw Ivan Volkov aim his mock flintlock pistol skyward, and panic gripped him.

"Scraps, get down!" Finn yelled, but the crack of the pistol immediately followed his words, and the bullet was faster than sound. Scraps was hit and his rotors were damaged, causing the robot to spin out of control, then crash into the snow between where Finn was pinned down and the advancing prefects. "Shit, I have to get him..."

Finn darted out of cover, but bullets slammed into his body and cracked his armor. He shielded his face with his vambraces, saving himself from taking a bullet to the head, but the impact stunned him and left him open. Then he felt Elara's hands around his waist and he was yanked back into cover just as a dragonfire round exploded where he'd been standing, engulfing the space with fire and scorching the ground black.

"You can't go out there, not until we've dealt with those prefects," Elara said, dousing flames that were clinging to his armor and webbing.

"I can't leave him!" Finn said. The memory of his robot pal, incapacitated in the snow, with nothing and no-one to protect him was unbearable. "He's saved me so many times before, I owe him the same!"

"I know, I want to save him too, but getting yourself killed won't help," Elara said. She turned to General Riley. "What do you have besides bullets? Explosives, stun grenades, smoke... anything?"

Riley shook his head. "We've already used it all," the general admitted solemnly. Another dragonfire round landed on the heap, forcing Riley deeper into cover, his beard and face scorched from the flames. "I hate to say it, but we have no choice but to go out there and fight."

"But that's suicide," Finn said. "They'll cut us down in a heartbeat."

"I agree," Riley said, smoke wisping from his singed hair. "But it's better than staying here and being burned to death."

A dragonfire round suddenly landed in the middle of them, streaking a curtain of fire across the heap and splitting off Private Reyes from the rest of the squad. The soldier cried out as flames lashed his body.

"Reyes, report!" Riley shouted, shielding his face from the heat. "Private!"

"I'm okay, sir," Reyes called back, his voice strained. "Don't worry about me!"

Finn squinted through the fire, but he could see that Reyes was far from okay. One side of the man's face had been badly burned, and an eye was ruined. Despite the pain that must have been wracking his body, Reyes then stood up and faced his general. Despite the dangers he had already confronted, Reyes man had never lost his cavalier sense of humor, but Finn also knew that when the situation demanded it, the private could be harder than a prefect's armor.

"Don't worry!" Reyes called out. "I've got this!"

The private picked up a prefect rifle that had fallen during their earlier firefight and held it in his off hand.

"Private, don't do anything stupid," Riley called out, trying to shuffle across the junk heap toward the soldier, but the fire beat him back.

"It's been an honor, sir," Reyes said, readying both weapons. He was positioned on top of the heap, like a soldier ready to climb out of a trench and charge the enemy line. "I don't give a fuck what you did before, sir. You've always been good to me."

"Reyes, get back here!" Riley yelled, still struggling to reach his man, but the flames and heat were too intense. "That's an order, damn it!"

"Kai, stop screwing around!" Thorne yelled. "This isn't the time for your bullshit."

"I always liked you, Mara," Reyes answered. "Make sure you get home, okay?"

"Kai!"

Thorne's desperate cry went unanswered, then Private Kai Reyes climbed to the summit of the junk heap, aimed his weapons at the prefects, and opened fire, while screaming at the top of his lungs like a man possessed. Bullets flew and the prefects were forced to close ranks, but the onslaught was unstoppable, and the human shield-wall began to crumble.

"He's doing it, we have to help him!" Finn shouted.

Finn jumped up and fired his laser, punching a hole through a prefect shield before being driven back. Thorne and Riley lifted their weapons and fired blind over the top of their cover, and Elara used her agility and accuracy to pick off prefects as they scrambled to maintain their formation in the face of a sudden blitzkrieg of gunfire. Within seconds, twelve prefects had been reduced to four.

"Fall back!" Juniper yelled. "Fall back now!"

Juniper turned and ran but Elara wasn't about to let her escape unchallenged. With bullets still flying in all directions, she climbed to the top of the junk heap and calmly aimed her rifle at the fleeing special prefect. Finn saw her draw in a breath, hold it for a moment, then squeeze the trigger. Juniper was hit in the back and went down hard, then Elara was back in cover, before the fractured remnants of the assaulting forces could tag her.

"Advance!" Riley ordered.

The general and Ensign Thorne scaled the mound of ground-up metal and opened fire with aimed shots that ripped through the remaining officers and forced the prosecutors to scatter and take cover. Finn looked for Juniper and saw the woman crawling toward the wall of prefects that were still desperately trying to hold back the mob of Metalhaven workers. He aimed his laser, but a group of armor-clad officers surrounded her and pulled Juniper into cover before he could get a shot off.

"She'll wait," Elara said. "She's not going anywhere."

"Medic!" Ensign Thorne shouted. "Medic, fast!"

The pilot was on top of the junk heap, crouched beside Private Reyes. The soldier was burned and bloody and not moving. Finn grabbed his medkit and was about to run to the soldier's aid when he spotted Scraps in the snow.

"Get him," Elara said, taking the medkit from Finn's hand. "I'll do what I can for your squadmate."

Finn nodded then ran out into open ground, risking being targeted by Herald and Inferno, but the two prosecutors and Ivan's bodyguard, Sloane Stewart, were nowhere to be seen. He scooped up Scraps without stopping then put on an extra burst of speed, keeping his head tucked and body taut, expecting to be shot at any moment, but not a single bullet was fired.

Placing Scraps onto a patch of ground that had been scorched clear of snow from a dragonfire round, he inspected the robot's oil-can body and found a neat bullet hole in the lower right quarter. Panic threatened to overwhelm him, but he'd learned to master his fears, and he calmly popped open the robot's chest compartment to inspect the damage, before laughing out loud with relief. The bullet had gone clean through, severing a wire between Scrap's power core and his primary system board.

"I don't know how you ended up being the smartest robot on the planet, considering how cheaply I built you," Finn said, while working to patch up the damage. "Though it does make battlefield first-aid a lot easier…"

Finn stripped the broken wires then twisted them together, causing sparks to fly and giving him an electric jolt for good measure. Then Scraps powered up and ran though his boot up sequence before his eyes glowed and life returned to his circuits.

"Ahh! Scraps shot! Scraps shot!" the robot screeched, flailing his arms and legs.

"Take it easy, pal, you're okay," Finn said, softly. Then he looked at the broken rotors that were still sprouted from the top of the robot's head. "Though, you won't be doing any flying for a little while."

Scraps jumped up onto his feet, twirled his rotors with his finger, scowling the whole time, before packing them away.

"Scraps broken," the robot said, forlornly.

"Damaged…" Finn corrected his buddy. "But I'll fix you up. I always do, don't I?"

Scraps smiled and nodded. "Yes-yes. Finn clever."

"Not as clever as you, pal," Finn replied, patting Scraps on the head.

"Fight over?" the robot asked.

"Not yet," Finn said. "But hopefully soon. This time, it was private Reyes that saved all our asses, and not you." He laughed. "But it's fine to give someone else a chance to shine, every once in a while."

He thought he'd get at least a giggle from Scraps, but the robot was looking toward the junk pile, his mechanical eyes sad. Finn picked him up and perched the robot on his shoulder before looking to where Elara, Riley and Thorne were attending to Private Reyes, but all of them were sat solemnly around the body, while the med-kit Finn had handed to Elara remained unopened. Finn massaged the tired muscles in his face then, with a sense of dread, he climbed the junk pile and knelt beside the body, alongside the others.

"He saved us," Riley grunted, the general's blood-soaked hand resting on Reyes' chest, which was riddled with bullet holes. "He was just a kid, goddamnit. He didn't deserve to die, especially protecting me."

"He did his duty," Elara said, though Finn recognized the ice-cold pragmatism of The Shadow as she spoke, rather the woman underneath the persona. "He did what you trained him to do. We should honor that. There will be plenty of time for grief later."

Scraps suddenly jumped down off Finn's shoulder and looked North. The robot opened his rear compartment and expanded his sensor dish, complete with fresh bullet hole.

"Skycar coming..." Scraps said, his metal eyes narrowed in concentration. "Damaged, but inside fence."

"Our skycar?" General Riley asked.

"Yes-yes!" Scraps said, suddenly certain. "Skycar made it. Arrive in ten min-mins!"

Riley nodded. "Then at least I'll get to take him home," the general said, looking again into the dead eyes of Private Reyes.

"Redeemer!"

The piercing cry cracked the air like thunder and Finn saw Ivan Volkov step forward, watched closely by his bodyguard and Tonya Duke.

"Come out and face me!" the Regent's son yelled. "The trial isn't over till I say it is!"

Finn looked into Elara's eyes, and he could read her thoughts like a worker logger. They didn't *need* to fight Herald and Inferno, they could easily wait for the skycar to arrive and escape into Metalhaven to rally the workers, but Ivan Volkov was right. The trial was not over until the prosecutors were dead, or they were.

"Here, take this," General Riley said, handing Elara his combat knife. Elara took the weapon and removed it from its sheath. The blade was nine inches long and jet black. "Now, go out and there and win your trial."

27
JUDGMENT DELIVERED

Ivan Volkov was in full view of the junk heap where Finn and the others had taken cover. The man's incessant pacing had carved a furrow into the snow and the Regent Successor seemed unconcerned that all hell was breaking loose only meters behind him, as the wall of prefects struggled to hold back the waves of Metalhaven workers crashing against it. Finn could have taken Ivan out with a single aimed shot from his laser cannon, but it wasn't enough to just kill the prosecutor and his companion, Tonya Duke. The people needed to see him best the golds in a contest of strength and skill. He needed to send a message and it was a message that no laser blast or bullet could deliver.

"*Redeemer!*" Ivan yelled. The man was sounding more unhinged by the moment. "I order you to face me!"

"Was he always this pissy when he didn't get his own way?" Thorne said. The ensign looked like she wanted to shoot Ivan as much as Finn did.

"Always," Finn said, recalling his numerous unhappy

encounters with the son of Zavetgrad's most senior Regent. "I used to make a point of opposing him every chance I got, but this time, I'm going to give that asshole exactly what he wants."

Finn climbed to the top of the junk pile and looked down at Ivan and the others. Sloane Stewart aimed her pistol at him, but Ivan angrily pushed her arm down to lower the weapon. It was a clear signal that his death wasn't all that the Regent Successor wanted. A bullet was quick, but impersonal, and Ivan wanted to wrap his fingers around Finn's throat and choke the life out of him with his bare hands. *Arrogant bastard...* Finn thought. *In nine weeks of training, he never beat me once inside the octagon...*

"If you want a fight, then throw down your pistol," Finn called out. "The same goes for your bodyguard and Inferno. No guns."

"I don't need a gun to kill you," Ivan snorted, drawing his mock flintlock pistol, and tossing it into the snow, where it vanished like a rock thrown into the sea.

"Ivan, this isn't wise," Stewart said. She had to raise her voice to be heard over the noise of the uprising, which meant that Finn could hear every word too. "It's not safe for you here. I have to get you away."

"Throw down your pistol," Ivan said, ignoring his bodyguard's warning. He turned to Inferno. "You too, close-range weapons only."

Inferno hesitated and looked to Stewart who was still clutching her pistol like it was a lifeline.

"Ivan, please," Stewart said, trying to speak more softly but there was no hope of privacy. "You are at risk here..."

"I said, throw down your weapon!" Ivan snapped.

The prosecutor tore the pistol from Stewart's hand and hurled it far across the yard. The Regent's son then glared at Tonya, and she reluctantly threw her custom-designed shotgun into one of the many junkpiles that filled yard four. Finn removed his laser cannon from its holster and set it down, then Elara climbed to the summit and stood alongside him, General Riley's combat knife angled toward their opponents.

"Prefect skycars coming!" Scraps said. He was perched on Ensign Thorne's shoulder, with his antenna disk extended.

"Reinforcements?" Finn asked.

"Maybe-maybe," Scraps shrugged. "Or rescue team."

Finn checked the horizon and saw a black skycar flying toward them from the North. At first, he assumed it was from the Special Prefecture, but the vehicle was trailing black smoke from its rear and was arriving from a point in the distance that didn't correspond to the Authority sector.

"Scraps, is that General's Riley's skycar?" Finn said, pointing to the black smear in the sky.

"Yes-yes!" Scraps replied, throwing up his hands. "Damaged, but okay."

"Will it get here before the Authority does?" Elara asked, but Scraps shook his head.

"Same time," the robot answered. "Five min-mins!"

"That's more than enough time," Elara said, swinging a few test cuts with the knife. "Killing Tonya Duke and Sloane Stewart won't take me more than a minute."

Elara set off toward the prosecutors that had hunted her across four of Metalhaven's thirteen yards, but Finn held her back. A key element of the trial was missing, and he needed to restore it before the fight could begin.

"Scraps, can you hack into the trial controller's computer and get those TVs back on?" Finn said, pointing to one of the many giant screens that were still hovering above the sector, their screens now black. "We need everyone to see us take down the prosecutors. We need them to see what real justice looks like."

Scraps nodded. "Yes-yes. Need bad-robot head."

"He means the head of a chief foreman," Finn said, noting Riley's confused frown. "There must be a dozen of them littered around here. Find one and plug Scraps in."

"On it," Thorne said, hurrying out ahead of the general.

"Redeemer!" Ivan roared. That Finn had kept the Regent's son waiting had further incensed the aristocrat. "I gave you a command, now obey it!"

"I'm coming, you impatient fuck!" Finn yelled back.

His outburst caused Elara to raise an eyebrow at him, and he realized he had fallen short of his former mentor's standards for self-control. Even so, despite training his mind and body to overcome the anger that had driven him to acts of carelessness in the past, he was done taking shit from Ivan Volkov.

"Stay focused, this is just like sparring in the octagon," Elara said, giving Finn one final lesson, as trainee and apprentice descended the slope toward the prosecutors. "Ivan Volkov is emotional and arrogant, so you must be calm and patient and let him come at you. Before long, he'll become frustrated and make a critical mistake. He always did."

"I've got this," Finn said. He wasn't worried about 'Herald', but there was one unknown factor giving him pause. "You be careful too. We've never seen Sloane Stewart fight, but I doubt they would have assigned her as bodyguard to a regent's son if she wasn't capable."

"I know her weakness," Elara said in a sinister, unconcerned tone. It was The Shadow talking, a side of Elara that always left Finn cold. "Prick Ivan and Sloane bleeds... So long as you take care of the Regent Successor, we won't have to worry about her."

Herald and Inferno moved out to face them and Finn and Elara stopped in front of the prosecutors. The distance between them was the same as the diameter of the octagonal training ring in the prosecutor barracks. *Old habits...* Finn thought. Sloane Stewart then moved to Herald's side, but the Regent Successor was quick to dismiss her.

"No, you protect Inferno," Ivan said, eyes remaining locked onto Finn.

"But Ivan, it is my duty to protect you," Stewart said, shocked by the request.

"It is your duty to do what I say!" Ivan snarled. "You are mine to command and you will do as I command." He grabbed Stewart's arm and shoved his bodyguard toward Inferno. "Make sure Tonya lives or you die."

Stewart staggered toward Inferno, and for a moment she was unsteady on her feet, before regaining her balance, but Finn could see that Ivan had hurt her deeply. Sloane Stewart wasn't only his bodyguard but his paramour. Finn understood the close connection that would have existed between them, yet while Stewart's affection for the regent's son was writ plain across her face, it seemed Ivan cared nothing at all for her in return.

Elara suddenly swept forward, taking advantage of

Stewart's distracted state, and attacking Tonya, who wasn't ready for such an aggressive assault. The prosecutor managed to parry and block with her armor, before Elara unbalanced her and sent the woman crashing to the ground. It would have been over then and there, if it were not for Sloane. Despite her earlier wobble, Ivan's paramour was now fully focused on Elara, and as the two clashed, it was apparent they were evenly matched. Tonya scrambled to her feet, her face flushed as red as her hair, and tried to attack, but Stewart blocked her at every turn, ensuring that the contest remained only between the bodyguard and Elara. Even after the derisory way in which Ivan had spoken to her, Stewart was doing his bidding and protecting Tonya from The Shadow, who everyone knew was by far her superior in combat.

"Sloane will take care of that traitor," Ivan said. To Finn's surprise, the prosecutor then threw down his glaive, and drew his rapier instead. "I'll take care of the traitor in front of me."

The glaive was a weapon that gave Ivan a significant reach advantage over Finn's baseball bat, and to discard it was another display of foolish arrogance, especially considering how frequently Finn had bested the regent's son in the ring.

"I should have killed you when I had the chance," Ivan continued, slashing the sword through the air. "I told Apex that you were a danger, but the fool wouldn't listen."

"I'm sure he'd be very sorry," Finn said, as the two began to circle one another. "Assuming he was still alive, of course."

Ivan snorted. "I didn't care about Dante Voss, or any of the prosecutors and apprentices. I am above them all!" The man aimed the needle-like point of his rapier at Finn's neck. "And I am above you most of all," he hissed. "You are a nobody from Metalhaven who was gifted a chance to become gold yet repaid the Authority's charity with betrayal. I will take your head, and once this petty rebellion has been crushed, display it on a pike in the middle of yard seven for all your former co-workers to see."

Finn shook his head at his former classmate. "You still don't get it, do you?" he said, using his bat to point to the mass of workers watching them from rooftops and terraces. "Metalhaven doesn't belong to you anymore, Ivan. And when I'm done, there will be nowhere in this entire city that is safe for golds like you."

Suddenly, the arena was bathed in a harsh light as the TV screens flickered on, showing a bright white screen with the word "Standby" written in plain letters in the center.

"What is this?" Ivan said, spittle flying from his mouth as he spat the words in anger. "These screens should not be active."

"Like I said, you're not in control here," Finn said. The white screen flickered and then Finn and Ivan were displayed larger than life across dozens of TVs, while the rest showed Elara, Inferno and Sloane Stewart. "What's the matter, Ivan? Afraid that everyone in the city will see me beat you?"

Ivan roared and charged at Finn, slashing the rapier at his face so fast that the blade was invisible. He dodged back and held up his bat, blocking the initial flurry of blows before dodging out of range, but Ivan was relentless, and continued to dance forward, thrusting, and lunging until the tip of his rapier slid between Finn's armor and drew blood. He hissed with pain and backed away, squeezing his throbbing shoulder, which was leaking blood onto his chrome armor.

"This isn't prosecutor training," Ivan said, flourishing his blade and spraying Finn's blood into the snow. "I was taught to kill before you were even out of the workhouse. Do you really think I'd reveal my true abilities inside the training ring, for the amusement of Dante Voss, and all the lesser golds? Your mentor should have taught you to never give your all in a fight that doesn't matter. I already know everything you can do but you know nothing about me." Ivan laughed, cruelly. "Well, you are about to find out."

Embarrassed and angry, Finn gritted his teeth and charged at Ivan, swinging the bat like it was a sledgehammer. Ivan jinked and dodged and spun past every swing, a nauseating grin stuck on the man's face, then when Finn's arms tired, the prosecutor stabbed him again, perfectly bisecting the armor plates on his left thigh. The pain was intense, and his leg gave way beneath him, but Ivan didn't move in to strike a killer blow. Instead, he stood and gloated.

"Perhaps you were right to let the people see this," Ivan said, grabbing the tip of the blade and flexing it, like an old schoolmaster testing the elasticity of a whipping cane. "Once they see me kill the great 'Redeemer', this rebellion will quickly lose steam. Then, when I take this blade and stab it through the cold heart of the legendary 'Shadow', no-one will dare stand up to the Authority again."

Anger flared inside him, and Finn couldn't contain it any longer. He pushed himself up, compelling his punctured muscles to work and charged again, but his attack was clumsy, and Ivan stepped aside and tripped him, sending Finn face-first into the snow. The sound of the man's laughter mocking him almost make him vomit, then he felt the thin blade perforate his armor and pierce the skin on his back. The cut wasn't deep, but the pain stole the breath from his lungs. Then, sensing that Ivan was close, Finn rolled over, ready to deflect the lunge he felt sure was coming, but instead Ivan kicked him in the crotch, and the incapacitating pain left him defenseless. Hunched double, and wheezing what little air he could manage through his teeth, Finn felt the cold blade of Ivan's rapier pressed to his throat.

"This is what it means to be gold," Ivan said, scoring a razor-thin cut across Finn's neck. He laughed. "At least you die where you belong, with all the rest of this diseased planet's junk."

Finn felt the blade cut deeper but he still couldn't move. Then just as Ivan was about to cut his throat, a blur of motion collided with the prosecutor and sent the man barreling across the yard. Finn rolled to his side and saw Elara on the ground, close to where Ivan had landed, dazed and bleeding from a cut to his head. Elara recovered quickly and switched her combat knife into a reverse grip, ready to plunge it into Ivan's chest.

"No!" Tonya screamed, charging at Elara, Scottish Dirk daggers held in each hand. "Get away from him, you bitch!"

Stewart called out a desperate warning, but it was too late. Elara had seen and heard Inferno coming, and instead of sinking the nine-inch blade into Ivan's flesh, she thrust it into Tonya's heart instead.

With his strength finally returning, Finn climbed to his knees and watched as the light began to leave Tonya's startled, terrified eyes. Elara yanked the knife from Inferno's chest and the prosecutor fell at her feet, dead.

"Kill her!" Ivan roared. Like Finn, the Regent Successor

was also on his knees, but now it was like Finn didn't exist. "Kill her, now!"

Sloane Stewart pulled a throwing dagger from a belt sheath and released it, but Finn was already running, and the dagger thudded into his chest plate before it could reach Elara. He landed hard, rolled through the fall, and was on his feet in time to intercept a second spinning dagger, which he deflected with his vambraces. A gust of air whipped past his face as Elara tackled Stewart before she could throw another blade.

Finn suddenly sensed Ivan behind him, and he spun around in time to catch the man's wrist and stop the knife. Stripping the blade, he headbutted the prosecutor and knocked him back two paces, but Ivan still managed to block his follow-up punches. It was like he was fighting a completely different man. The apprentice he'd known in training had been holding so much back that Finn had no idea how to beat the real Ivan. He was about to attack again when he remembered Elara's advice. *"Ivan Volkov is emotional and arrogant, so you must be calm and patient and let him come at you. Before long, he'll become frustrated and make a critical mistake. He always did."*

Finn had an idea, but it repulsed him. Even so, it was the best and perhaps only way he could win. Backing away from Ivan, he sidestepped until the dead body of Tonya Duke was between them. She was lying on her back, eyes wide and staring blankly up, blood caking her prosecutor armor. Ivan tried not to look but it was impossible, and with each glance, he could practically hear the man's black heart crack, like brittle glass.

"She's better off dead than with a bastard like you," Finn

said, and Ivan recoiled from him as if he'd spat in the man's face. "What was it you said? *I don't care about any of the prosecutors and apprentices. I am above them all!*" Finn laughed. "I'm glad she died before she found out what a piece of shit you really are."

Ivan let out of roar of primal rage and came at Finn with his knife pulled back high above his head, like a common thug. Finn waited, letting the prosecutor come to him, parrying or dodging each frenzied attack, while biding his time and waiting for the one perfect opportunity to strike. Then it came. Ivan's temper boiled over and the man overreached, allowing Finn to slide under his attack and draw his knife across the Regent Successor's gut, below his armored tunic. Ivan staggered forward a few paces then dropped to his knees, his hand pressed to the wound, which was leaking blood through his fingers. Finn turned and switched his knife into a reverse grip, ready to make the killing blow, when bullets bit into the ground in front of him and he dove for cover. The thrum of a skycar's rotors filled the sky and the craft dropped into yard four so rapidly Finn thought it was crashing.

Sloane Stewart ran to Ivan and pulled the man up, calling to the prefects that were piling out of the skycar.

"Medic! Medic! Help him!"

Finn and Elara were caught out in the open, but before the special prefects could draw a bead on them, more gunfire crackled, this time from the top of the junk heap, where General Riley and Ensign Thorne were still camped out. The officers were forced to retreat, but Stewart struggled on, protecting Ivan Volkov with her own body.

"Help him!" Stewart yelled. "By order of Maxim Volkov, you must not let this man die!"

Prefects braved the onslaught of bullets and three were shot and killed before Ivan was finally wrestled into the skycar. Sloane turned and looked Elara dead in the eyes, as if cursing her, then grabbed a handrail and pulled herself on to the sill of the skycar.

"No, you don't…" Elara hissed.

She drew back her arm then launched the nine-inch black blade, which sunk into Stewart's back with an organic thud, like a butcher chopping meat. Ivan's bodyguard and paramour arched her back, trying desperately to pull the knife free, but it was impaled too deeply, and soon her strength failed her. Stewart's fingers slipping from the handrail and as the skycar lifted off the ground, Ivan's bodyguard and paramour fell into the snow, beside the body of Tonya Duke.

"No! Get her!" Ivan yelled from the back of the skycar, kicking and screaming, but the prefects held him like a vice. "Don't leave her! She's all I have!"

The skycar door was slammed shut and bullets pockmarked the metal as Riley and Thorne continued their assault. Then Finn saw someone running toward the opposite side of the vehicle, her yellow hair stretched out horizontally behind her like a fine silk flag. Finn switched his grip and threw his knife with all his strength, but Juniper Jones had leapt inside the skycar before the blade could find its target, and the weapon sank into a scrap pile and was lost. The skycar climbed higher, chased by more bullets, which chipped away at its armor and damaged its engines, forcing the craft to limp away, barely twenty meters off the ground. Yet escape it did, taking Ivan Volkov and Juniper Jones with it.

The prefect encirclement folded, and the Authority forces were overrun and trampled beneath the bootheels of hundreds of workers. Chromes stormed into the yard, seizing weapons from fallen officers and firing them into the air in celebration, and before Finn knew it, he and Elara had been hoisted into the air on a sea of hands, to deafening cries of "Metal and Blood! Metal and Blood!"

28

NEW METALHAVEN

General Riley's skycar touched down in the center of yard four, sporting a few extra dents and bullet holes from overzealous Metalhaven workers who had taken pot-shots at it en-route, mistaking it for a prefect vehicle. The downdraught from its rotors helped to clear a space and finally give Finn and Elara some room to breathe. They had been carried half-way around yard four and back, and still the chants of Metal and Blood rang out across the entire sector. It was euphoric, but also exhausting.

"I had wondered if they'd ever put you down," General Riley said, using the landed skycar to support his powerful but battle-weary frame.

"Me too, but I'm glad they did because it was starting to make me feel nauseous," Finn replied.

"I have to admit I had my doubts about this plan, and I'm still struggling to believe you actually pulled it off," Riley added. He sighed and looked at the army of workers in the yard, laughing and dancing and even drinking, courtesy of hundreds of freshly pulled pints that were pouring out of the nearby recovery centers. "But seeing is believing. Metalhaven has fallen."

"Now, we have to make certain it stays this way," Elara said. "The Authority will act quickly, and we have to be ready."

Elara was the only person in the entire sector who had not been swept up in the emotion of their victory, and Finn suspected this had something to do with the escape of Ivan Volkov and Juniper Jones. Finn could empathize, though while it soured his own mood to know they had gotten away, those darker feelings were more than offset by the joy he felt knowing that Elara was safe.

"And they call me the gruff one," Riley said, offering Elara a half-smile, which she did not return. "But you're right of course, which is why Ensign Thorne and I need to leave. We have to let Haven know what happened and prepare them for what comes next."

A trio of workers pushed their way through the crowd, an act that would have normally started a fight had they been in a recovery center, but despite the explosive combination of Metalhaven workers and ale, the mood remained jubilant. Finn recognized Briggs and Xia, the Metals who'd helped them once they'd arrived in the sector, and he was glad to see that Trip was with them too.

"How did you get here?" Finn said, clasping hands with the former Metalhaven worker. "Last I saw, you were starting a riot inside a beer factory!"

"And as much fun as that was, I wouldn't miss this for all the ale in Makehaven," Trip replied, grinning like a buffoon. Finn could smell the beer on his breath, and the thickness of the fumes suggested it was more than his customary three pints.

"Briggs, gather all the other Metals in this sector and have them put together squads of defenders from the most capable and willing workers," Elara said, remaining laser focused on what needed to be done to secure their victory. "Once we have armed men and women on every gate and entrance in the sector, I need you to raid the prefect hub and gather as many weapons as you can."

"Yes, ma'am, but don't worry, I'm already on it," Briggs said, straightening to attention. "This sector is ours and those bastard golds aren't getting it back."

It took Finn a moment to process what had just happened, then he realized it made perfect sense that Briggs would already know Elara, a fellow Metal. The fact that Briggs had called her "ma'am" was more revealing, however. It showed the level of respect and authority that Elara already held inside the covert organization and hinted at a wider role for her to come.

"In the meantime, we'll clear the sector of bodies and collect all the fallen weapons," Trip said. Finn saw that the dead were already being piled into a pit not far from where they were standing, and that black smoke had begun to rise from it. "It doesn't feel right to burn the chromes alongside the golds, but we have nowhere else to put them."

"They're only shells now, so it doesn't matter," Elara said, coldly. *The Shadow speaking again...* Finn thought. "But make sure you collect their identification cards and record every last man and woman that died here. They should be remembered as heroes, today and in all the days to come."

"We'll make sure it's done," Trip said, and he nodded to Xia who hustled away into the crowd.

The smoke from the first pyre, which consisted solely of dead officers wearing the black carapace armor of the special prefecture began wafting past Finn's face. He was used to the acrid taste of charred metal in the air, but the smell of burning flesh was something much more visceral and unpleasant.

"I hope they smell this in the Authority sector," Briggs said, idly watching the plumes of black smoke billow into the murky sky. "It'll let those bastards know what's coming for them, especially once we free the other colors."

"We don't have the numbers or the training to take over Stonehaven, Seedhaven or any of the other work sectors," Elara said.

"But what if the general can bring more fighters from Haven?" Trip asked.

"Elara is right, we don't have the numbers to take the entire city, even with my squads," Riley said, and Trip chest's deflated like a leaky balloon. "We could only take Metalhaven because it was a perfect storm of opportunities, but we don't need to free the other sectors to bring down the Authority."

"Then how?" Finn asked.

Riley looked to Elara, and it seemed the two had an intrinsic understanding of what needed to be done.

"To bring down the Authority, we need to attack their leadership," Elara said. "That means taking the Authority sector, but also achieving something that is arguably even more challenging."

Finn raised an eyebrow. "There is something more challenging than taking over the Authority sector?"

"The key to control of Zavetgrad is the Regents," Elara said. Her tone remained darkly sinister, and it was clear whatever she was about to propose had been at the back of her mind for some time. "But to capture the Regents, we have to assault their sub-oceanic villa complex."

This time it was Riley who raised an eyebrow. The general may have already known that expanding upon their victory would require attacking the Authority sector, but Elara's bold suggestion appeared to have surprised even him.

"No-one in Zavetgrad has ever seen inside that complex, not even the other golds," Riley grunted. "The Regents are escorted out by their own personal force of bodyguards then put into the charge of the prefecture. Everyone else, their servants, worker robots, and support staff, are all taken there as infants and are raised, live and die without ever seeing the sun."

"Then we'll be the first outsiders to see it," Elara said, coolly undeterred.

Riley grunted a laugh. "Pen was right about you. You are ambitious."

"I prefer determined," Elara replied. "And no-one has ever gotten inside the villa complex because no-one has ever tried."

"Oh, we've tried, and we've failed too," Riley said, with a knowing smirk. "But something tells me that you will be different."

"Whatever we do, we'll need a way to stay in contact with you back in Haven," Finn said, focusing on the here and now. "But no more cloak and dagger shit. I need to be able to dial you up, like you were in the next building."

"You could probably reach Haven using that transmitter tower," Trip said, pointing to the tallest building surrounding yard four. It was also the only building that didn't have workers partying on the rooftops, and Finn knew exactly why.

"Gene banks are like the real banks of the pre-war world," Finn said. "Everything is locked up tight, especially the entrances to the upper floors." He had a thought and smiled. "It sounds like a job for Captain Scraps."

Finn looked for his robot then had a mild panic as he couldn't immediately see him. Eventually, he spotted Scraps on the shoulder of a Chief Foreman robot that was standing upright and appeared to be activated, though the top of the machine's cranial section was flipped open like a hatch.

"Hey, pal, I have a job for you that's more important than what you're doing." Finn said, leading the group over to where the robot was working. Then he frowned. "What are you doing, anyway?"

"Wait-wait!" Scraps said, as sparks exploded from the top of the foreman's head, like an electrical volcanic eruption. "Almost done!"

"Almost done doing what?" Finn asked.

Scraps didn't answer then slammed the top of the foreman's head shut, before leaping onto Finn's shoulder and steadying himself by grabbing a tuft of his hair. The foreman's primary power core then hummed into life and its mechanical eyes glowed and fixed themselves onto Finn. Instinctively, he reached for his laser cannon and was about to blow the robot's head clean off when the machine inexplicably smiled at him.

"Hello, sir, how are you today?" the foreman said, in a cheery tone that reminded Finn of Scraps. "The weather is a bit bleak, isn't it?" the robot continued, peering up at the black, smokey sky. "But the forecast for tomorrow is clear, won't that be nice?"

"What the flying fuck is this?!" Trip said, pointing a pistol at the robot.

"Please do not shoot me in the head," the robot said. "It would impair my ability to function, and I live to function!"

Trip looked to Finn, and he just shook his head before lowering his laser cannon and looking at the robot perched on his shoulder.

"What the hell did you do?" Finn asked. "I've never heard a foreman say please before, and why it is talking about the weather?"

"Scraps re-programmed bad robot to make it good robot!" Scraps answered. "Chiefy now a Metal. Chiefy re-program all other bad robots and make them good, like Scraps!"

"*Chiefy?*" Elara said, scowling at the foreman, who simply waved back, still in good cheer, despite the less than warm reception it had received.

"Yes, Chiefy help Briggs and Trip," Scraps said. "Chiefy good robot!"

"Wait, are you saying that you re-programmed this machine so that it's now on our side?" Finn asked, and Scraps nodded. "And that 'Chiefy' will re-program all of the other surviving foremen to join us too?", he added, and Scraps nodded again.

"Chiefy already doing it," Scraps explained. "Sixty-two bad robots still in Metalhaven. Soon, sixty-two good robots!"

Finn laughed and soon the others were joining in. "You're a genius, Scraps, have I ever told you that?"

Scraps shrugged. "Scraps clever! Finn makes him so!"

"I don't think I can take the credit, but thanks," Finn said.

"Hey, I don't suppose you can do something to the skycar's nav so we can get over the border fence without being shot to pieces?" Ensign Thorne wondered. Thorne had been working on minor repairs to the damaged craft, and Finn hadn't noticed the pilot join the group.

"Already done!" Scraps said, smiling. "Chiefy helped. Chiefy clever too."

Thorne scowled at the re-programmed robot then at her skycar. "You've already done it, like just now?"

"Yes-yes," Scraps said. "Done it before, so already know how."

"He's right, it's how I got out of Haven in the first place," Finn said, trying to set Thorne's mind at ease. "Though that did require strapping an evaluator robot's head to the console."

"No head needed," Scraps said. "Unless pilot-Thorne want one?"

"No!" Thorne said, holding up both hands. "I definitely do not want a disembodied robot head in my cockpit."

"Okay-kay," Scraps shrugged. He then looked at the mass of twisted robot parts littering the floor of yard four. "Plenty to go around."

"We're good, thank you Scraps," Riley cut in. The man seemed anxious to leave, though unlike Thorne, it didn't seem to have anything to do with avoiding severed robot heads. "And since you've already sorted out the nav, we should leave. I have a lot to report."

Riley walked up to Finn and plucked the captain's bars from Scraps' oil-can body. He put them into his pocket, before removing a single silver star from his own uniform and placing that into the center of Scraps' body instead.

"Stay safe, General Scraps," Riley said, and the little robot's face lit up. "And look after Finn and Elara. I will be in contact with you all again soon."

Scraps saluted and Riley returned the salute, before patting the robot on the head with genuine affection. Finn said his goodbyes, which felt oddly final, then the general climbed into the skycar alongside Ensign Thorne, who was wearing her aviator sunglasses, despite the thick black fog of smoke that was wallowing around the yard. The rotors spun into life, blowing the area around the vehicle clear of the foul-tasting fumes from the pyre, then the skycar lifted off the ground and climbed sharply above Metalhaven before speeding away in the direction of the Davis Strait and, eventually, Haven.

"Do you need help with the transmitter?" Briggs asked, once the dust had settled. "I can probably spare one or two men to help, but I need most of my Metals to co-ordinate the defense of the sector."

"No, we've got this," Finn said, looking at Scraps and the latest addition to their group, the foreman called Chiefy. "I suggest we use the top-floor offices of the gene bank as our base of operations in Metalhaven, so meet us there when you're done."

"Yes, sir," Briggs replied, and for once Finn didn't flinch at the use of an honorific when addressing him. He was starting to get used to it.

Briggs and Trip departed to continue their work and Finn peered at the transmitter tower on top of the gene bank, which rose a hundred meters into the ash-darkened sky.

"Can you get us to that rooftop, pal?" Finn asked.

"Yes-yes," Scraps said, unconcerned, before pointing to the reprogrammed foreman. "Chiefy clever *and* strong. Doors no problem for Chiefy."

The foreman robot smiled and waved as Scraps explained its capabilities, which only made Finn feel even more uncomfortable. He'd never seen a foreman do either of those things, and it seemed fundamentally wrong, like snow feeling hot to the touch.

"Then lead the way," Finn said, partly so that the robot would stop looking at him. "We need to make a call."

The walk to the gene bank took longer than expected because every worker they passed would stop to thank them or say, "fuck the Authority" or even just drunkenly offer them a swig of beer from their half-empty glasses. Like being called 'sir', Finn was getting used to the attention, and he and Elara both nodded and smiled and talked to the workers who stopped them, despite feeling a pressing need to be elsewhere. He imagined it was how Pen felt most days, when promenading the inner walkways of Haven, and he wondered if he was becoming as much a public figure as he was a freedom fighter. That sat awkwardly with him too, but he chose to believe he would grow used to it, and would be happy to do so, because it meant he would have survived the many trials of a different kind that were still to come.

Finally, they reached the gene bank and Chiefy smashed open the door with ease. The reception area, normally filled with the cries and screams of those being forced to undergo medical procedures that stole their DNA, was eerily quiet. A pair of horn-rimmed glasses sat on the desk, along with a half-drunk cup of coffee. The computer was even still switched on.

"They sure left in a hurry," Finn commented, finding it bizarre to walk freely through the foyer without being stopped by prefects.

"Having your sector overrun by the angry mob has a way of motivating people," Elara commented. Now that they were alone, she allowed herself a slight smile.

The doors to some of the ground-floor examination rooms and procedure rooms were still open, and Finn wandered into one. It reminded him of the room where the Metalhaven Head Prefect Victor Roth had forced him to undergo a TESA procedure without anesthetic. The pain of having a needle shoved into his scrotum was still more intense than anything he'd felt before or since, and it made his blood run cold. He'd hoped to see Victor Roth inside the crucible, but his reckoning with the sadistic head prefect would have to wait.

Finn unplugged the storage freezers before he left, so that the collected seed samples would all spoil, then found the door to the bank of elevators and pressed the call button. The panel flashed red and demanded an ID.

"Scraps, I think this is more your domain than Chiefy's," Finn said, stepping back so that the little robot could put his incredible hacking skills to use.

Within seconds, Scraps had bypassed the security and the lift doors opened with a tuneful ping. He stepped inside and held the doors for Elara and the foreman, before hitting the button for the top floor. Banal, instrumental music played inside the car as it lifted them high above Metalhaven. It made an already surreal experience even more dreamlike.

Exiting on the top floor, which housed the executive offices for the golds that administered the gene bank, Finn checked a floor map on the wall then led the party to the stairwell that would bring them out on the roof. Chiefy employed his robotic might to good effect, smashing down doors and breaking locks that would have required a laser cutter to bypass otherwise, and before long Finn was stepping out into the snowy air. A hundred meters up, it felt even colder than on the ground, but the smoke from the pyres was at least thinner so that the taste of death was less intense on his tongue.

He headed to the antenna, icy wind lashing his face, then climbed onto its base and looked out across Metalhaven. The height should have made him feel queasy, but not this time. His sector was free, with armed chromes guarding every way in and out, and patrolling the rooftops so that even skycars couldn't approach without risk of being shot out of the sky. It didn't feel like it should have been possible, yet he knew it was real. And now that it had been proven the Authority could be resisted and beaten, he had an unswerving belief that the rest of Zavetgrad could be freed too. All it took was Metal and Blood.

"You can feel it too, can't you?" Elara said, joining him on the antenna platform. "There's an energy in this sector now, and do you know what it is?"

Finn shrugged. "Anger? Faith?"

"Hope..." Elara replied. "Hope is what the Authority took from the workers so long ago that everyone forgot what it felt like. Now, they remember, and they won't forget again."

Finn turned to Elara and tried to summon the courage to

say the words he'd practiced in his mind, should he ever see her again, alive. The truth was, he'd rather fight a hundred Ivan Volkovs than tell Elara how he felt.

"I don't expect you to forgive me, and I'm not asking you to," Finn said, his voice catching in his throat. "I'm just glad you're alive. Besides Scraps, you're all I have."

Elara smiled, and The Shadow was finally in the background. "You have more than you think," she said, gesturing to Metalhaven, spread out beneath them. "You have an entire sector now, with tens of thousands of people who owe their freedom to you."

"I don't want it," Finn laughed. "I don't want any of it." He took Elara's hands, calloused, and covered in blood, but warm. "All I want is you."

Elara smiled again then placed her hand at the base of Finn's neck, causing electricity to race through his body. Then she eased him closer, and he closed he eyes, so that all he could feel was the press of her lips against his.

"Sir, sir!"

Chiefy's strident cry split them apart like a lightning strike and Finn glowered at the foreman as it practically skipped toward him.

"Sir, great news, I have successfully tapped into the radio tower!" Chiefy said, throwing his hands up in the air, in the same ways Scraps did when he was excited.

"Seriously? Could you have not waited one fucking minute to tell me that?" Finn said, still glowering at the robot, though Elara was choking back laughter.

"I could have, sir, but why?" Chiefy asked. "Were you doing something important?"

Finn opened his mouth but there was no answer he could

give that would not lead to further questions, and even more embarrassment.

"No, Chiefy, you're right," Finn said, accepting that the moment, as fleeting as it was, had gone. "And since you have it working, let's see if we can send a message..."

Finn and Elara jumped down beside the antenna's control panel and observed as the two robots tuned the system into Haven's frequency. A screen rose up from inside the control panel, but the display was blank, save for three dots that pulsed and rippled across the middle of the screen.

"Maybe she's not home?" Elara said, whimsically.

"If she's not, then we're in trouble," Finn said.

Suddenly, the screen flashed, and the face of Principal Penelope Everhart appeared. She was wearing night clothes, and her hair was tousled up on top of her head.

"Do you have any idea what time it is, Will?" Pen said, rubbing her eyes. "The Pit had better be on fire, or I'm finding myself a new general."

"Hi Pen, it's not General Riley, it's me," Finn said. The day had just gotten stranger. "I'm just using Riley's private channel, that's all."

Pen squinted then rubbed her eyes again. "Finn?"

"Yes, ma'am," Finn replied, smiling.

"Where the hell are you?"

"I'm on top of a gene bank in Metalhaven," Finn said, realizing that the situation would require a little explanation. "There's probably too much to go through right now, but all you need to know is that the sector is ours."

"You actually, did it?" Pen said. She was patting the side of her face, as if trying to test if she was awake or dreaming. "You took over Metalhaven from the Authority?"

"We did," Finn said, scarcely able to believe it himself.

"And Elara?" Pen asked, tentatively.

Finn stepped aside and Elara took his place. He'd never seen her look nervous before, without her many shields in place, but he understood why, because Pen was Elara's biological mother. The two had never met. Like every worker born in Zavetgrad, Elara was the produce of stolen seed, implanted forcibly into a surrogate that either carried the child or was executed for violating the law. Yet to see them looking at each other, it was obvious to Finn they shared a connection that transcended mere DNA.

"Hello, ma'am," Elara said, timidly. "It's good to finally meet you."

Pen beamed a smile back at her that was so warm it lit up the dark rooftop more brightly than any fire could have done.

"It's good to meet you too," Pen said, smoothing down her messy hair. "And you can stop with the 'ma'am' business, right now. It's Pen, okay?"

Elara smiled and nodded. "Yes... Pen."

"And what of Will?" Pen asked. "General Riley, I mean."

"He's on his way back to you now," Finn said, stepping into the frame behind Elara. "We lost Reyes and Kellan, but Ensign Thorne made it."

Pen nodded solemnly. "I will ensure their sacrifice is not forgotten."

"I'm sure General Riley will explain everything once he's back, but I just wanted to call, and ask you to save this frequency," Finn continued. "Metalhaven is ours, but it's only the beginning."

"What did you have in mind for your next move?" Pen asked, though she was now looking at Elara.

"Now, we show the Authority what real justice looks like," Elara said. "The Regents like their trials. For decades they've used them to keep us afraid and under control. The trials are their power, and I'm going to take that power away and use it against them." Elara drew in a breath of the ice-cold air and her emerald eyes hardened. The Shadow had returned. "Seven work sectors, seven Regents. I'm going to find them and drag them out of their villas. Then, when they're on their knees on the golden bricks of the Authority central square, all of Zavetgrad will finally see justice done."

Pen nodded. "And then?"

Elara looked up and Finn followed the line of her gaze all the way to the Nimbus Space Citadel that was home to the Authority's leader, Gideon Alexander Reznikov.

"Then, we aim higher…"

The end (to be continued).

CONTINUE THE STORY

Continue the story in book #4 of the Metal and Blood series, Justice of Metalhaven. Available from Amazon in Kindle, paperback and audiobook formats, and in Kindle Unlimited.

ALSO BY G J OGDEN

Sa'Nerra Universe

Omega Taskforce

Descendants of War

Scavenger Universe

Star Scavengers

Star Guardians

Standalone series

The Aternien Wars

The Contingency War

Darkspace Renegade

The Planetsider Trilogy

G J Ogden's newsletter: Click here to sign-up

ABOUT THE AUTHOR

At school, I was asked to write down the jobs I wanted to do as a "grown up". Number one was astronaut and number two was a PC games journalist. I only managed to achieve one of those goals (I'll let you guess which), but these two very different career options still neatly sum up my lifelong interests in science, space, and the unknown.

School also steered me in the direction of a science-focused education over literature and writing, which influenced my decision to study physics at Manchester University. What this degree taught me is that I didn't like studying physics and instead enjoyed writing, which is why you're reading this book! The lesson? School can't tell you who you are.

When not writing, I enjoy spending time with my family, playing Warhammer 40K, and indulging in as much Sci-Fi as possible.

Printed in Great Britain
by Amazon